CW01638497

DEEP WATER

Nicola Kelsall

Little Studio
Publishing Company

DEEP WATER

First published as an eBook 2023

Copyright Nicola Kelsall © 2023

Cover Illustration by Nicola Kelsall © 2023

ISBN: 978-0-9956685-5-3

All rights reserved.

No part of this publication may be reproduced, stored in a retrieval system, or transmitted, in any form or by any means, without the prior permission in writing of the publisher, nor be otherwise circulated in any form of binding or cover other than that in which it is published and without a similar condition including this condition being imposed on the subsequent purchaser.

All the characters appearing in this book, apart from those in the public domain, are entirely fictitious. Any resemblance to any real persons either living or dead is purely coincidental.

Many thanks to all my friends and family who have inadvertently inspired the content of this book, and a special 'thank you' to Fiona at Fiona McIntyre Designs, for her work on the cover design.

"Smooth seas do not make skilful sailors."

Franklin D. Roosevelt

Chapter 1

'OK... so... are you listening?'

'Yes...' Briony was standing by the open door to our sitting room. She flicked her long sleek brown hair over one shoulder and leaned her head against the doorframe. She was watching me with mild curiosity – one eyebrow raised, her large pale blue eyes steady and unblinking. 'Go on then...'

'OK....' I cleared my throat nervously and read to her:

'She turned her impassive, unremitting gaze from the cold, dead eyes and the pale, lifeless body lying prostrate on the sloping mudstone riverbank, and studied the purple stain of the darkening sky across the gaping, greedy mouth of the estuary. The last remnants of a fiery winter sunset ebbed quickly away into the chill of the encroaching night. Noisily, the turgid, swirling water slapped relentlessly, turning the shale and stones over and over and over again in a never-ending, remorseless clawing motion. Soon it would be dark, and the tidal current would be merciless in its journey along the fast-flowing river, and this sorry, wretched soul would be carried away, dragged silently to a watery grave, and no one would miss them – no one would know... or even care..."

'So, what do you think?' I asked in hopeful anticipation.

'Um, well...yeah...'

'What's that supposed to mean?'

'Well, it's...er...quite good...maybe needs a little tweaking.'

And there was I, thinking I had the best EVER opening paragraph to my new novel EVER written in the history of Crime Fiction.

'What's wrong with it, then?' I said, irritably.

'It's just a bit…you know…flowery.'

'FLOWERY!'

'Yep.'

Talk about deflating a person's ego, which by the way is more sensitive than Briony would appreciate, given that she seems to think I am emotionally stunted (I AM NOT EMOTIONALLY STUNTED, just in case you're already taking sides.)

I looked at the expression on Briony's little heart-shaped face and thought how insensitive *she* was being, for someone with such a sweet-looking face. Those big baby-blue eyes might fool some people, but she can really stick the knife in if she wants to.

'I'm sorry, Alex, but you did ask my opinion…' She regarded me, clear-eyed, tight-lipped, with the slightly chilling gaze of a Chucky doll.

There are times when I wonder whether I made a bit of a mistake suggesting that Briony should move in with me. It's not turning out to be as mutually satisfying as I'd hoped, or as convivial. Maybe it would have been better to put off this living together business until we're in our 40's... Because, by then, we could hopefully be able to afford a bigger house, better holidays, and a cleaning person, and a nice, big garden, and my own private study …These things might mitigate the constant irritations, such as space-invading and total lack of orderliness. I don't mean to carp, but sometimes our flat looks like a squalid student rental. Briony doesn't seem to have any inherent house-keeping skills that I can see. I was recently forced to introduce a rota for various jobs around the house out of sheer exasperation. She didn't take to the idea too well, but there is a limit to how many times I can tolerate dried-on Chocorocks left on bowls all day (which incidentally, sets like concrete in minutes, especially if left on windowsills in full sunlight), or thick clumps of her long fine hair clogging up the plugholes in the shower and in hairbrushes lying on the kitchen table (perilously close to the open butter dish), or worse – a surplus of cat poos threatening to overflow the litter tray. I mean, Mr Catkins isn't even **my** *cat, for God's sake! I only said she could bring him if he pooped outside. I don't really like cats much – too hairy and demanding. Give me a goldfish any day. Xavier and Xander are perfect pets. They just swim around looking pretty and non-threatening – quite good company really. Anyway, I think I've been quite magnanimous accepting Briony's fiendish feline, along with her own annoying habits. I have tried to overlook her little foibles and eccentricities, but as my mother says, "you really shouldn't cast dirt into the well that gives you water", and I do think she has a point.*

'I'm going out for a bit,' she said, smiling. The smile had the faint whiff of pity about it.

'Where?'

'Not sure. It's a shame to stay inside on a sunny Saturday. I might cycle down to the park.'

She was gone almost as soon as she'd said it. This seems to happen quite a lot these days – before I've even had time to consider the idea of joining her, she's gone. I'm beginning to wonder if she really wants a boyfriend any more. Perhaps she was being serious when she said she was feeling 'stifled' a few weeks ago. Come to think of it, she wasn't laughing along with me at the time, but really – how could I take her seriously when she was standing there, stark naked, flapping her arms about like that? If I remember rightly, all I'd done was ask her if she would mind *not* leaving talcum powder all over the bathroom floor for me to slip on, and potentially die a tragic and completely preventable death.

'Seventy-three percent of accidents happen in the home environment', I told her, – 'and did you know, it costs the NHS forty-five million pounds a year? And these are all preventable accidents. Just imagine how much money they would have if people just thought more about what they were doing. People just don't use their common sense.'

'Alex, you are *insufferable*, sometimes,' she said at the time.

She went out for quite a long time that day. I was still speaking when she shut the front door. She can be quite rude if she's in one of her moods. But you have to take the rough with the smooth I suppose. No relationship is perfect, is it? My mate, Jacob, says you have to learn to be tolerant and willing to compromise, if you want a relationship to last. I think I'm pretty good at both those things, actually. Briony disagrees, of course. Jacob isn't really the best person to give out advice, though. He's the last person to consider someone else's feelings but we've got each other's backs, as they say. I've had to cover for him on more than one occasion. In fact, it's probably down to me that his wife, Lucy, hasn't left him yet. Five years have passed since they tied the knot and Jacob has settled down quite a lot since the early days. Lucy used to blame me for his bad behaviour, since I was still single and fancy-free, but to be honest, it was always Jacob who was the rebellious one.

'You're leading him astray,' she used to complain to me, if we came back drunk to their place, – 'you can't carry on like students now…'

When she gave him an ultimatum, I told him we needed to find a different way to go boozing without the fallout afterwards. That's when we came up with the simple plan to tell her he was away on sales weekends once a month. It was so easy to start with. She never suspected a thing, especially since he was always getting lots of commission for his sales job anyway. 'It's like falling off a log,' Jacob used to joke. Ah, those were the days! But we're both 35 now – a bit long in the tooth for all that. My word is my bond, though. I will never let on to Lucy about what we got up to and that's how I've helped Jacob and Lucy to stay together all this time, by being a loyal friend – which I value above everything else. Mind you, I don't envy Jacob one bit – Lucy is not what you'd call a 'catch' by any stretch of the imagination. I don't want to sound unkind, but when my mother saw her, she described poor Lucy as having "less personality than a stick of celery". It's true that Lucy does not possess much in the way of conversation skills, but obviously, that's how Jacob likes it. There's no accounting for taste, is there? Sometimes I question my own relationship with Briony and whether or not we're really right for each other. We're like chalk and cheese, and I'm not really sure where the glue that holds us together, actually resides. Are we just too lazy to make a change? Is the passion we first felt for each other dead or just gone to ground for a bit? These are the questions that occupy my mind in the small hours, when I can't get to sleep, and I'm wondering how it is that some people have ambition in bucket loads, and others, like me, seem to lack it completely. Time for another heart to heart with my old friend Jacob, I think.

'I'll get these,' he said. We often meet at the *Malt and Shovel* in town – it's a sort of second home. We sat down on the well-worn stools at the end of the bar where we could see ourselves in the mirrored backsplash behind the spirits.

'Cripes, we're getting older, aren't we!' said Jacob, fingering his greying hair. 'You're getting a bit thin on top, mate,' he said, perusing the crown of my head and slapping me on the back.

'Well, at least being blond, it's not as obvious as yours,' I said, feeling a bit miffed.

'Ah, well, you can't hold back time,' he said, taking a swig of beer. 'So, what's the latest?'

'You have to promise not to laugh…'

'OK…I'm intrigued.' He sounded a bit insincere.

'Well…'

'Don't tell me – you've taken up some weird hobby, like growing Armenian cucumbers, or Cheese Rolling, or Underwater Hockey…'

'None of the above. I'm training to be a Special Constable.'

'Really?' Jacob looked incredulous.

'It's not *that* unusual!'

'I'm just a bit surprised, that's all. How can you fit it in with work?'

'It's fine – you only have to do four hours a week.'

'What made you decide to do that, then? Was it the uniform?' Jacob was smirking, – 'because you know, Alex, you don't have to get a job to dress up in your spare time you know!'

'It's for research purposes, Jacob. I need to gather information from the inside – for my book.' *(This was only half the truth. Briony has been suggesting that I should get out more and find a way to meet more people, given that my social circle is very small – well, basically consisting of one person. I don't know if Jacob minds that he is my one and only friend – I mean, that's a bit of a responsibility, isn't it?)*

'Oh, yeah – your book! I forgot. When do I get to read it, then?'

'When it's finished and not before.'

'Can't I help with editing or something?'

'No. I've decided not to show it to anyone. It will suppress my creativity – I don't want any negative comments. Briony has already put me off a bit.'

Jacob nodded in fake recognition. 'So, how's it going with her, then? Any better?'

'Not really…'

'Did you try any of the things I suggested?'

'Um, well, a bit…'

'Alex! You need to listen to what I've been telling you. You need to relax more about stuff, you know. You'll just piss her off going on about her being untidy all the time and criticising her every move. You need to choose your battles carefully, you know.'

'I know, but she can be so annoying. I mean, just the other day I found ALL the towels had been used up and there were NO clean ones in the cupboard! And, get this, her cat actually crapped on our doormat because Briony was too lazy to clean out the tray. And another thing, I went to look for some string to tie up the passenger door on my car, because she is always banging it too hard, and now it doesn't close properly…and I found it on her dressing table all cut up to make cat toys.'

Jacob was looking at me in an odd way, and then just laughed his head off. 'Mate, you really do need to chillax a bit! Jesus!'

'Do you think I'm being unreasonable?'

'You're just…' he wiped the tears from his eyes, – 'I don't know… you're just Alex, I guess. Maybe living with someone just isn't for you.'

I fell asleep on the sofa when I got back to the flat. These days, four pints of beer is enough for me. My phone rang, suddenly waking me up. It was getting dark, and I realised I was still on my own in the flat. On the phone, Briony's voice was hard to hear above a lot of talking and general noise going on in the background.

'What was that?' I asked her to repeat whatever it was she was saying.

'I'm staying out this evening,' she was saying above the cacophony.

'Oh, I thought we were going to watch that film this evening – the one you said you really wanted to watch…'

'Oh sorry, Alex. Which film was that? Oh, never mind – look, I'm with my friend Jilly and she asked me to go along to a girl's night. I'll be back late so don't wait up.' Then she was gone. I tossed the phone down, irritated and slightly bemused. Oh well, Alex, I thought, you'll have to eat alone again, and drink this nice Rioja all by yourself, just like last Saturday. In fact, now I think about it, this is the fourth Saturday in a row…something's not right. I pondered on this sad and now obvious truth. My girlfriend was slipping away from me, and I didn't know what to do about it. I rummaged in the fridge for the microwavable curry I knew was lurking somewhere on the verge of its sell-by date and opened the bottle of red I had planned to share with her this evening. I suppose I'd saved some money by not getting a takeaway for the two of us, and I could watch whatever I liked for a change, but, still, I felt a dark cloud encroaching, an unpleasant sense of impending gloominess and misgiving. Mr Catkins jumped onto my lap and stared at me with his clear, penetrating malachite eyes – he knows something, I'm sure of it.

I only drank one glass of the wine – drinking alone isn't really particularly fun, and to be honest, it's a bit of a lonely thing to do. I suddenly had a horrible feeling that if I didn't stop myself from downing the whole bottle, I could start a trend that I really, really don't think would be a good idea right now. I've seen what can happen to people who just slide into a depressed state of mind and drinking like that becomes a habit they can't stop. Anyway, I needed to keep a clear head for my writing, which, by the way, is the one thing about my life that I *am* really happy about. The rest of it isn't going too well. I'm bored with my job at Anderson & Sons. The world of bespoke kitchens is not exactly riveting. I just fell into this job by accident when I was looking for a stop gap four years ago, and someone I knew just happened to be leaving and they put a word in for me. I really should be making more of an effort to look for something more stimulating, but it pays well, and I've been told I'm good at it, which is mostly true. I wish I could be more ambitious, though – I mean, I'm getting older, and you can get written off if you don't achieve your full potential by forty. That's what people say, isn't it? Briony says I'm 'stagnating' and need to 'push' myself more. At Christmas, she bought me a book called '*Cut the Crap and Get Shit Done*'. I think she was hoping it would be motivational. I just found it depressing – I don't even have the motivation to follow the motivational tasks, so if I can't even find the mental energy to think about why "*success is the child of audacity*", or "*if you think you are too small to make a difference, try sleeping with a mosquito*", then I'm stuffed, because ambition is as elusive to me as understanding the universe. I'm just not that kind of person. That's another reason why Briony gets frustrated, I suppose. Her favourite quote is: "***Life is not measured by the breaths you take, but by the moments that take your breath away***". Briony like quotes. She puts up little signs with hearts and pithy mottos all over our flat. She has scatter cushions with things like, "***Whatever Makes You Happy – DO THAT!***" and "***When I'm Sad, I Go To My Happy Place!***". I noticed the other day she must have bought a new one. It says on it: "***The Grass is Always Greener When You Water it***". I'm not sure what this is supposed to mean, but I have a nagging feeling that something ominous is about to happen. I turned it round so I couldn't see it and went to bed early.

Tomorrow I'll go to *my* '***Happy Place***' and carry on writing my novel. At least I can find some solace there. It will take my mind off Briony and her weird standoffish behaviour.

Chapter 2

'Is your brushed white oak flooring sustainable?' One of our long-standing customers, Mrs Bedlington-Clarke, was on the phone again this morning. Alice was patiently explaining that *all* our wood is sustainable and thorough checks are made on purchasing. 'But how do you know?' she persisted.

'Because,' said Alice, carefully, – 'it's certified by the FSC…'

'And who are they?' Alice rolled her eyes and gave me a look of exasperation.

'The Forest Stewardship Council, Mrs Bedlington-Clarke – they ensure that the forests are being managed to strict environmental, social and economic standards…'

'But how do we know these people are doing their job properly? I've heard that there's a lot of fraudulent activity going on with some of these timber companies – you can't trust them.'

'Give it to me…' I said, motioning to Alice to hand over the phone. 'Ah, Mrs Bedlington-Clarke – how nice to hear from you again. Now, let me assure you that we do all we can to check our supply chain. We are in the same position as every other company here in the UK. We do our very best.'

'Very well,' she said, – 'I suppose I'll have to accept what you say, but I'm *not* convinced. There's something else I'd like to discuss with you, Alexander…'

'It's Alex – please call me Alex…'

'I'm not very happy with the colour of the tiles at Butler's Court, Alexander. They'll have to be changed.'

'You chose the colour yourself, Mrs Bedlington-Clarke…'

'Did I? Well, I've decided I don't like them – they're sludgy. I want them changed to *Moonstone Grey*.'

'The customer is always right,' I said to Alice once I'd put the phone down. She puffed out her rouged pink cheeks at the worn-out cliché and exhaled loudly.

'Mrs BC is such a *pain,* Alex. She's rung four times today already.'

'Just remember, Alice – customers like Mrs B.C. are our bread and butter. We have to do our best to keep them happy.'

Alice gave me a sulky stare and got her hand-mirror out to touch up her sugar-pink lipstick. Her brown, curly hair was tied up with a leopard print scarf and gold clips on either side. She wears far too much makeup in my view. I mean, she's only nineteen and quite pretty without all that foundation and stuff plastered on her face. I made the mistake of saying so once. I won't do that again in a hurry. Old Mr Anderson made me apologise to her and told me to keep my personal opinions to myself in future. Talk about humiliating! Mr Anderson is a bit of an old duffer – he has some very old-fashioned views about how to run a company, and his son, Declan, isn't much better. I've tried to suggest the odd thing to them, but they're very set in their ways. Only the other day, I asked Mr Anderson if we could have a decent coffee machine in the foyer for our customers. He looked at me as if I'd suggested handing them a tenner each as they came through the door.

'Are you serious, Alexander?' he said, scowling at me from beneath his white, bushy eyebrows – his smooth bald head glinting under the unforgiving strip-lights of our showroom. 'We don't need gimmicks like that to entice people! Our work speaks for itself. Good grief, you'll be suggesting piped pop music next…'

Then Declan joined in: 'Those fancy coffee machines are expensive, Alex. It's not practical. Dishing out free coffee won't sell our products any better. It'll just lose us money. Things are tight enough as it is!' Old Mr Anderson coughed and shot Declan a look. 'All I'm saying Alex, is that we don't think it'll be worth the outlay.'

I decided I should probably keep shtum about my ideas after this exchange. They just don't want to move with the times, and it shows. I'm loath to tell them how busy their rival company, Craftisan Bespoke Kitchens, is. Briony and I went there a few weeks ago to check it out. Everything about it was better, brighter, friendlier, more modern. I picked up their brochure and brought it to show Mr Anderson, thinking he would be interested to see it. I got that wrong too. 'I don't give a monkey's what they're doing over there,' he said crossly, – 'they can't touch us on quality – not in a million years. A fancy brochure doesn't change that fact.' He flicked it into the bin in disgust.

'You're wasted in that place,' Briony told me later. 'They're never going to listen.'

At 1 o'clock we *all* go for lunch at the same time. That's another thing that old Mr Anderson refuses to change. I mean, who shuts for an hour at lunchtime nowadays? I don't think I know any other shops that do that. We've had loads of complaints about it, and I reckon we've lost customers to Craftisan because of that too.

My phone pinged with a WhatsApp message at ten minutes to one. Surprised, I fished it out of my back trouser pocket and quickly checked it, out of Declan and Mr Anderson's eyesight. It was from Briony, which is unusual during the day – she's pretty busy in her own job.

'Hi! Fancy getting lunch? Fosters? I can be there in 15…x'

Fosters is a pub about half way between Briony's office and Anderson & Sons – a convenient meeting place – not that we go there very often. Usually, I take a sandwich to work to save money, and Briony has lunch with her mates from work most days. She was already at the bar when I went in.

'What would you like?' she said.

'Just a half of IPA. Thanks…'

'What do you fancy to eat? I'm having salad and a cheese omelette.'

'Oh, well, I might as well have the same – sounds good.'

She seemed different somehow, to how she'd been in the morning. More…I don't know…more efficient – brighter and more with-it. In the morning she'd hardly spoken. She'd seemed distracted and disorganised. She almost forgot to feed the cat, which was quite unlike her. Now she was smiling happily and organizing me in her slightly bossy, managing way – more herself. It felt more familiar to me – the Briony I'm used to.

'Let's sit by the window,' she suggested, putting her lime and soda down on the little round table and flinging her jacket over the back of a chair. While we waited for our food to come, she checked her emails on her phone. 'Sorry Alex, I just need to answer something…'

Part of the reason I don't suggest lunchtime meetups is because Briony spends a good deal of time on her phone. She's in PR – a small firm with big ideas called *Zenith* (the 'i' in the Zenith logo is a line drawing of a mountain). Briony spends most of their time in meetings, as far as I can gather. Anyway, she seems incapable of switching off during break times. It's pretty annoying. I looked out of the window at the people going by while I waited for her to finish whatever it was that was *so* urgent. I looked out at the busy street and wondered why was it, that other young couples always look so much happier and together than Briony and me? I watched a young man grab his girlfriend's hand – they were laughing and joking. Their eyes were locked together. They were oblivious to everyone else around them. I looked across at Briony, immersed in email-checking, her lips pursed in concentration and her finger stabbing at the little keypad on her phone. Finally, she put her phone down. The food came and she began a conversation about holidays. She asked me what I thought about going away for a week in Devon.

'Mandy at work says we could have her family cottage at Hope Cove in two weeks' time. Someone cancelled. She can let us have it for half price, Alex. What do you think?'

'Oh, right…' I was thrown by her sudden need for an instant answer. 'Well, I'm not sure if I can get that week off at such short notice, Briony. You know what Mr Anderson is like.'

'Yes, I do.' She was looking at me intently, willing me to just say 'yes'.

'It's difficult. You know how they like to plan ahead – I had to put in for my holidays ten months ago.'

'I know, Alex – but it's time you took a stand, it really is! You let them walk all over you. You've been there for four years now. Just *tell* them it's what you're doing! It's not as if it makes a scrap of difference when you go on holiday, does it! The Andersons are always there – they never go away *anywhere!* Come on, Alex, this is a chance to have a nice week away, and it won't cost us much at all. You know you're always worrying about the cost of things… And that's another thing – you've been on the same salary for two years. You need to take control of your life, Alex. Be more assertive. Good things *don't* come to those who wait – that's cobblers.'

'Alright. I'll ask Mr Anderson about it this afternoon, but I can't make promises, Briony. Anyway, how come you can just take off at short notice like this?'

'Jen swapped a week with me – she said it suited her better.'

'Well, that was lucky.'

'Not luck, Alex – it's called friendship. You really need to get away from the Andersons. It's not doing you any good staying there. You're turning into a fossil, just like them.' She finished her food and got up to go. Her smile had faded, and she was obviously displeased with my lack of enthusiasm. 'Tell them!' she said, bossily, pushing her chair roughly under the table and grabbing her coat. 'I need to go. See you later.'

'Have you arranged for re-fitting Mrs Bedlington-Clarke's tiles yet?' asked Declan in the afternoon, – 'it's a bit of a priority, Alex…'

'Oh, yes. I'll get onto it.'

Honestly, I don't know why we have to jump to Mrs B.C.'s requests as if our lives depended on it. I've often wondered what her hold over the Company is. It's not as if she owns hundreds of properties and employs us for huge amounts of work. She only has a small block of flats – on the outskirts of Putney. It's not even particularly smart. There are a lot of things about this Company that I don't understand very well. It's crying out to have some money spent on it, but old Mr Anderson refuses to spend a penny more than he has to. For instance, I can't believe they still make that medicated toilet paper – it's like using a Brillo pad on your bum, for God's sake! I'd rather hold it in till I get home. Alice said she looked it up once, and you can buy an original roll of it from the 1950's on an antiques website for twelve quid. One of the lads bought a roll of maximum grit sandpaper from *Toolstation Ltd* and swapped it for a laugh. He put it in the men's loos on the loo-roll holder. Mr Anderson went ballistic. That lad nearly lost his job. It goes without saying that the Andersons don't have much of a sense of humour. More recently, Alice had the audacity to ask them for a more comfortable chair to sit on. They finally acquiesced when she informed them that she could always go to the Health & Safety Executive and ask them for one. The following week, Mr Anderson purchased a second-hand adjustable swivel chair off Facebook Market Place in a lurid shade of mauve PVC. He presented it to her as if it had been bequeathed by Thomas Jefferson himself.

Anyway, today, I think I designed my best kitchen so far – a fantastically simple but stylish layout in forest green with light oak wood trim and flooring, ice-white quartz worktops and handle-less drawers and cupboards – just as the client requested. Mr Anderson doesn't approve of no handles, even though they've been around since the 1960's. He says kitchens like that have no personality. 'Good design,' he says, – 'is all in the detail. That's what makes it come to life, Alexander!'

Chapter 3

Briony has given me an ultimatum: if I don't tell the Andersons by Friday that I'm going on holiday in a week's time, she will go without me. Since it's Friday tomorrow, I'm really under the cosh. To be fair, I have been prevaricating. The trouble is, I know it'll be a 'no' and I'm just putting off the evil moment. There's a bit of an atmosphere in our flat right now – even the cat has noticed. He's been avoiding Briony as much as I have. Only this morning he exited the kitchen through the cat flap at an unusually spritely pace, just as Briony came in to make her extra strong coffee. Even her resting face has a scowl on it. Cats are very sensitive to people's moods – I read about it when I was trying to find out more about cats to impress

Briony in the early days. I secretly ordered a magazine called *Puss in Boots* and one called *My Purrfect Cat,* to try and understand them. The former turned out to be nothing to do with cats (I've still got it somewhere, hidden in my underwear drawer). Anyway, in *My Purrfect Cat,* there was a really good article by Dr somebody or other – she'd done some experiments showing different human expressions to a succession of cats, monitoring their reactions. The study concluded that cats definitely prefer a smiley face to a cross face, which is what I told Briony while we ate our toast. I was really just trying to make conversation, since there was deadly silence apart from the crunching noises while we ate, and to be honest, I was getting a bit fed up with her lack of social interaction. I know she's annoyed about the holiday thing, but she doesn't understand how difficult things are at work at the moment. We've got several deadlines to wrestle with, and supply issues, not to mention the fact that Mrs B.C.'s replacement tiles were the wrong colour and had to be removed *again.* Mr Anderson has been in a foul mood all week, so it just hasn't been the right time to approach him. I must say, the idea of a holiday is very appealing – I could do with a break, I really could. Anyway, on top of a difficult week, my mother has decided to come and see us on Saturday. She wants to take us out for tea and go to the theatre in the evening. She's got tickets (without asking, which has put Briony on edge already). She does this sometimes – just decides we will accompany her to something. Last time was about two months ago, and my mother wanted to go to visit Berkeley Castle. Luckily there's plenty of space there and one doesn't have to be squished up next to someone as prickly as my mother. Unfortunately, her approach to meeting new people is to assume they are guilty until proven innocent, and she is still viewing Briony with a good deal of suspicion. We've been together for eighteen months, so it's hardly in its embryonic stage. I don't think my mother will ever approve of any of my girlfriends – I'm 'the only child of a jealous and possessive mother', according to Briony. She refers to her as the 'Munster-In-Law', which I have pointed out she isn't, as we aren't married, but Briony just rolls her eyes and says that 'for the purposes of *descriptive cataloguing*', it's fine. Anyway, I feel it's a bit harsh.

'Your mother,' says Briony, – 'is so passive aggressive – she's practically got a PhD in it.'

I can't say I really see it myself. Briony gets quite frustrated when I don't understand what she means. When we were at Berkeley Castle the other week, it was a nice sunny day and all my mother said to her was, 'You should cover up Briony dear – this sun can damage pallid skin.' And then, when we were in the café, Briony ordered a cappuccino which came with a biscotti biscuit. 'Oh,' said my mother, – 'they're very hard, aren't they? I suppose *you* dunk them, do you?' Strangely, instead of answering my mother in a normal way, Briony related the story of King Edward's gruesome murder at the castle in 1327, involving a fetid, airless dungeon and a red-hot poker. Later that evening, Briony said she thought I was probably on the spectrum, because anyone else would be able to 'see what *that* woman was up to, *Alexander!*' She only calls me that when she's angry. I said I was sorry, but I really thought she was overreacting, and that my mother didn't mean any harm. 'She's just making conversation,' I said, – 'I really don't see what's wrong with asking if you want to dunk a frigging biscuit!' The atmosphere was pretty frosty for a couple of days. Then, Briony announced that she wasn't going to let someone's negative energy 'penetrate her aura'. She told me she'd been reading a book called *Don't Kill My Vibe*, and that it was really helping her to 'grow as a person'. She certainly seemed a lot happier, thank goodness. She did try to get me to read it too. 'It'll open your eyes, Alex,' she said. 'You'll be able to recognise the people in your life who aren't healthy for your karma, and then you can protect yourself from them.' I didn't like to say it, but the only negative person I'd come into contact with in the last two days was her. Anyway, the positive energy didn't last long. Someone at work stole an idea she'd had and passed it off as their own. She came home fuming about it, drank a whole bottle of wine and then cried all evening, saying she was going to 'castrate Fergus, the bastard, with a spoon, barbeque his balls and feed them to the cat'. I thought it best not to suggest she re-read the section in *Don't Kill My Vibe,* about 'visualising your aura-shield and letting the bad arrows of harm bounce back off'. Instead, I made her a big mug of sweet tea and let her go to sleep on me, which wasn't as romantic as it sounds, since I woke up with a dead arm the next day and a bad headache. I reckon I'd absorbed all *her* bad karma in the night. She woke up feeling fine saying it was a new day and that she was going for a refreshing run before breakfast. I went to work with a thick head, a worryingly dysfunctional left arm and the inability to stop yawning.

When Friday came, I galvanised what little courage I have when it comes to confrontations and asked the 'old fossil' if I could see him for a minute of his time. Mr Anderson's office is a shrine to the 1930's – he still has a frog-green, leather-topped, mahogany desk with a Bakelite lamp sitting next to it, and a tatty brown tub-chair – the seat of which must have served four generations of Andersons' behinds and has a permanent dip where all the leather has flaked off. The dingy room smells of old tobacco and polished wood, and there's a faint aroma of hair oil. I sat down on the only other available chair.

'Well then Alexander, what did you want to see me about?' Piles of drawings and papers on his desk half-obscured Mr Anderson's face as he sat down in the old tub chair which threatened to swallow him up.

'I, er… I know it's a bit short notice…but, well…I, um…I'd like – if you don't mind…'

'Spit it out, lad!'

'I want to go away next week…'

'Oh, well, I don't think we can spare you – which day?'

'Not a day, Mr Anderson – it would be for, um…for a whole week…'

'A WEEK! You what? You are joking, aren't you? I cannot possibly agree to that, as you well know.'

'Right. I thought that would be the case. My girlfriend wants to go away on a holiday and hoped you would be amenable…'

'We can't start letting staff have holidays willy-nilly, Alexander! Everyone would want to do it, wouldn't they! This company has to run like clockwork. I need to be able to rely on my employees to be 100 percent focussed on their work, not swanning off on holiday every five minutes.'

'Well, to be fair, Mr Anderson, I haven't had a holiday since Christmas, and I was only going to swap it with the one I've taken in August…'

He was scowling more than usual, and his face looked quite purply, so I didn't persist. As predicted, Mr Anderson's position regarding holiday requests was as immovable as a barnacle on a groyne. I decided not to relate this to Briony just yet. I needed to consider my options, and being berated by an angry and disappointed girlfriend wasn't the favoured one.

I left his office with my tail between my legs and went back to my desk in the open-plan design area.

'So, what's going on, then?' asked my colleague, Steve, seeing my unusually disgruntled face.

'I attempted to move a mountain,' I said, sarcastically.

'Oh?'

'I asked for time off next week – an unscheduled holiday.'

'Ah, well, I bet that didn't go down well.'

'Like a bucket of cold sick.'

'Hmm – well, you should have known that would happen.'

'I did, and I still did it because my girlfriend's been putting pressure on me...'

'Women, eh! What are you going to do now, then?'

'I'll have to fess up – tell her I failed to be the commanding, forceful, successful man she wants me to be – that I'm a pathetic excuse for a partner and not worthy of her dwindling admiration and respect…'

'Oh, dear…' Steve sounded genuinely sorry for me. 'Couldn't you just pretend to be ill? Then she'll never know, and you'll retain your hitherto alpha-male status. In her eyes, you'll be a confident, assertive, sex-God, Alex!'

'Keep your voice down, Steve!' I said, looking round. Alice was on the phone, so wasn't listening. Declan appeared to be away from the shop floor, and Mr Anderson was still in his office.

'They can't prove anything, Alex – just tell them you're ill and then go on holiday,' he said, more quietly this time.

'That's not something I would feel comfortable doing.'

'You're too honest. I did it a couple of months ago…'

'Really?'

'Good grief! I had no idea.'

'It's what loads of people do, Alex,' said Steve, laughing. 'You need to grow a pair.'

'Well, that was an eyeopener', I thought, as I let myself into the flat after work. I genuinely had no idea that Steve pulled sickies. I really did feel quite stupid now. Briony was still out – probably having Friday drinks after work with her lairy friends. What was I going to tell her? It's not my style to lie or even be economic with the truth. I decided to shower, get changed, and meet up with Jacob at the *Shovel,* before the inevitable Spanish Inquisition.

'You're scared of her, aren't you!' said Jacob, grinning.

'No! Not exactly…'

'Look, Alex, you can't go on like this – it's not working, is it? You're not happy.'

'I don't know…What am I going to do about this bloody holiday she wants to go on?'

'Look, to be honest, she can't expect you to just take time off work – that's not the real world, is it? You've got two choices. You can pull a sickie yourself or tell her it's not possible.'

'She said she'll go anyway…'

'So? Let her, Alex! You can't just jump to her demands like that. Stand up to her! Man alive!'

'You don't know her – she'll have a face like thunder all next week. She'll be impossible to live with.'

'Well, tell her to get lost, then, Alex – she's the one who's being unreasonable.'

Everything had seemed very black and white at the pub. Somehow, by the time I got home around 9pm, I didn't have the same conviction as I'd had bantering away with Jacob, while swigging back several beers. I needed to eat something too. Briony arrived shortly after me.

'There's a pizza in the freezer we can have,' she said, – 'if you want to share it.' She went and switched the oven on.

'So,' she said, opening a big bag of crisps and putting a couple of beers out on the table, – 'do I need to organise someone to feed the cat next week?'

Chapter 4

Suffice to say, I have been in the doghouse as expected. At the weekend, Briony made an excuse to duck out of coming to the theatre with my mother. I actually think she would have enjoyed the play, although my mother's sister got the wrong tickets. My mother said she'd asked my aunt to get tickets for *As you like it*, but for some unfathomable reason, she bought tickets for a rather controversial play called *Cock,* instead. I don't think my mother enjoyed it very much. She said she needed a stiff drink afterwards. We had supper beforehand at the *Ivy,* which was very good and made up for the rather taxing theatre experience.

'I was hoping to see a comedy,' said my mother on the way back to Richmond in the taxi.

'Well, there were some funny bits…'

'I didn't notice,' she said, glumly. I changed the subject and asked her how the re-configuration of her garden was going. I was tempted to stay overnight at her house, primarily to avoid the cold war going on in our flat, but I had my police training the next day, so I drove home and went to bed before Briony got in. I didn't sleep very well, though – probably subconsciously waiting for Briony to get home, which she didn't. Mr Catkins wasn't happy about this either and showed his disgust by attempting to use my leg as a scratching post while I was eating my breakfast muesli.

I tried not to dwell too much on why Briony didn't come home last night, because the only acceptable explanation would be that she stayed with one of her friends. I did text her the previous evening to ask if she was alright, but at this point there was no response. Last night, I hadn't wanted to give her the impression that I didn't care if she'd been abducted, or fallen in the canal drunk, or was lying in hospital injured or suffering from amnesia or something. Anyway, she did finally respond with a brief text saying; '*I'm fine – see you later*'. You'd think, wouldn't you, that she could have written something a bit more illuminating. I wish I hadn't bothered to be concerned about her now, as she's obviously still annoyed with me.

At least the police think I'm doing pretty well with the training course. Today, we covered some more of the personal safety stuff. I'm getting quite good at the '*elbow strike and finger in the eye*' move. Unfortunately, when we went on to the next set of combat moves, I followed the instructions for the '*knee strike to the groin*' a bit too keenly, and our instructor had to sit down for twenty minutes to recover. He said I was supposed to wait for him to pick up his shield pad first. Anyway, it gave us all time to get to know each other better over a cup of tea. There are six of us altogether – two women and four blokes. Last week, I discovered that some women can be tougher than they look when I chose Kate with the short blonde hair and small stature as my sparring partner – she wiped the floor with me. Sharon is older – probably about forty-five, and to be honest, she's a bit scary-looking. None of the chaps wanted to have her as their opponent, not least in case she fell on them. I got to know her better this week though, and actually she's not really an ex-wrestler (that's what Rick said). Rick is a bit of a wind-up merchant. The other two are twins and very serious – Leo and Theo. Luckily, they aren't identical because that could get very complicated, although their personalities are completely interchangeable. They have no sense of humour at all. Rick reckons they're both a few sandwiches short of a picnic, but I think it's a bit soon to make such a damning judgement. He reckons they misunderstood the meaning of 'Special' in Special Constable when they applied for the training, because when they were asked on the first day why they applied, they both said it was because they wanted to be 'respected and appreciated members of society'. 'I rest my case', whispered Rick, who was sitting beside me. I can't remember what I said in response to the same question, but I think I said I wanted to be a useful member of my community, or something like that. Rick said his dad had bet him that he wouldn't stick at it for more than six months, so he thought he'd prove him wrong. Then he said that half his family were in the police and that he'd been resisting the inevitable. 'It's in my blood,' he said., – 'which is actually blue…' He then showed everyone his arm tattoo depicting a dripping sword with blue drops of blood. 'They ran out of red dye,' he explained to me later. 'I thought it looked cool at seventeen…'

'Why don't you train to be a full-time police officer?' I asked him at the end of the session. He told me he wasn't ready to commit totally, plus he has a girlfriend who doesn't want him to.

Kate said she liked the idea of doing something more exciting than sitting at a computer screen all day and she wanted to get fit. 'She's already fit,' said Rick, under his breath. When the police training officer asked Sharon, she said something that changed everyone's view of her. She said she'd been caring for her mother for ten years and was desperate to get out of the house and meet other people.

Once our instructor, Jim, had recovered from his injury, we all went back to self-defence tactics, which in my opinion, could be very useful whether you're a police officer or not. I have been in some quite dodgy situations in the past, and I could really have done with knowing a bit more about how to handle a potential attacker. It would certainly have been more impressive where Briony's concerned, if I had been able to throw a convincing punch at the thieving scumbag who stole her bag last year, instead of freezing on the spot and shouting 'stop thief' from a safe distance. Not long after, I'm sure I heard Briony on the phone to her friend Jen, saying that a 'chocolate fireguard' was more useful. And then there was the time that she watched the Judo Championships on the TV and tried out a move on me which practically broke my arm. My right elbow still isn't right. She said that if we had another war, I'd probably be amongst the first to perish, and then laughed hysterically. She's not the most sympathetic of girlfriends, I must say. I've been contemplating recently asking her what she sees in me, because I'm not sure she really has my best interests at heart. Perhaps it will be a good idea for Briony to go away for a while. She might even realise she's missing me – it could be a good re-set for our flagging relationship.

'How did it go?' she asked when I got back home in the afternoon. She seemed to be in a better mood.

'I'll show you if you like – we've been doing self-defence. I could show you some useful tips, Briony. You never know when you might need to defend yourself…'

'OK,' she said, pushing the sofa back to make room. 'Come on – show me some moves, you bad boy!' She was smiling in a slightly odd way.

'Let me just get into position,' I said.

'Who's the attacker, and who's the victim?' she said, looking steely-eyed.

'Um, well, for this exercise, obviously you're the victim and I'm going to show you how to stop me from grabbing you from behind…are you ready?'

Sometimes I feel as if Briony is a stranger to me. I had no idea she was so good at fighting. She was so quick, I didn't have a chance to explain to her what to do, and now I'm nursing a great big egg on my head.

'Sorry, Alex,' she said, bringing me a bag of frozen onion rings, – 'this is all I could find.'

'Why didn't you tell me you already had training yourself?'

'It didn't come up,' she grinned.

'It came up just before you threw me against the coffee table…'

'I didn't mean you to bang your head, Alex – that was an accident…' She did have the temerity to look a little sheepish.

'I could have permanent brain damage,' I said, feeling the swollen lump on the side of my head.

'Keep the bag on it,' she said, – 'and don't worry – it'll go down in a few days. I'll make something nice for dinner,' she said in an attempt to mollify me.

So, now I have to go to work with a massive swelling on my head. Great. Not only have I failed dismally to impress Briony, but I've allowed her to – no, *encouraged* her, to physically harm me. What an idiot! Can things get any worse?

I don't think having your girlfriend pitying you is very good for one's ego, or for a successful relationship. I went to work on Monday feeling quite disheartened by the whole situation. The first thing Alice said to me, was: – 'Oh my God! Alex! Is that a brain tumour?' I quickly disabused her of her absurd hypothesis.

'No, Alice – I fell and banged my head.' I did not elaborate – it's bad enough having a reputation at home for being a 'twerp', without people at work thinking the same thing.

'That's a nasty bump,' said Steve.

'I don't think you should meet any clients for a couple of days,' said Mr Anderson, – 'we don't want to alarm people.'

'What does he mean by that?' I said to Steve, when he'd gone.

'Well, it does look quite bad…did it really happen when you fell? I mean, you know – that girlfriend of yours sounds a bit, you know – a bit on the feisty side…'

I stared at him for a second or two. 'What? No!'

'…because you can get help, you know, Alex. You did say she was quite aggressive…'

'Not aggressive, Steve – *assertive!* There's a difference. Anyway, the answer is 'NO'!'

Mrs B.C. rang up again about her tiles. The two fitters who do all our work have now refused to go back there.

'I simply can't understand why those men are being so unhelpful,' she said, when I took the phone from an exasperated Alice. They said they can't re-do the tiling in the time I've allocated, Alexander. I think they're being very difficult about it.'

'What exactly were you asking the men to do, Mrs Bedlington-Clarke?'

'I simply told them they had to finish by tomorrow afternoon. I've got an important viewing – it's already been arranged…'

'Well, the trouble is,' I said, taking a deep breath, – 'is that they had to remove all the old tiles and prepare the wall – that takes much longer than just installing new ones…'

'I've already waited a week, Alexander.'

'I know, but they do have other jobs…' This was plainly the wrong thing to say.

'I'd like to speak to Terence, please.'

'Mr Anderson is busy at the moment – shall I get him to ring you back?'

'No. I wish to speak to him straight away. Go and fetch him, Alexander.'

'I told you,' Alice said, – 'she's on the warpath. You'll have to tell him that Dave and Pete have walked out on her as well.'

'Can't you?' I said, weakly. 'I've already got a headache.'

'Sorry, I'm busy,' she said, answering the other phone.

'I've had a terrible day,' I said, phoning Jacob, after walking to my car. 'Fancy a beer?'

'Bloody hell, mate! What happened to you?' said Jacob as I walked into the bar, – 'that's a stonking Tom Cruise you've got there on your head!'

'It throbs like hell.'

'You make my life seem so dull,' said Jacob, when I told him about my weekend.

'What do you think I should do?'

'About what?'

'About Briony, of course.'

'Dunno, mate. I could ask Lucy…'

'She'll probably think Briony's better off without me.'

'Hmm, maybe…'

'Thanks! I wasn't expecting you to agree.'

'Look, Alex – maybe you're flogging a dead horse. There are plenty of other women out there, you know. It's not as if you're a gargoyle or anything. Lucy thinks you're pretty shagable.'

'Oh, does she? Right…'

'You just need to dress a bit differently.'

'What do you mean?'

'Well, just, you know – jumpers are not exactly the height of fashion, Alex.' He looked me up and down, and took a swig of beer, – 'if you want the honest truth.'

'Not really.'

'And those jeans are out of the ark, my friend. You need to go shopping and get some up-to-date gear. I'm surprised Briony hasn't taken you in hand.'

'She did try.'

'Ah…'

'I hate shopping.'

'It shows,' said Jacob, sniggering. 'You need cheering up,' he said. 'I tell you what, we haven't been on a good old bender since you met Briony. How about next weekend? Briony's away then, isn't she? Get yourself to the shops and buy something to wear that doesn't make you look like a shop dummy in the Edinburgh Woollen Mill. You need to get with the times again, Alex.'

When I got home, I looked in the long mirror in the hallway and realised Jacob was right. I really should make more of an effort. Perhaps Briony's interest in me could be rekindled if I looked a bit more trendy. It's true, I've fallen by the wayside when it comes to keeping up with what's fashionable. It's never been a particularly important part of my life, but I suppose, if women want their partners to look relatively with-it, I could try a bit harder. I decided to take Jacob's advice on board and go shopping after work the next day.

Chapter 5

Something is going on at work, but I don't know what it is. Mr Anderson and Declan have been arguing and there's a tense atmosphere. Steve reckons the Company might be in trouble. Old Mr Anderson certainly seems to be on a short fuse at the moment. Steve was told to improve his turn-around times on his jobs yesterday. He wasn't happy.

'I can't go any faster without cutting corners,' he complained. 'I thought they wanted good quality design! Something is up, Alex. We might have to start looking for new jobs soon…'

'That's a bit premature,' I said to him, – 'I mean, we don't know what the problem is.'

'Mark my words, Alex, something's up and it's not good. I've noticed a drop in the bigger jobs – we've mostly been getting lower end work – cheaper materials and smaller kitchens. Haven't you noticed?'

'Well, I suppose so, but times are difficult right now, aren't they? The property market has slowed up and the cost of living is rising…'

'It's not just that, Alex. We are losing out to Craftisan – it's obvious. Our talents are wasted here, Alex. I'm seriously considering moving on.'

Alice hasn't been her usual self either. I think Declan has been quite short with her a few times this week and she's got a face like a wet weekend. I tried cheering her up yesterday, but it fell a bit flat. She normally likes my bad jokes but this time she told me off for being childish. All I said was 'what do you call a fish with no eyes?' When I said, 'a fsh', she said I should 'grow up'.

Pete and Dave agreed to go back to Mrs B.C.'s flats after a long discussion which involved a substantial bribe – I overheard Mr Anderson telling them that he would pay them overtime rates to compensate them for the inconvenience of having to go back twice. They were told to refer Mrs B.C. to him rather than engage in conversation with her, which would 'not be very constructive'. That's an understatement, I can tell you! Dave told me what happened on-site. I wish I'd been there! Apparently, the old bat was having a purple fit when they said they were knocking off for the weekend and the job wasn't finished. She tried locking them in the bathroom, but they just took the door off its hinges. 'Sorry Mrs, but it's not our fault this job's late,' Pete told her as they stepped over the door now lying on the hall floor. 'We've got homes to go to.' Then, apparently, she told them she was going to ring Mr Anderson, who would not hesitate to sack them on the spot. Dave laughed and told her to go ahead since he could find twenty other jobs that would probably pay better, and he wouldn't have to deal with such 'fucking awful clients!'.

'Oh, my God! You didn't say that?' said Alice at coffee break, as we listened to Dave regaling us with the sorry saga.

'He did,' said Pete. 'You should've seen 'er face!'

'What did Mr Anderson say?' I asked, intrigued to know how this whole appalling disaster was rectified. I mean, how could we recover from Dave telling Mrs B.C. how awful she is? Surely, she would go elsewhere, now?

'Well,' said Pete, grinning, – 'he told her that Dave was suffering with his mental health and asked her to make allowances for 'im.'

Dave gave a rueful smile, – 'I *am* suffering with me mental health working here!'

By Friday, the bump on my head had receded sufficiently to be covered over by strategically placed hair. It has been a very difficult week at work, and it was a relief to go home, despite the fact that Briony was still in an odd mood. She was packing her suitcase when I got in.

'You don't know what you'll be missing!' she said, smiling to herself.

'Well, no, I don't, but I'm sure you'll enjoy yourself.'

'I will,' she said, sounding particularly pleased with herself.

It occurred to me that I hadn't really asked her what she'd be doing all by herself in a cottage on the Devon coast for a whole week.

'What do you plan to do while you're there?' I said, as I watched her pack her best underwear and a rather racy new swimsuit I hadn't seen before.

'Oh, this and that,' she said, evasively. 'To be honest, Alex, I'll just be really glad to get away from these four walls for a bit.'

'Oh, right…'

'You'll remember to feed Mr Catkins, won't you? And don't forget to brush him. I don't want him to be all matted when I come back.'

'Are you going to be alone there?'

'Not sure. I've asked a couple of friends if they'd like to join me, but it depends if they can get away. Don't worry, Alex – I'll be good!'

What did she mean by that? Why would she need to be 'good'? I'm not sure I liked the sound of this trip now – only people who aren't usually good, say things like that, don't they?

'I'll miss you,' I said, as she shoved the last of her stuff into a bag-for-life. She grabbed a bottle of vodka and some tins of diet coke from the fridge on her way out. 'Message me when you get there…' I said as she gave me a very cursory kiss on the cheek and threw her bags into the back of her mini. She got in, waved briefly and drove off up the road without so much as a backward glance. I went back into the flat and suddenly it felt very empty and dismal. Mr Catkins yowled for some food and wound himself in and out of my legs.

'It's just you and me now,' I said to him. He gave me a disinterested look, gobbled his pouch of smelly salmon-meat and exited back out through the cat flap.

I decided I wasn't going to let Briony's lacklustre attitude get me down. I put on some loud R&B, had a hot shower and got changed into my new cool clothes. I poured myself a double Jack Daniels and strutted about for a bit, getting into the Friday night mood. I was ready to party like a twenty-year-old. I've still got the moves, I told myself. I caught a glimpse of myself in the glass panel of the sideboard. I ran my fingers through my hair and gave it a foppish flick at the front. 'Yeah, you *can* look cool, Alex – because you're worth it,' I said to my reflection as I danced a little dance.

'Who the hell are you talking to?' said a voice behind me, and I nearly jumped out of my skin.

'SHIT! Jacob! You nearly gave me a heart attack!'

'Sorry – the door was open, so I just came in. Looking good, my friend!' Jacob assessed my appearance briefly and then demanded a drink himself.

'To old times and new!' he said, clanking his tumbler against mine.

'What did you tell Lucy?'

'The truth – that I was off out to cheer up my old mate, Alex, and I'd be staying out. She doesn't mind me going out occasionally – she just doesn't want to see me again until I'm sober.'

'Fair enough. I can relate…'

‘'What do you mean?’

‘Well. Last time we went out on the town you fell in that trench where they were laying new gas pipes, and it took four of us to pull you out, if you remember!’

‘I don’t remember falling in, but I do remember the next morning when I woke up,’ he laughed. ‘Lucy nearly killed me for ruining all the bed sheets and the living room carpet…’

‘Really?’

‘Yeah! I was covered in orange clay, and I just staggered into the house and went to bed fully clothed, boots and all! Completely ruined the sheets, and the mattress still has a body-shaped orange stain on it – we couldn’t get it out. The footprints across the carpet were the worst. I had to hire a Rug Doctor three times – took me ages to get back into Lucy’s good books.’

‘Do you remember that time we went camping in Wales and that mate of yours from school went for a slash in the night…’

‘Oh, Christ, that was funny, wasn’t it! He woke up the next morning in someone else’s tent. Hahahahah! They called Security, didn’t they? Poor old Hugh – he didn’t know what was going on. Probably still pissed at that time of the morning and they were trying to roll him out of their tent. He was a big lad though…’

‘So, where shall we go first, Jacob?’

‘Well, I’m starving – let’s get some grub at *Spoons* and then decide.’

It was lunchtime on Saturday before I could even face dragging myself off the bed and propelling my reluctant body towards the bathroom. I staggered to the kitchen and gulped down a pint of water and an Alka Seltzer, two Ibuprofen and a Paracetamol. Jacob lay across the sofa, one leg on the carpet, his previously pristine white shirt decorated with food stains and stinking of beer. He already had grey stubble appearing on his jawline. I decided to leave him for a bit and took some more water back to the comforting refuge of my duvet. It was only then that I realised there was someone else in my bed and I nearly dropped my glass. *Shit! Who was it? OK, Alex, be cool, be relaxed, don't make a mountain out of a molehill… but this IS a mountain! Oh crap! What have I done? Right, you need to stay calm…* I didn't remember anything about this. I couldn't see who it was as they had the covers up over their face. I looked around for evidence and saw a blue skirt and cream top dangling over the end of the bed. Still no memory. I could hear breathing now – soft and regular, and I could just see some blond hair on Briony's pillow…*Briony's pillow! Oh my God! What did I do last night? Shit, shit, SHIT!* I went back into the lounge and shook Jacob awake.

'Fuck's sake, Alex!'

'Wake up, Jacob, this is *really* serious…'

He blinked and sat up. 'Oh, man, I feel rough…'

'There's a woman in my bed, Jacob!'

'Oh, really? Good for you mate.'

'NO, NO, NO, it isn't! What am I going to do?'

'Make us all some coffee?' he suggested.

'How did this happen?'

Jacob laughed. 'Well, how do you think!'

'No, I mean…I can't remember, Jacob. I can't remember anything after we left the nightclub.'

'Neither do I, to be honest.'

'Well, do you have any idea *who* that is in there?' I said, pointing desperately at the door to the bedroom.

'Not a clue, mate.'

'If I go and hide outside somewhere, could you get rid of her for me?'

'What, dressed like that?' he said looking at me standing there in my SpongeBob boxers and nothing else. 'You'll scare the children! Anyway, Alex, don't be such a wuss. Just be cool. She might be the woman of your dreams…actually, look at the time – I need to go – Lucy will be wondering where I've got to. I need to get home and get showered. I'll call you later,' he laughed. And disappeared down the hall, banging the door on the way out.

Chapter 6

'Where is he?' A small cross face was staring at me. She came out of the bedroom, now dressed, and was pulling her long blond hair back into a sleek ponytail.

'I'm sorry?'

'Jacob – where is he?'

'Um, I don't know…'

'Thought he'd make an exit, did he? Before I woke up? Scumbag! You're all the same – get what you want and then piss off. Well, he's not getting away with it this time.'

'I don't understand…'

'Well, let me explain – boy meets girl, they have a few too many drinks, boy invites girl back to his place…'

'I know all that – but you were in *my* bed…I'm sorry…what's your name?'

'Maggie. You should probably put some clothes on, by the way. Those shorts are giving me double vision.'

'Oh, yes…look, I've made some coffee. Help yourself while I do that.' I left her in the kitchen and quickly pulled on a tracksuit. When I returned, she'd calmed down a bit and asked if she could make some toast. 'So,' I began again, – 'please tell me why you were in my bed?'

'I didn't know it was yours – Jacob said it was his place. I waited for him, but he went to sleep on the sofa – snoring like an old man, he was.'

'Where was I then?'

'In the bathroom. I thought you'd never come out. I was dying for a pee. Anyway, I just thought I might as well get my head down – I didn't fancy getting a taxi at 2am on my own.'

'Right…so, um, nothing happened, then?'

'What? Oh, you don't remember?' She gave me a cheeky grin.

'No…'

'You danced naked outside, and you were singing 'Dancing Queen', and all the neighbours were looking out of their windows…'

'Oh, God!' I put my head in my hands.

'Hahahahah! I got you there, didn't I!'

'You mean, you're kidding?'

'Course I am! Don't worry – all you did was throw up in the bathroom and then get into bed. You're a terrible duvet-hogger though. I bet your wife gets annoyed!'

'I don't have a wife – you mean my girlfriend. Anyway, how do you know I've got a girlfriend?'

'You don't have to be Sherlock Holmes, love – this flat's full of girly stuff – look at all these cushions everywhere! And you've got a cat.'

'That doesn't mean anything! Lots of blokes have cats.'

'They're usually gay.'

'Rubbish! Anyway, you'll have to get off soon, won't you? I've got stuff to do.'

'OK, well, thanks for the toast and coffee. Tell Jacob I'm gonna come looking for him, though!'

Good grief, that was far too stressful. I made myself another coffee and went back to bed for a bit. I tried to message Jacob, but it went straight to his answer phone. I'm definitely getting too old for nights out like that. Thank God it wasn't me behaving so recklessly. Well, more like a total cad, actually. Jacob's going to get himself into hot water if he doesn't rein it in. If Lucy finds out, he'll swing for it – he can be such an idiot. My phone rang while I was in the shower. I could see it was Jacob's home number, which was a bit odd. I rang it back once I was dressed.

'I think I must have left my phone at your flat, Alex. Could you check?' He sounded pretty cheesed off.

I looked everywhere but couldn't find it and rang him back. 'Sorry mate, it's not here. Have you tried ringing it?'

'Yes, but I think I might have put it on silent.'

'Oh well, maybe you should check the nightclub…'

'Did that.'

'You were pretty drunk last night – it could be anywhere.'

'Yeah, well, I've only got myself to blame.'

'That girl – she's called Maggie by the way, said it was you she was with, not me. She wasn't too happy with you, Jacob. She said she's going to track you down…'

'How? She probably doesn't know anything about me. I'll be fine. What does she look like?'

'Can't you remember anything about her?'

'No, I really can't!'

'Did you give her your surname?'

'I don't know…'

'Well, that's all she needs, Jacob.'

'Oh, shit! Well, I'll just deny everything. Anyway, right now I need to find my phone.'

'OK, I'll let you know if it turns up.'

After I'd put the phone down, it occurred to me how easy it is these days to find someone on social media. Or, he might have told her where he works. Oh, well, it's his lookout. It was time for me to get on with my novel now I had the flat to myself. I needed to make the most of Briony's absence. No time like the present to get on with the creative process of writing without any distractions. Perfect.

I read my next excerpt out to myself, just like Claire from my Authors Group advised, last time we met. She's full of tips and good advice for budding authors like myself. It helps you to notice any mistakes or problems if you read it out loud, apparently. I don't mean to brag, but I haven't really found anything wrong yet. Mr Catkins was stretched out on the sofa nearby, so I had an audience of sorts. He certainly seemed to be listening to me. I'm not sure if cats flatten their ears for improved hearing or for some other reason, but I felt that he was taking it all in, even if his facial expression looked a bit pained. I think that mushed up salmon dinner might be a bit rich for him. Anyway, any audience is better than none:

'She slipped silently into the dark shadows along the towpath, where creatures of the night secreted themselves within the rustling foliage, occasionally making sudden unexpected noises strange and jarring to

her ears. She quickly navigated the walkway by moonlight which cast an eery glow along the rough ground. A cat's luminous green eyes watched her from a high mossy wall up ahead. Its long stripey tail twitched as she approached and the cat waited for her to find the hidden gate, stiff and rusty with lack of use. She ducked under the overgrown ivy and broken, rotting trellis and felt her way along the damp crumbling wall until she found the door – the door to all the secrets and lies that had shaped her miserable life until now.

'What do you think Mr C.? I've put you in my novel! It's only a bit part, but you never know, it could be developed into something more substantial if you play your cards right.' Mr Catkins yawned, closed his eyes, and then farted – an eye-watering silent but deadly one that was quite beyond the pale. If cats could smile, I'm sure I saw a glimpse of one lingering smugly on his fluffy chops. What have things come to that not even the cat is impressed with my wordsmithiness. I've come to realise that to be a successful writer, one has to sacrifice all hope of praise in any form and go marching on steadfastly believing in one's innate ability and aptitude for the task in hand. You cannot be dissuaded from reaching the holy grail – the culmination of all your endeavours. As the ubiquitous Virgil said, 'fortune favours the bold'. 'So, Mr Catkins, I will not be diverted from my mission to become an author, by your pathetic attempt to distract me with your uncouth and foul-smelling vapours. I will simply apply this bulldog clip to my nose, and all will be well.'

OK, so maybe that wasn't the best idea I've ever had. Those clips are brutal. My nose was as red as a beetroot and throbbing like hell. I couldn't write another word. 'Now look what you've done,' I said to the now gently snoring cat. 'How is a person supposed to get any work done round here?' The truth was, that I was finding it hard to focus. Briony's breakfast bowl still sat on the draining board in the kitchen – the spoon welded to the glutinous dregs at the bottom. In the bedroom, her vast collection of female primping and grooming accessories, taking up most of the available space, mocked me from their crowded shelves, and in the lounge, her fleecy blanket, furry slippers, and an open book lay abandoned on the rug. And, to make things worse, Briony had just sent me some photos on WhatsApp, of her frolicking about in the sea, having a great time without me. And who, I wondered, was taking these photos? AND – *that* swimming costume was barely covering anything. I don't want to sound old-fashioned, but I've seen more cloth on a peg-doll. I sent her a photo of Mr Catkins asleep on her slippers in the hope that she might feel a pang of guilt, at least. While I was contemplating the irksome nature of Briony's holiday snaps, my mother rang and left a message. Something about my cousin's wedding coming up. I'll have to listen to it again. I wasn't really paying attention yesterday. I hate these family things – everyone always wants to know when I'm going to 'settle down' and how my 'career's going' and whether I'm investing my money 'wisely'. My mother doesn't help things either. Last time someone asked about Briony, she told them my girlfriend was 'rather flighty' and not the sort to 'stay the course'. When I challenged her about this, she said that long flowing hair was a sign of blatant hedonism, and it wasn't to be trusted. I said to her, 'what about Jesus, then? And Albert Einstein?' She told me I was being obtuse. 'On your head be it,' she said, imperiously. I sometimes think my mother is a bit unhinged, but I'm not one for confrontation, and she *is* getting on a bit. I wouldn't want to be responsible for her early demise, so I try not to antagonise her too much. Briony says I'm a coward, and that I should speak my mind and not let her get away with the things she says. She's probably right, but my mother's got me over a barrel, since she owns my flat. She doesn't let me forget about it either.

I went to bed feeling very dissatisfied with my life. I tried not to look at the photos Briony sent, but I couldn't help it. Perhaps my mother is right about her – Briony does look as if she doesn't have a care in the world, swanning about in 'Devon heaven', flaunting her shapely body at all and sundry. The message she sent with the photos merely said, 'bet you wish you were here!' Not even a kiss or a heart emoji. My headache returned as I turned out the light, just to top things off.

The self-defence training continued on Sunday, with special emphasis on restraint. Speed seems to be key when it comes to restraining a suspect. It was a very enjoyable training session – I particularly liked the bit where you get to cuff the felon and read them their rights. Leo and Theo were a bit slow on the uptake and didn't quite understand that there's a technique to safely manhandling a person and that you can't just shove them to the ground and sit on them. In fact, Jim had to tell Leo to stop throttling his brother as that would count as 'unreasonable force, and hadn't he seen the news recently?' We had good fun doing the role- playing. To be honest it made me think what fun it must be to try and dodge the police with a bag full of loot from the local supermarket (a Tesco bag full of potatoes in this instance). 'I grabbed it in a rush to get out of the house', explained Jim, – 'we're having Gratin Dauphinois for supper.' I must say, Jim's sophisticated food choice took me by surprise. He seems such a gruff sort of chap. Just goes to show, you can't judge a book by its cover. When it was my turn to be the thief, I thought I'd be quite good at running away, and that Sharon would struggle to keep up, but how wrong I was. Sharon must have unseen talents because she caught up with me straight away. She did apologise for being so over-enthusiastic and nearly knocking me unconscious. Jim was quite concerned for a minute or two, until I regained my equilibrium. 'Perhaps a bit less brute force,' he advised Sharon, once I'd stood up and staggered to a chair.

'Sorry,' said Sharon to Jim, – 'I was visualising my poor mum being burgled and I was trying to imagine that Alex was a vicious thieving scumbag, so I went for him. Sorry Alex.'

'No worries,' I said, nursing the second lump on my head starting to appear on the opposite side. 'It's all part of the training.'

'I'll get you an ice pack,' said Kate, disappearing into the kitchen and returning with a blue cloth ice-pad. She wrapped it carefully round my head and tied it on with her belt. I had to sit it out for the rest of the afternoon and just watch everyone else which was a bit humiliating. Plus, I looked like a right plonker, as Rick rightly observed. Anyway, at the end of the day, Kate suggested we went for a drink at the local, round the corner. Jim came along too and regaled us with lots of stories about other recruits and some of the disasters and funny things that had happened over the years. At 8pm, we realised it was getting late, and we hadn't eaten, so we all went our separate ways to go home. Kate was going the same way as me, so we wandered along the road together until we reached her house.

'So, you live in there?' I said, when we got to a large, very attractive Georgian three-story house.

'Yes. Is that so unexpected?'

'Um, no, of course not.' I felt a bit daft. 'I suppose I thought… well… you're quite young. I mean, I'm still in a flat. I haven't graduated to more than one floor yet.'

She laughed. 'To be honest, it's not really mine. I share it with my brother and sister and my parents. Basically, I'm still living at home, to my shame.'

'Oh, I'm sure that's fine. Whatever's right for you.' I wasn't sure how to react.

'It's terrible really,' she said. 'I should have moved out several years ago! By the way, can I have my belt back, please?'

'Oh, no – I've been wearing this the whole time! Thanks a bunch! I must look like a total idiot!'

Kate laughed again, and I noticed what nice teeth she had, and what pretty green eyes she had. In fact, Rick was quite right, what he said about her being 'really fit'.

'How's your head now?' she asked.

'OK, apart from looking like one of the Ferengi from Star Trek…'

'You're a bit better-looking than that,' she said with a smile, as she went through her gate and off up the path.

When I lay my poor battered head down on my pillow to go to sleep that night, I felt an unsettling niggle in my bones. I closed my eyes and contemplated Virgil's quote about being bold. As I drifted off, a Star Trek Ferengi with a huge head appeared and told me I was going 'where no man had been before'. The boundless, desolate galaxy lay before me – an unexplored, vast and frightening place. He told me I should be careful out there in case I was 'phasered' by the humans – an unreliable and primitive species. 'Watch out for their women,' he hissed, – 'they are extremely dangerous, and they take no prisoners.'

Chapter 7

Since the weekend, I've been making quite good headway with my novel. My protagonist is shaping up nicely, if I say so myself, turning into a very complex and troubled woman. Briony asked me a few weeks ago if I'd based her on anyone I know. I told her that my character is an amalgamation of several people I know – a sort of composite of their worst aspects. She narrowed her eyes and asked me outright if any of these composite elements were her. I told her 'of course not! That would be relationship suicide!' She seemed to accept what I said. Secretly though, I have imbued my murderess with a few of Briony's traits, but I don't think she'll ever know. I've had a few more photos – Briony eating ice-cream, Briony sunbathing on a rock, Briony sipping a cocktail, Briony dancing in a nightclub…a bit odd, that – I mean, who goes to a nightclub on their own? Anyway, I've distracted myself with writing and working to avoid thinking about it. The atmosphere at the office is still quite tense – Declan seems to have gone away somewhere, so it's just old Mr Anderson, and he's been in his office most of the time. I asked Alice if she knew anything, as she sits at the reception desk (the hub of the office comings and goings), but she doesn't seem to know anything about it. She does know other things though – like the fact that Jacob and I were out on the town at the weekend, partying.

'I saw you two at the Rave Club,' said Alice, sniggering. 'You two were totally smashed!'

'Why didn't you come and say 'hi'?'

'Well, I was going to but when I looked for you, you'd gone. Your mate was with my friend Maggie. I was a bit annoyed actually – she just buggered off without saying anything.'

'Have you heard from her?' I asked, slightly warily.

'Yeah, I did. She wanted to know if I knew where Jacob lived. She's got his phone.'

'Oh, I see…'

'So, where does he live then?'

'Um, he moved recently. I think he's at his dad's…'

'Oh, well, maybe you could find out.'

'I could, or Maggie could just give it to you, and I can get it back to him – how about that?'

'Well, I think she'll say 'no' to that – she told me that Jacob was a lying worm and that when she finds him, she'll put his balls in a mincer and feed them to her dog.'

'Nice!' said Steve, who was standing next to me, – 'she sounds like a right bunny-boiler. He should maybe change his name, or even emigrate…'

'For goodness' sake,' I said, – 'people should just calm down! It was a drunken one-night stand – not even that, in fact, because nothing happened…'

'How do you know?' said Alice, gawping.

'Because, well – she was in my bed…' They all looked at me waiting for some big revelation. 'I didn't even know she was there, OK! Not until the morning…'

'That's what you say!' said Steve, grinning.

'Oh, Gawd! All I'm saying is that Jacob didn't promise anything – he was pissed and off his head and so was she, and NOTHING HAPPENED!'

'Well, Maggie is upset, so he should apologise.'

Oh cripes! Well, I can't ring him to warn him. I can't go to his house, that's for sure. Lucy would wonder why. I'm really not keen on this perpetual role I have of covering for him. I'm getting too long in the tooth. Why can't he just settle down? He's got a nice wife who cares about him, an OK job, a comfortable home – what more could he ask for? If he's not careful he's going to mess everything up. If this girl decided to go and cause trouble, Lucy might never forgive him.

After work, I drove over to his work and parked along the road. I waited for him to drive out of the carpark and waved him down. I told him to meet me at the usual place.

We sat at the bar in the *Shovel* with a couple of beers and mulled over the situation.

'You'll just have to get a new phone, I suppose – kind of a wake-up call Jacob, isn't it…'

'He looked at me and sighed. 'You're right, Alex. I need to grow up. It's been fun, though, hasn't it!' he grinned.

'I don't know, Jacob – you're the one who fools around.'

'Well, I think I've finally got to accept the choices I've made, Alex, and stop messing around. Lucy deserves better.' He actually looked like he meant it.

'Well, that's really good – I'm glad for you.'

'You should think about tying the knot. It's not so bad, you know.'

'She's gone on holiday without me, Jacob. I'm not sure if she's by herself either.'

'Oh… When's she due back?'

'Sunday.'

'Why don't you go and surprise her, then? You could drive down tomorrow after work. It's a win-win, Alex. If she's on her own, then it's all good, and you can have a nice weekend. If not, well, then at least you'll know.'

'That feels very underhand…'

'No, it isn't! You're going down to surprise her – like any romantic lovelorn bloke would do if he was missing his girlfriend. Aren't you?'

'What?'

'Missing Briony?'

'Um, I suppose so…'

Jacob rolled his eyes. 'I can't help you, then. I mean, you must know how you feel about her, don't you?'

I looked into the bottom of my beer glass for inspiration. None came.

'OK, well, like I said, I can't help you. You'll have to make up your mind one way or the other. By the way, I've been meaning to ask – what happened to you?' Jacob was frowning at the still obvious bulge on the side of my head.

'Hand to hand combat.'

'Blimey, I don't remember getting into any fights the other night…'

'No…it was at police training – role-playing. I was the tealeaf – I had to run away. We were doing safe restraining.'

He looked at my head again. 'I guess your policeman wasn't much cop, then!' He said, laughing loudly at his own joke.

'It was a woman…'

Jacob laughed even harder. 'Oh, Alex, you need to come to the gym with me and do some working out, mate! That's shameful!'

'OK, OK, you can stop now,' I said. 'Sharon is actually pretty strong – she'd give *you* a run for your money.'

'No way – look at these guns, my friend…' he said, flexing his extremely muscular right bicep in my face. 'Seriously Alex, you should come with me – Tuesday nights are the best – that's when the women's hockey team go to work out.'

I rolled my eyes. 'You're relentless, Jacob.'

He grinned. 'Got to get some inspiration from somewhere…'

'I'm not sure I want to embarrass myself in front of a load of super-fit women.'

'Come on Alex, you're getting a bit flabby – I'll help you. You can't let *Slammer Sharon* get the better of you. You'll be a laughingstock!'

'Too late for that,' I said, thinking about Kate's belt and what a plonker I must have looked.

Mr Catkins was waiting to be fed when I got home, and there was a message on my answer phone. I pressed the 'play' button.

'Alexander, dear – it's your mother here…I'm still waiting to hear from you about your cousin's wedding… ' She sounded a bit cheesed off. I rang her back and apologised for my late response. Cousin Harry's wedding is next month, and she wanted to make sure I didn't miss the fitting date for the kilt and usher's suit I'll be wearing. Why Harry wants us all to wear kilts when we're not even Scottish is beyond me. This is obviously his fiancée Julia's idea, and he's just gone along with it. We're all going to look like idiots, if you ask me. I mean, none of us has ever worn a kilt before, for heaven's sake! My mother thinks it's OK because her own mother was half Scottish, and apparently that's enough of a connection, especially since they had their honeymoon on Skye. 'Anyway', she said, – 'anyone can wear the Black Watch tartan. You'll look very handsome.' I sighed loudly. Honestly, if I'd known about it sooner, I'd have tried to talk Harry out of it. Too late now, unfortunately. The other thing she asked about was Briony, and whether she would be attending or not, given that she wasn't always very 'reliable'.

'Of course she'll be there!' I protested. 'She's already bought her outfit.' This was an outright lie, and I instantly regretted it.

'What does it look like?' said my mother, without missing a beat.

'Um, I don't know – I haven't seen it,' I faltered.

'Hmm,' said my mother, – 'I was very disappointed she didn't come to the theatre with us the other night.'

'I told you she was otherwise engaged, Mother. She was sorry to miss you – she loves the theatre…' (another fib.) Steve's comment that I should 'grow a pair' flashed through my mind. 'She does have other commitments, you know – she's got a very important job,' I said. 'She can't just drop everything to accommodate …other people.' I stopped shy of saying 'you', but my mother's sharp intake of breath was enough for me to know it didn't go unnoticed.

'Well, Alexander,' she said, crisply, – 'I hope she can fit Harry and Julia's wedding into her busy schedule. It would be a shame if she was absent on his *special* day.' She emphasised 'special' just to be sure I got the message.

'Don't worry, Mother – all will be well!'

'I hope so, Alexander.'

I have no idea whether Briony will agree to come with me or not, the way things are at the moment. I decided at lunch time today, to go down to Devon after work, as Jacob suggested. There's a rumour going around at work that Anderson's is in trouble financially. Steve obviously thinks that's the case – he's already been applying for jobs elsewhere. I suddenly feel quite sorry for old Mr Anderson. This company has been his whole life and the thing is, there aren't many businesses like this any more, where the service is of such a high standard and has the personal touch. Bespoke design is expensive though, and in these difficult times, perhaps it can't survive. Steve thinks the writing is on the wall. As he says, times have changed, and Anderson's hasn't. He says people want everything cheaper and don't care about quality. But something inside me doesn't want this to be the case. Surely the Craftisans of this world can't be allowed to be the only option for people? Quality products can succeed – I mean, look at Savill Row, Rolls-Royce, Cartier, Selfridges…they don't cut corners or use cheap materials, do they? I bet no one suggests to Jimmy Choo that he uses chicken foot skin to save money. The more I think about it, the more I want to do something about it. It's all in the marketing – you can't just rely on word-of-mouth like the old man seems to think. But how am I going to get him to listen? And, what if it's too late? There certainly seems to be an odd atmosphere at work. Declan is still away, and Mr Anderson practically lives in his office at the moment.

Just before the end of the afternoon we were all very surprised to see Mrs Bedlington-Clarke striding across the shop floor towards Mr Anderson's office. She barely acknowledged us and looked like she was in a foul mood. We heard his door open and close abruptly and then muffled raised voices from within.

'What's going on, Alice?' I asked.

'Well, I'm not sure, but Mrs B.C. rang earlier and was really rude.'

'Nothing new there…'

'No, but she said she urgently needed to speak with Mr Anderson. When I asked her if it was about the tiling, she said 'no it wasn't' – she said it was with regard to the Company. That's all.'

'Why would she want to see him about that, I wonder?'

'Because,' said Steve, – 'she's a major shareholder. Didn't you know?'

'No,' I said. 'Blimey! How do you know?'

'Ah,' said Steve, tapping his nose and winking, – 'I have my sources.'

'Well, what else can your sources tell us, then?' I said, slightly irritated.

'Only that it's been the case for, like, forever…that's why everyone has to be nice to the old bat…'

'Oh, I see.' It all made sense now. Of course! Now my mind was working overtime, trying to second-guess the situation at the Company and what the solution might be – all a waste of time because I still have no idea what's going on.

Anyway, when we all went home, the two of them were still holed up in that stuffy old office.

The drive down to Devon in the evening sunshine should have been an enjoyable experience, but it seems everyone else on the planet had the same idea. I finally got to Mandy's cottage at around 10pm to find Briony's mini outside, but no one in. I texted her but there was no answer, so I went and found a pub nearby to wait for her to contact me. Three pints of beer and two hours later, when she still hadn't responded, I realised this wasn't such a great idea after all. At closing time, I wandered back to the cottage and texted again. Still nothing. Realising by now that I would have to find somewhere to stay overnight, I began to feel annoyed that I'd listened to Jacob's stupid suggestion. Feeling dejected, I imagined Briony laughing and having fun at some nightclub miles away, while I was stuck here wondering what the hell to do next. Then it began to pour with rain – just my luck when I hadn't bothered to bring a coat. I was now over the limit and couldn't drive anywhere. Briony's holiday cottage lay in darkness with no apparent way to enter without smashing a window or jimmying the door locks. Then I spied an open window above the porch roof. What luck! It would be so simple… if I could just find a ladder or something…

'YOU UTTER AND COMPLETE BLOODY IDIOT!' A familiar voice was complaining loudly, as I slowly woke up from a weird dream about falling through space and then crashing onto a strange, spikey mass…

'Where am I?' I heard myself saying. A blurry face floated in front of me and then came sharply into focus. A searing pain in my leg shook me out of my semi-conscious state. 'Ow!' I yelled, – 'my leg hurts like hell!'

'That's because for some crazy reason, you were doing a George Mallory impersonation. What on earth were you doing up there, Alex?'

'Breaking and entering. I was trying to avoid sleeping in my car. Where were you, anyway? I've been trying to call you all evening…'

'Try and lie still,' said a voice, – 'and take these painkillers.' The paramedic handed me a plastic cup of lukewarm water. The ambulance ride to the hospital was not a smooth one. Every time we went over a bump it jarred my leg. It was an agonising journey. I felt sick and I cursed my own foolishness with every painful jolt.

'We must be there soon…' I moaned pathetically.

'Five minutes,' said Briony. I looked at her and realised she was dressed in very little. 'I didn't have time to get dressed properly,' she said. 'I thought you were dead, Alex! You were out cold! Thank God you landed in the shrubbery.'

'Why didn't you answer the door?'

'Because, you idiot, that wasn't *my* door.'

'But your car…'

'Mandy's neighbours let people park in their driveway because her cottage doesn't have space.'

'So, you were in the whole time?'

'Yes. I went to bed early and read my book. My phone was in the kitchen, so I didn't get your messages. Sorry, Alex, but you should have let me know beforehand…'

'I wanted to surprise you…'

'You certainly did that!' said the Paramedic.

Chapter 8

'Sorry for being such an idiot,' I said to Briony as the nurses strapped an ankle brace to my left leg and told me how lucky I was to only have a bad sprain. I didn't feel lucky, though – I felt unbelievably stupid.

'I've ordered a taxi,' said Briony, – 'I don't know what we're going to do about your car, though. I'll have to move it – I can't believe you parked it right across the neighbour's front door!'

'I used it to climb up…'

''Well, it's going to have to stay down here now, unless you can get Jacob or someone to come down and drive it back for you.'

'I'll ask him.'

'You won't be able to go to work for a few days.'

'Probably a blessing…'

'Why?'

'I think something serious is going on – there's definitely a problem.'

'Oh, right…'

'In fact, Briony, I might need your expert PR advice at some point.'

While we waited for our taxi, I told her what Steve had said about the Company.

'I want to save it from the scrap heap, Briony.'

'That's very admirable, Alex, but is it really worth the trouble?'

'I think it is…'

'Where would you get the money from? It might need a *lot* of money. You don't have any…so I can't see how you could really do much…'

'Well, I haven't got very far yet. Until I know what's going on, I can't plan anything. Everyone's dying to know at work, but the Andersons haven't said a word.'

'Why don't you just ask the old fossil outright? You've all got a right to know if the Company's about to fold, Alex.'

'Hmm – well, I suppose I've got nothing to lose…'

'Exactly.'

When we got back to the cottage, dawn was breaking. I swallowed down some more painkillers and we tried to sleep for a few hours.

'I'm getting up,' said Briony around 9.30am. 'I can't sleep.'

'Do you think it would be wrong to shoot at those birds outside the window? They're so noisy…'

'We're not used to it, living in the city,' said Briony, – 'let's go down to the harbour and get some breakfast. Can you walk?'

Briony drove us down and I limped along into the little café where we sat looking out to sea. 'It is really nice here, isn't it?' I said, – 'I'm sorry I couldn't come down earlier. Why don't we arrange to do something in August? We could go abroad for a week somewhere…'

'Maybe,' said Briony, vaguely.

'Don't sound too enthusiastic, will you!'

'Sorry, Alex, I'm just a bit, you know, unsure about my plans at the moment…'

'Right. Well let me know when you've decided.'

Suddenly, a young man wearing torn, faded jeans, with sun-bleached curly hair and a deep tan, bounced excitedly over to us. Briony jumped up and hugged him like a long-lost friend. They chatted for a bit until I cleared my throat loudly. Briony turned round and belatedly introduced us to each other. 'I'm Fin. Findlay Connor,' he said holding out his hand. He smiled widely and asked me about my leg, laughing uproariously when Briony told him how it happened. Then he asked me where my parrot was, thinking himself very witty. I smiled weakly and asked him if his shark tooth necklace was real.

'Oh, yeah,' he said, – 'it's a Megalodon – fossilised – about three and a half million years old. They were three times bigger than a Great White! Awesome, isn't it! It's a

Hawaiian symbol of masculinity going back centuries – they believe if you wear one, you'll be protected from the dangers of the sea.'

'Wow,' said Briony, stroking its smooth surface against Fin's blond furry chest hairs, whilst gazing up at him wide-eyed and gushing about how knowledgeable he was.

I bit my tongue and continued to smile benignly like a mindless fool. 'Your coffee will go cold,' I said to the besotted Briony, in the hope that she would stop ogling him like an infatuated teenager.

'I'd better be going,' said Fin, sensing his time was up. 'Keep in touch, B.' He flashed another smile.

'Who was that?' I said, – 'you seemed very friendly.'

'Oh, just someone I met when I came down. He's good fun – and so interesting. He knows so much about the sea, Alex. He comes from five generations of fishermen – isn't that amazing! I mean, the connection to the ocean and the daily struggle to survive on the open water – it's so romantic, don't you think?'

'Um, not really.'

'I wish I'd been brought up by the sea,' she said wistfully. 'People here are so, I don't know… *real…*'

'Shall we order some food? I'm starving,' I said.

'Oh, yes. And then, we could sit outside, Alex – it's so nice to feel the salty air on your face and watch the waves breaking on the shoreline.'

Good grief! That bloke's had a strange effect on Briony. He's turned her head good and proper. She'll be reciting Alfred Lord Tennyson next. And I strongly disagree with Briony about him being 'real'! His stupid shark's tooth might be, but those gnashers of his didn't look remotely natural to me…

I watched Fin high fiving someone in the distance as he weaved his toned, nut-brown beach-body between the crowds of people on the beach.

'Is that who took the photos of you?' I asked.

'Um, yes, it was,' said Briony, biting into her bacon sandwich. I looked at her, waiting for an explanation, but none came.

'So, what's the deal with him, then?' Briony gazed at me, looking slightly puzzled. 'Is he just a friend?' I asked, pointedly.

Briony grinned. 'You're jealous, Alex!'

'No, well, yes, I suppose so – I mean you seemed very keen just now…'

Briony laughed. 'You're funny,' she said, taking another bite.

'Well?' I persisted.

'He's just a friend, like you said, Alex.' She smiled a little secret smile to herself, and I was none the wiser.

'Do you think you'll be able to swim with your gammy leg?' she asked after a long silence.

'I can try. I brought my swimming shorts with me.'

'Great!'

We spent the afternoon on the beach, going in and out of the sea and dozing in the sun. I tried not to think about Briony's new so-called 'friend', but even when we were making out, I couldn't relax. I kept seeing his irritating, grinning brown face in my mind's eye. I tried replacing him with random objects like a banana skin or a bag of prunes. Beyonce twerking in a black leather thong worked much better, but I still couldn't get rid of the image of his smirking face entirely. Later, at the cottage, Briony commented that I seemed a little distant. I made the excuse that my leg was still painful. She seemed to accept this and was almost sympathetic.

'Don't worry, Alex, it'll get better in a day or two. You've been in the wars recently, poor boy – good job I'm here to kiss it all better! Let's make some popcorn and watch a film. Mandy's got some good DVD's – your choice!' she said, smiling sweetly.

Sunday was spent lying around in bed and going out for a long, lazy lunch down the coast at a pub famous for its crab sandwiches. It would have been a lovely way to spend our last couple of hours there, if Fin hadn't turned up unexpectedly at the same pub. He came over as soon as he saw us, in response to Briony's annoyingly over-enthusiastic invitation.

'Alright, mate?' said Fin, sitting down next to Briony, – 'still lame?'

'It's improved,' I replied, struggling to smile back at his irritating face. I spent the next hour and a half being subjected to an endless supply of fishing anecdotes and tall tales of derring-do. Briony was in his thrall. I honestly don't think they would have noticed if I'd gone to the bar and not bothered to come back. However, I wasn't going to let this bag of wind get the better of me. I mean, some of the things he was saying were plainly absurd. For instance, and I quote; "...we were heading into this *massive* storm..." *(Why would a boat deliberately sail into a storm? Particularly a 'massive' one! Plainly nonsense.)* And another; "...this absolutely *enormous* squid, twice the size of my 30ft trawler, smashed into us broadside and nearly capsized the boat..." *(Really? I don't think so! Hardly anyone has ever seen a giant squid in action and the largest ever seen was around 40ft long – I know because I used to read the* **Guinness Book of Records** *at bedtime.)* He continued with this kind of boastful bollocks for longer than I cared to remember. When I could get a word in edgeways, I asked him when he was going out on his boat again, and 'was it soon?' It went over his head completely, and even when I butted in again and told him we lived in Surbiton near Fishponds Park, which probably didn't contain any fish, but I'd seen some ducks flying around there, he just looked confused and carried on.

'Oh right...anyway B, you *have* to come out on my boat sometime – it'll be *awesome!* Oh, and you, Alex,' he said, as an obvious afterthought.

'I thought he was *NEVER* going to leave!' I said to Briony, when Fin finally made a move to go, saying he had some engine parts that needed lubricating. 'Why was he here? I mean, he must have known we were going to be here...'

'Well, I did mention it to him, but I didn't think he would have time to come as he has such a lot to do on his boat.

His life is *so* cool, don't you think? Imagine not having to sit at a desk, or answer emails or phone calls! I wish I could just sail away somewhere and leave all that behind me. I sometimes wonder what the point is, of me spending my life in a job I don't really care about. The idea of just stepping into a new carefree life is so wonderful – wouldn't that be bliss, Alex! Just think how amazing that would be!'

'So, you'd rather get drowned in the sea and eaten by a shark, then? Or sit on a freezing stone wall in the biting wind mending nets for hours? Come on, Briony, it's not a life you'd actually want, is it?'

'Well, OK, but it still sounds more exciting than my life. By the way, why were you going on about Surbiton? That was so boring and, well, random…'

At home, Mr Catkins initially seemed pleased to see us, then went and sulked in a corner.

'Aw, my poor little furball,' said Briony, scooping him up into her arms and fussing over him. Didn't that mean old Alex leave you enough food?'

'Of course I did!' I said, – 'can't you see how fat he is?' She ignored me and carried on telling him how much she'd missed him. Since I was redundant, I went and got into a nice hot bath and soaked my aching leg. I reflected on what a weird weekend I'd had. It didn't really turn out quite as I'd hoped. For one thing I didn't expect to have to spend half of it in the company of an irritating interloper. What on earth did Briony see in him? Apart from being good at catching fish (and that's debatable), his only other attributes were his tanned abs. Maybe that's the key…I need to go down to Jacob's gym and get some. The hot water was so soporific I dozed off, only to be jolted out of it half an hour later by Briony banging on the door and shouting at me.

'What on earth is it?'

'You've got some explaining to do when you come out of there, Alex Philpot!' she yelled.

She was waiting for me in the bedroom when I entered with trepidation. *(What on earth could she be talking about?)*

'Alex. What. Is. THIS?' she said, holding something shiny up in the air between her thumb and forefinger. She held the object aloft with a look of disdain and fury on her face and glared at me.

'I don't know what you're referring to…'

'THIS, Alex – THIS!!' She shook the object in my face, and I realised it was a silver bracelet with some things dangling from it. 'It's a lucky charm bracelet, Alex…'

'Oh, I see…'

'Only it's not bringing you any luck right now!'

'I don't know what you mean…'

'It was IN OUR BED, Alex! On *my* side of the bed. I have never owned such a thing, so my question to you, is: WHO THE HELL WAS IN OUR BED WHILE I WAS AWAY?!'

'Oh, yes, I see now…I can explain, Briony…'

Sleeping on the sofa was a most uncomfortable experience as it's not long enough. I had to rest my boot brace on the arm and in the end, I slept on the rug instead, where I could at least stretch out. As you can probably guess, Briony did not accept my side of the story, so I am now persona non grata in my own flat – a very sorry state of affairs, I can tell you. It was too late to ring Jacob and make him explain things last night. Mind you, he couldn't remember anything anyway. I will have to get hold of Maggie as soon as possible or my life won't be worth living.

I hobbled into work looking like I'd had a very rough night, which I had.

'Oh, dear…' Alice said, when she saw me.

'Don't ask,' I said, grumpily. 'But I need to ask *you* something…Please could you get hold of your friend Maggie? It's urgent.'

'Oooh, that sounds intriguing…'

'Can you do it today?'

'I'll try. What shall I say?'

'Just that I need to speak to her or I'm dead meat.'

'Oh, dear…' said Steve, when I sat down at my desk. 'Bad weekend?'

'The worst…'

'OK.' Steve decided it was in his best interest not to pursue it.

'I've got an interview later,' he told me at coffee break. Guess where?'

'Not Craftisan?'

'Yep.'

'Oh.'

'I know what you're going to say, Alex, but beggars can't be choosers. I've got a family to think about.'

I tried to immerse myself in a new design idea for a client we've just taken on, but it was really hard to feel motivated. Just after lunch, Mr Anderson suddenly appeared and beckoned me into his office.

'What happened to you?' he said, looking at my booted foot.

'Tripped on the stairs,' I lied. 'Just a bad sprain.'

'Right. Would you like a coffee, Alex?'

'No thank you,' I said hastily. I'd have to be literally dying of thirst before a cup of that disgusting liquid would pass my lips.

'Fair enough,' he said, and sat down heavily in his tub chair. 'Now then, Alexander,' he began, – 'I have to inform you of rather sad news, I'm afraid. You're the first person to know, so I'd like you to keep it under your hat until tomorrow, but we are selling the Company. As from next week it'll be going on the market. We will keep you on full pay for one month, after which time we don't know what the outcome will be. It might be the case that a new owner can be found who is willing to keep the current staff on, but there is no guarantee. I'm sorry, Alexander, but I tried my best to keep things going. It's difficult times….' He trailed off and I could see he was upset.

'My life's going from bad to worse,' I complained to Jacob in the pub after work. 'Briony's refusing to speak to me, my job's about to end and my mother is forcing me to wear the most ridiculous wedding attire known to man….and on top of all that, I'm hobbling about like Long John Silver. Oh, and Briony got herself a new love interest while she was away….'

'Really? That was quick work! So, are you two splitting up, then?'

'Not exactly, but it's not looking good at the moment. I mean, I can't compete with this guy, Fin – she's besotted.'

'What you need to do my friend, is sew a few seeds of doubt in her mind and she'll soon come round.'

'I tried that, but she didn't take the bait.'

'What did you say to her?'

'Well, I asked her if she'd noticed his fisherman's claw-hands or the strong smell of old haddock on his clothes, but she just ignored me and said I was being childish. Anyway, worse than that – she thinks Maggie was with me that night – she found her bracelet in our bed.'

'Well, I can't tell Briony that she was with me – Lucy will go ballistic!'

'You've dropped me right in it, Jacob!'

'Sorry, mate…'

'You'll have to tell Briony, Jacob! Seriously! I've been trying to get hold of Maggie as well...'

'Oh, God...' Jacob put his head in his hands. 'I'm going to be toast!'

'I'm going to call Briony now and you have to tell her the truth, OK?'

'OK.'

Whether Briony believed him or not was hard to tell. I could hear her noncommittal response on the other end of the line.

'Well?' I said, after the call.

'She just said, 'OK'.'

'Is that all?'

'Yep.'

'Well, hopefully I can go home safely now and not get my head bitten off. By the way, you know how you're supposed to be my best mate?'

'Er, yes...I suppose so...'

'I need a huge favour – my car is stuck down in Devon. I couldn't drive it back because of my ankle...I'll pay you, obviously...'

Jacob puffed out his cheeks and reluctantly said, 'OK.'

'By the way, I tied up the passenger door with string last week, because it doesn't work, in case you wondered why it doesn't open…'

'Right…you should get that fixed…'

'I know. Thanks for doing this for me.'

Chapter 9

'£550,000!' exclaimed Steve at morning break time.

'That includes the building…'

'Where will you get that much money from, Alex?'

'Not sure yet…'

'I think you're crazy!'

'Well, maybe I am. If I do, would you consider staying?'

'I don't know, Alex. To be honest Craftisan pay better…'

'Well, I'd be in a position to improve on it…'

'I've already accepted their offer. Look, Alex, you've never run a business before – you don't know anything about it – how will you manage?'

'Well, I know what I want to improve on – I think I could make a real difference to Anderson's future.'

'Will you still call it Anderson's?'

'I think so – I mean, Philpot doesn't have the same ring to it, does it! Anyway, they've built up a good reputation. We just need to capitalise on that.'

'Have you told anyone else?'

'No, not yet – I haven't thought it through properly, or secured the money – don't mention it to anyone yet, will you, Steve?'

'No problem, but I still think you're mad.'

I've been thinking all week about how to get the money to buy Anderson's. My mother is the obvious source of financial support, but I ejected that idea as soon as it dared enter my head. I tried to talk to Briony about it but she's still off with me, even though Jacob explained about Maggie. I don't think she really believes us. Maggie has proved impossible to get hold of – Alice says she's on holiday and won't be back for two weeks. I don't know why that means she can't pick up the phone and call me. I think she's enjoying the drama and all the fuss she's caused.

Police training has been more successful this week. At least I haven't sustained any injuries or embarrassed myself. By the weekend I was able to ditch the boot and almost walk normally again. We covered appropriate use of tasers and PAVA spray but using substitutes, of course. The thought of Leo and Theo being let loose with the real thing is quite a frightening prospect. They were far too eager to pull the triggers on their tasers. Thank goodness it was only foam that was released, or we'd all have been blinded for a week.

I can't count the number of times Jim told them to give the felon (in this case, Rick) reasonable opportunity to comply with the order to put his hands where they could be seen or some such instruction. They seemed to completely ignore the fact that tasers should NOT be aimed at the face or head of the intended target. Rick was most put out about the state of his hair afterwards, which he said was 'ruined' when he was meant to be going out on a date with his girlfriend later on. I must say, there are a few people I'd love to blast with a taser if I ever got the chance – Fisherman Fin comes immediately to mind, followed in quick succession by anyone in a kilt.

After training, we all went to the pub and Jim told us a few more stories about misuse of firearms. According to him, an entertaining but worryingly high number of incidents have occurred in Surbiton alone, over the last two years. It makes you wonder how there aren't more fatalities. Leo and Theo left early, and I asked him what his thoughts were on their suitability to carry a weapon. Jim's reaction was slightly unprofessional – he just laughed his head off, but I had to agree with him. Neither of them has the slightest idea how to deploy their weapons safely. Even using handcuffs seems to confound them. Leo had to be told that cuffing himself to the offender would likely end in tears and the aim was to not only restrict the prisoner's ability to assault a member of the public, but also to protect the officer from further harm. Leo responded by saying that if the offender assaulted him, he'd just spray them in the eyes, to which Jim replied that it wouldn't be within the accepted safe distance of one metre, and he would probably blind himself as well as the prisoner. 'Well, what if I taser him, then?' said Leo, – 'that would stop him.' We all looked at him in disbelief.

'Tasering someone you're attached to would be a really bad idea…' said Jim, seriously understating the possible consequences of such a ridiculous scenario. If nothing else, the twins provide us with a good laugh on a dull day. Kate got the giggles after that and couldn't stop.

'This place cheers me up after a boring week at my desk,' she said, – 'it really does!'

'You should seriously consider policing as a career,' Jim told her, – 'I reckon it would suit you. You've got all the right skills.'

'Aw, thanks, boss,' she said, – 'I'll think about it.' She winked at me and smiled. I'm not sure why she did that, but Rick noticed and elbowed me in the ribs, saying, 'You're in there, mate! You should ask her out.'

'Oh, well, um, no – I've got a girlfriend – she lives with me…'

'You've never mentioned it,' he said, – 'what's she like?'

'Well, she's quite a serious sort of person, I suppose. Very direct. She doesn't suffer fools gladly – and she loves her cat, probably more than me, and she works quite hard…'

'Right,' said Rick, – 'well, she sounds like a right laugh!' As an afterthought I told him she was very pretty and quite stylish, which sounded even worse somehow. I realised afterwards as I walked home, that maybe I didn't feel the same way about Briony as I used to. I mean, I'd just described her as if she was a slightly aloof well-turned-out aunt who came to visit occasionally. Perhaps the shine really has gone off this relationship.

'You're in the doldrums, that's all,' said Steve. It was Monday morning, and everyone knew about the Company's plight. Old Mr Anderson had sent everyone an email on Friday, just in time to ruin the weekend for them.

'I've been thinking about what you said, Alex…'

'About what?'

'Saving Anderson's.'

'Oh, really?'

'Yes. I think you might have a point. In fact, I've been putting some figures together for an initial discussion with you. It's worth considering some options. What do you think?'

Steve and I spent two hours after work discussing the pros and cons of buying Anderson's and what we'd do to transform it, or 'drag it into the 21st century kicking and screaming' as Steve said. We were on the same page entirely. It was the most exhilarating thing that's happened in such a long time, I'd forgotten what that felt like.

I was buzzing by the time I got home and couldn't wait to tell Briony about our plans.

When I opened the front door, I knew straight away that the flat was empty, and when I saw Mr Catkin's food dishes were gone, along with his bed and litter tray, I realised she wasn't just out somewhere. There was a note on the kitchen top which I opened with a heavy heart. It didn't say much, but it said enough.

Alex – I need some space. I don't know whether we are really compatible any more. I think we want different things. I've gone away for the weekend to think things through. I'll be at Mandy's place, and I've got Mr Catkins with me, in case you were wondering where he was. Don't call me – I need to work things out by myself. Bx

I opened a bottle of beer and sat down in front of the TV for a bit, thinking about Briony's note. It wasn't exactly a surprise – I've been thinking the same thing, but she got there before me, of course.

'What do you think?' I said to my fish swimming aimlessly in their tank. 'Have we come to the end of the road? Do I want that to be the case?' They just stared out at me with their expressionless eyes and gormless faces. Findlay, being practically a fish himself, would be smirking his way through a pint of cider at the Sailor's Tryst with Briony hanging on his every word by now. They'd probably be planning a trip out to sea tomorrow so he could show her the ropes and his tackle…Perhaps she'll invite him back to her cosy cottage afterwards. I hoped Mr Catkins would lacerate his stupid face with a swift swipe of a well-aimed claw. I made a conscious decision to stop tormenting myself. It wouldn't do me any good. She obviously thinks I'm not exciting enough. Well, I'll give her something to be amazed by when she comes back. Steve and I are going places. She won't believe it when she finds out. I immersed myself in writing my book for the rest of the evening. In fact, I've had a bit of an epiphany – I need to create the murderer in my own image so I can *really* write from the heart. It'll be more realistic that way – more believable. I decided to change my protagonist to a man: A jealous, enraged, frustrated man. A man who feels life is against him, that he's not good enough, not successful enough – a man who drew the short straw, who is thwarted in love and can't get a break. Now I really think I have made significant progress with my story. I'm at the crucial part where the murder takes place and, I have to say, I did really enjoy writing this bit:

'It wasn't something he'd considered before – the idea of closure by elimination. But the anger and loathing had eaten away at his soul over these last few years, and a plan had slowly revealed itself to him. Now, the plan was no longer a plan – it was a crusade, a quest for deliverance, which he'd set in motion, and there was no turning back. He felt a strange sense of calm when he thought about the next part of his life. He would begin a new chapter, a new dawn. Was it really possible to have a spiritual re-birth and start again? He'd dreamed of such a thing for so long, and now it was within his grasp. He wanted to obliterate the past – expunge it from his mind, and this would be the moment, the final act of retribution. He was as ready now as he ever would be. He smiled softly to himself as he took the knife from its simple wooden box and held it up to the light of the window. It glinted brightly as he turned it over in his hand. He took one last look at it, before he placed it carefully back inside. Dropping it into the rucksack waiting on the kitchen table, he closed the zip and threw the bag over his shoulder. The person he saw reflected in the mirror as he paused in the hallway would be a changed man on his return. He gazed briefly at himself – the blue-eyed blond-headed boy his mother had adored as a child had become hard and cynical with age and torment. His expression, bleak and hollow-eyed, stared back at him, willing him on to do what needed to be done. He opened the door and stepped outside where he would become synonymous with the dark, deserted night.'

In the morning, I got the train into the city to meet my cousin Harry at McDuff's for the dreaded fitting. Despite my reluctance to be as enthusiastic as him about it all, it was good fun and took my mind off Briony. There were five of us being measured up; Harry, his brother Patrick, my Uncle Frank (his dad), and Harry's Best Man, Jack.

'So great to see you,' said Harry, slapping me on the back. Uncle Frank did the same, and then asked how my mother was.

'Same as ever,' I said. He gave me a knowing smile. 'Well, it'll be great to have all the family together, won't it!'

'Yes, it will,' I said, knowing that it would be anything but. My mother frequently rubs the others up the wrong way. Still, I can't let it bother me. You can't choose your relatives, as they say. During the fitting, I told them about my plans to go into a partnership with Steve and what we were hoping to do. Uncle Frank took me aside for half an hour and, to my astonishment and enormous gratitude, he offered to guarantee my half of the money.

'I know you won't want to ask your mother, Alex, but your father would have helped you to do this – I know he would. So, I'm going to do it on his behalf. Your mother doesn't need to know. OK?'

'Wow! Yes – thank you so much. I don't know what to say!'

'All I want, is to be able to check the agreement and go over the figures before you agree to buy, Alex. And then, I'll leave you to get on with it. Of course, I can advise you any time you need. We can discuss details later, but this is what your father would have wanted, and he would have been supportive – I've no doubt about that.'

Back at Harry's parent's house, over dinner, his mother Lauren asked me about Briony, and if she would be coming to the wedding. I knew my mother must have said something to her. I decided to be honest about it.

'I'm not sure. Things aren't going well between us at the moment.'

'Oh, I'm sorry to hear that, Alex,' she said, diplomatically.

'Plenty more fish in the sea…' said Frank.

'Frank!' Lauren said, frowning at him.

'I'm only saying…'

'You don't know how right you are,' I said. 'I'm going to concentrate on my business plans for now, anyway.'

'Quite right,' said Frank, – 'can't let these women folk distract us, can we!' Lauren rolled her mascara-clad eyes and instructed him to serve coffee. He winked at me and disappeared into the kitchen.

'Julia's friends will be pleased to learn there's a single available man at the wedding,' said Harry, grinning.

'My mother will be as well…'

'Oh, so not a fan of Briony's, then?'

'No, but that's no surprise. I don't think anyone would be right.'

'Your mother is a tricky customer…'

'You can say that again, Harry. By the way, just out of interest – why are we wearing kilts?'

'Julia's idea. I'm just going along with it. Gotta keep 'em happy! Now, I vote us lads all go down to the Frog and Fiddle. What do you think?'

I caught the last train home and went to straight to bed. For the first time in ages, I fell quickly into a deep, contented sleep. Uncle Frank had changed the course of my life, just like that! Now all I had to do was make sure it was going to be successful and that I didn't make a massive pig's ear of it. No pressure at all, then…

The only good thing about Briony's absence, was that I could make some more decent headway on my novel. Having the time to spend getting into the mind-set of a cold-blooded killer like my main character has been really useful. With everything that's going on in my own life right now, I think I can really identify with his motives and get into his head. So, now I'm at the point where my protagonist has committed the final act of murder and I'm going to go back in time to write the back story and all about what led up to this terrible crime. I am wondering whether to change the murder scene. Jealousy is a powerful and dangerous emotion, especially when it comes to relationships. I'm doing my best not to let Fisherman Fin get under my skin too much, but I can see how, if I allowed myself to dwell on it, my imagination would run wild and it would be possible, given the right circumstances, to bludgeon him to death with a fishing mallet and feed him to the seagulls, or I could wait until he falls asleep drunk on rum or whatever it is that sailors drink these days, roll him up on one of his rotting fishing nets and cast him out to sea like a giant chorizo. I was really enjoying this game of fifty ways to kill a cuckold, when the phone rang. It was my mother wanting to know how I'd got on at McDuff's.

'Splendid!' I said, – 'it was a great success.'

'Oh, good,' she said, a little taken aback by my unusual over-enthusiasm for clothes-shopping. 'In fact, it was a most exhilarating experience, mother.'

'Now you're being silly!' she said, tutting. 'How was your Uncle Frank?'

'Very well. He was on good form.'

'And your aunt?'

'She was fine. They all asked after you.'

'I wanted to ask you, Alexander, what colour Briony's outfit is – for the wedding? I don't want to be too similar.'

'Oh, well, I'm not sure…I don't know if she's even coming, Mum…'

'Oh, really?' My mother sounded almost cheerful. 'Why?'

'We're not getting on very well right now.'

'Well, I'm not surprised, Alexander. I've always thought she wouldn't stay the course – girls like her have no loyalty – no integrity, Alexander. You need to find someone who is more sincere in their intentions, not a flibbertigibbet…'

'I think that's quite uncalled for Mum – she's not like that…'

'I'll make my own mind up about that, Alexander, and we'll say no more about it.'

When my mother rang off, I noticed there was a message on the answer phone:

'Do you know why Briony isn't answering her phone, Alex? Please can you call us?' Briony's mother's voice rang out in the particularly shrill way of a worried mother. I summoned up the courage to call her back, and she answered immediately. 'We can't get hold of her, Alex. I know she's in Devon, but she's usually quite good at returning my calls…'

'I don't know why she isn't answering – she's not answering mine either.'

'Well, that's not surprising, is it Alex? Under the circumstances.' She sounded tense and accusatory.

'You know *she's* got someone else, don't you?' I said, trying to defend myself.

'No, I didn't. Are you sure about that?'

'Look, I'm sorry, but I didn't want to be the one to tell you. Really, I didn't. He's a fisherman called Findlay Connor. She likes him because he's a free spirit, unlike me, who, according to her, is 'a stagnating old fossil'.'

'Well, if you hear anything, please call us at once, Alex!'

'Of course.'

I've always got on alright with Briony's parents. I think they quite liked me. Until now, of course. Briony will kill me for telling them about Findlay when she finds out, but I don't see why I should be getting the blame. Anyway, it might all be a storm in a teacup. As Shakespeare said, "*The course of true love never did run smooth*".

I went back to inventing ways to dispatch my victim with renewed vigour and then decided I was in exactly the right mood to write the murder scene for my book:

'His entire body prickled with the tension and anticipation of what he was about to do. He held out his hand in front of him and watched it tremble with nerves. He willed it to stop. 'Mind over matter – that's the key,' he told himself. 'Just stop and breathe. Take stock. There's no rush…' Hiding next to a row of overflowing bins behind a disused storage unit, he listened out for the familiar sound of the footfall of the man he'd waited half a lifetime to confront. Soon, the erratic clunk-clack of cowboy boots weaving along the pavement signalled that the old bastard was approaching the ally-way, just as he always did. Just as Axel's younger self remembered. The sound of it made him instantly nauseous. It was burned into his brain like a hot iron branding a Longhorn. As a young boy, he heard it from his bedroom window up in the eves – the sound travelling along the road from the late-night drinking sessions in the local pub. He knew the drill – an endless repeat of the same scenario every Friday and Saturday night, sometimes more frequently: faltering footsteps, door key fumbling, staggered clumping up the stairs, shouting, screaming, banging, then the horrible silence when he lay awake wondering if his mother would be alive or dead in the morning.

The sound of the heavy boots came nearer, and he saw the silhouette of the now bent old man as he steadied himself against the wall at the entrance to the narrow lane. He saw his chance and he briskly followed behind. It was the look on his father's face that threw him. The murdering old bastard actually smiled at him in recognition, until he realised that the strange feeling in his stomach was his haemoglobin flowing away from his ravaged body like an open tap.'

Later on in the day, Jacob turned up with my car and we sat and watched the cricket on TV for a bit. I decided to tell him about my plan to go into business with Steve.

'I hope you know what you're doing – I've heard some bad stories about partnerships that go wrong, Alex. You need to be really careful.'

'I know. It's OK, though – my Uncle Frank is helping me. He's a retired lawyer. Steve is a good egg – we should be able to work most things out.'

'Well, good luck with it, mate – it's about time you got out of the rut you've been in. What does Briony think?'

'Ah, well…I don't know. She's not here.'

'Oh. Where is she, then?'

'In Devon. Probably cosying up with a bloke she's only just met who she thinks is the best thing since pickled herring.'

'Oh dear. Well, I always thought she wasn't right for you…'

'What do you mean by that?'

'Well, you know, she *is* a bit stuck up…'

'Not really, Jacob – she's just a bit more serious than us – probably more mature.'

'Well, she's not much fun, is she?'

'Life isn't just about having a laugh, Jacob…I mean, you can't tell me Lucy's a laugh a minute…'

'No, true enough – well, she used to be when we first met.'

'People change, Jacob – except maybe you haven't!'

'Well, I'm going to have to grow up now. I just found out that Lucy's pregnant. She's known for ages but didn't tell me.'

'Oh, cripes! Really? I mean, um, well done! That's amazing, Jacob! Congratulations!'

'I don't know, Alex – I'm terrified, truth be told! I'm not ready to be a dad…'

'Well, you've been together for ages now. You'll get used to it – you haven't got much choice anyway! Whether you like it or not, it's happening. When's the due date?'

'December some time.' Jacob looked worried.

I couldn't help grinning at him. 'No more clubbing and boozing for you, then!'

'Do you fancy coming to the gym with me? We could go now and have a drink after…'

The gym is never my favourite place – too many sweaty bodies and testosterone flying around. Still, I thought I ought to show willing, and I did feel better afterwards. We both showered and made our way to the Shovel which was quite busy for a Sunday.

'We've got a party going on,' said the barman.

'Shall we go somewhere else?' I said to Jacob.

'No, it's fine. I don't mind a bit of noise. So, what are you going to do now?' he said when we sat down by the window.

'About what?'

'Briony!'

'Oh, I don't know. Nothing, I suppose.'

'Can I suggest something?'

'Your last suggestion got me into a load of trouble, if you remember. My ankle is still aching and swollen up like a marrow.'

'Well, I didn't tell you to climb on someone's roof, did I? Or to fall off it, either!'

'No, obviously not…'

'Anyway, at least you found out what she was up to, didn't you?'

'Um, well, not exactly…I still don't know what's going on between them. She's being so elusive.'

'Well, I reckon that tells you everything you need to know, Alex. She's having a fling with Fin, and you'll just have to move on with your life…'

'Yes, perhaps you're right.'

'I am. Fancy another beer?'

Chapter 10

The thing is, I'm not ready to tell Briony to go yet. I'm going to do it in my own time. Anyway, I've got to focus on the business plan. Steve and I had such a lot to discuss this week, I've got figures and ideas coming out of my ears. When we told old Mr Anderson, he was really chuffed –

surprised but obviously pleased. He asked if we would keep the staff on, but Steve says it would be better to have a clean slate. He reckons they won't be able to take instructions from us – particularly Alice. We told Mr Anderson we didn't know yet. Uncle Frank suggested we get someone to negotiate the sale on our behalf to keep things professional and avoid any pressure to agree to things we shouldn't be agreeing to. Steve and I are making plans and I wish I could tell Briony all about it. She still hasn't come back and it's now Wednesday. I rang her work eventually and they said they were expecting her in on Tuesday but hadn't seen her. Now I'm starting to worry that she was serious about jacking everything in. It's not like her to fail to turn up to work. I rang her parents, and they had no idea where she was. Then I rang Mandy, and she told me Briony was supposed to be out of the cottage on Monday morning. She asked her cleaning lady to go round and check it out, promising to get back to me.

Mr Anderson has started to clear the office of all the old paperwork and years of junk that's been hanging around. He asked me to help him shred a lot of it and take it to the tip. It's not really in my contract to be a dog's body, but I felt sorry for him. Declan seems to have disappeared completely just as there's loads of work to do clearing the place up. Annoyingly, I cut my hand on a broken mirror and got blood all over the back seat of my car before I realised. I think it's time to get rid of my car anyway. It's not worth anything much. Amongst the rubbish I found a brass letter opener which old Anderson obviously didn't want, but it was quite a nice thing. I kept it as a sort of keepsake and slipped it into the glove compartment. Anyway, now I'm going to be a Business Owner, I'd better buy something a bit more impressive than my very old Renault. That's what Jacob says, anyway.

It's hard to focus on work with all this worry. She's probably just swanning around with that idiot on her arm and ignoring her phone, or worse – maybe they've run away together to escape everyone and create a new life together. A life unfettered by trivial things like working and paying bills. I can just imagine what he's saying to her: *'Don't go back to that boring existence with your loser boyfriend. Stay here with me and be wild and free. We can live off the land and the sea – we only need each other, Babe. Let's take off and leave it all behind…(or some such other bollocks).* I pictured them sailing off into the orange sunset, wind in their hair, the setting sun on their smug faces…

'Alexander…' I was abruptly distracted from these odious imaginings by Mrs B.C. bending over me at my desk.

'Oh, hello Mrs Bedlington-Clarke – how are you today?' I stood up and pushed my chair back.

'Well, Alexander, that is a very good question.' She eyeballed me from beneath her stiffly coiffed hairdo. 'I'd like to discuss your plans, if you have a moment…' She looked down at a half-eaten biscuit sitting on my latest drawing next to the coffee cup holding the corner down. I quickly removed the biscuit and asked if she'd like to step into Mr Anderson's office. 'Where is Steven?' she enquired.

'Oh, he's out measuring up somewhere. Would you like a coffee?' I asked.

'No, thank you.'

'So, how can I help?' I motioned for her to take a seat and sat down myself in old Anderson's tub chair behind his desk.

'Don't get too comfortable there, Alexander,' she admonished me, – 'you're not in charge yet!'

'Oh, yes – sorry…'

'I just want to ask you a few questions about how you intend to run things if you take over. You may not know it yet, but I own 60% of this business. My late husband, Alfred Bedlington-Clarke, founded this Company, you know, along with Terrence, who was his very good friend – they met at Edinburgh university when they were studying architecture together.'

'Oh, right…'

'Of course, Terrence makes all the decisions about managing the Company, Alexander, but I hold the purse strings.'

'I see.'

'I haven't been happy about the Company's dwindling profits, Alexander. I have great hopes for you and Steven though.'

'Do you?'

'Of course! However, in order for me to agree to sell, I need to discuss a few things first.'

'Um, I think we should wait for Steve to participate in any discussions about the future of Anderson's, Mrs

Bedlington-Clarke, much as I would love to hear your thoughts…'

'Very well, Alexander. I'm sure that's quite correct, but if I could leave you with one little thing to talk to him about, that would be most helpful.'

When Steven came back into the office later on, I grabbed him straight away to tell him about the peculiar request Mrs B.C. had made.

'You're kidding me!' he said, spluttering out a mouthful of tea.

'I know! It's bizarre isn't it!'

'So, where does she want us to put this ginormous statue of her late husband, then?'

'Right by the front entrance so people see it as soon as they enter the building.'

'And…she wants us to re-name the Company, '*Bedlington-Clarke'*. She wants it stamped on every kitchen cupboard and work surface.'

'I suppose it sounds better than 'Philpot Pratt'…couldn't we just agree to it and then do what we like?'

'Hmm…I'm not sure where we would stand on post-agreement default. Frank says we might end up being in breach of contract.'

'Sounds like we're a bit stuffed, then. We'll have to sleep on it.'

Mandy rang me in the evening with worrying news. Apparently all Briony's things are still in the house, and the housekeeper, Mrs Parker, said that she'd had to feed a rather grumpy and hungry cat, as well as clean out his litter tray. It beggars belief, really. Fancy going off like that and leaving poor old Mr Catkins to fend for himself. It just shows you how selfish and thoughtless she's being. I suppose I should consider the unlikely prospect of our relationship surviving this state of affairs. It's staring me in the face. I decided to bury myself in writing my novel in the evening, just to get my mind off everything. It's quite useful in a way though, to feel aggrieved like this, and rejected by Briony. I can use these emotions to write something powerful and gripping.

I wrote 5,000 words in two evenings and it felt amazing. I was mid-flow last night when Mandy rang me again.

'Alex, I'm really worried about Briony. No one has heard anything from her. We can't get her on her phone. We need to call the police.'

'Oh, well, I suppose that might be a good idea…'

'What on earth do you mean by '*might*'? She's been missing for three days now, Alex! Aren't you concerned?'

'Well, she's probably just gone off with a man that she met the other week – a fisherman called Findlay Connor. She was very smitten and talking a lot about being free from her boring life and chucking it all in…'

'But something might have happened to her – we need to call the police right away! I can't believe you're not worried about her!'

'Well, to be honest, I'm pretty pissed off with her if you must know. If she wants to go off gallivanting, that's her look out…'

'Alex, be serious! I'm going to call the police right now. There's no way she would have gone off and left Mr Catkins like that. You should know that at least!'

I think it's an overreaction on Mandy's part to call the fuzz. Briony will be mortified when she finds out. Oh, well, better to be safe than sorry, I guess. I went back to writing a bit more of my book before bedtime and was particularly pleased with the last paragraph:

The river, as still as a millpond, shone in the moonlight like thick, black glass. The night was eerily silent, broken only by the splash of water against his feet. The bag was heavier than he'd imagined it would be, and he struggled to drag it down the uneven, muddy riverbank. Axel tried to hide himself within the shadows of the trees which clung to the shoreline like wispy stick men, leafless and sparce. He felt vulnerable and anxious. Someone might see his dark shape moving in the dim light. He needed to hurry. Sliding the bag down into the water, he pulled it behind him. The holes he'd stabbed into the plastic soon began to suck in the ice-cold water. He pushed it further out and then watched it slowly start to sink. He instantly regretted tying the bulky bag with white string, which stood out sharply in the bright light of the moon. Making his way back up the bank, Axel hid behind a tree and watched it finally disappear beneath the surface. Like a log, it rolled and tipped before it dropped to the riverbed and found its resting place. Relieved, he quickly returned to his car. Sweat had broken out on his brow. He wiped it quickly away with his sleeve. Lifting each foot, he removed the carrier bags he'd tied to his ankles and put them inside another bag. He would have to make his way home again along the narrow country roads to avoid any cameras, where it would be very unlikely that he would meet any people at 3am in the morning. At his house, he parked at the front instead of driving onto the gravel, to avoid making any unnecessary noise. He would clean the wheels in the morning when no one would think twice about it, especially since the wet weather was creating a lot of mud on vehicles everywhere. He would need to get rid of the plastic bags he'd used to walk on the muddy ground by the river and take his clothes and gloves to the tip. By the time anyone could check, these things would be long-gone, mushed up with thousands of other bits of detritus and tons of household waste. Axel thought about what he had done and surprised himself that he felt no remorse. There was no sudden pang of regret or creeping realisation of the enormity of his crime. In his mind his actions were clearly justified. His only fear was the possibility of being caught. He'd planned everything meticulously and gone over every step many times. It was watertight. He smiled when he thought about the use of that word 'watertight'. How apt it was! How perfectly pertinent. He would sleep soundly for the rest of the night and awake refreshed – his new life ahead of him with nothing to cloud his thoughts or darken his mood.'

Before I left the house this morning, Mandy rang me again to say the police wanted to speak to me about Briony. Obviously, they are taking her disappearance seriously. I must say, I *am* beginning to worry a bit. Mrs Parker rang me last night and asked me to come down tomorrow to pick up Mr Catkins. Apparently, he's been tormenting her pet budgie, Cyril, and she's worried about her feathered friend's 'mental health'. She said she can't take the risk of letting him out of his cage for fear of him being gobbled up, or worse. I've never understood the attraction of keeping a bird as a pet. They make loads of noise pecking at their irritating bells and mirrors, and if you let them out, they fly around all over the house, pooing on your furniture. I suppose some people feel they're conversing with them if they can squawk back at you with a '*hello pretty boy'* or something, but you'd get a better conversation from Alexa and at least she can tell jokes. I noticed, while I ate my muesli this morning, that one of my fish has developed an unsightly bulge. I suppose even keeping fish isn't plain sailing.

The police rang me at work, which was a bit embarrassing since I hadn't told anyone except Steve. Alice was most intrigued and was itching to know what it was all about. Steve said I should tell her, or she'd make her own mind up about it and before you could say 'knife', I'd be branded as a 'wanted' man, so I told them all at morning coffee break.

'Oh, no!' said Alice. 'How terrible! I hope she's found soon!'

'Well, I'm not sure Briony is actually a missing person in the strict sense…' I said to her, – 'she was talking about leaving the rat race and being a free agent before she went missing, you know…'

'Oh, right. Still, it's a bit strange not to contact anyone at all, isn't it?'

'Have you seen anything of your friend Maggie?' I said, changing the subject.

'Not for ages. She's still mad at Jacob, though.'

'I don't get it. Why doesn't she just forget about it and let bygones be bygones?'

'Oh, she's terrible like that – she'll carry a grudge till doomsday!'

'Oh, great! Well, Jacob's wife is pregnant, so I think she should just leave him alone now. Also, I've got her bracelet which she left at my flat, so if she wants it back, I'll do a swap with his phone. Will you let her know, please Alice?'

'OK, I'll tell her when she comes back form Corfu.'

'I wouldn't mind a holiday,' said Steve, – 'Things are going to get pretty busy for us soon. You've got one booked haven't you, Alex?'

'Yes, but things are all a bit up in the air – I don't know if I should take one, to be honest…'

'I'm not going to enjoy my holiday now,' said Alice, – 'I've probably got to look for another job, haven't I?'

'Um, well, there's a lot to sort out, Alice. I'm afraid,' I said, playing for time. 'We will know more next week. We'll be informing everyone here about their redundancy packages.'

'I won't get anything because I'm too young and I've only been here two years…'

'Well, let's just see what happens next week, Alice.'

'This is going to be quite difficult,' said Steve, later on. 'It's not great, is it? Giving people notice, I mean.'

'I know. I don't like it either. Maybe we could give Alice something anyway – you know, for goodwill.'

'Yes, I don't see why not.'

'I don't want to lose the fitters, though, Alex. They're very skilled and we have a good working relationship. We need to make sure they don't walk.'

'Yes, agreed. Do you want to give them the heads up that they'll keep their jobs but tell them to keep it under their hats until next week when we can make everything official?'

'Will do.'

'How long have Pete and Dave been with us?'

'About fifteen years…'

'Ok. I'll speak to the negotiator chap tomorrow. I think Frank said he's called Gordon.'

There are so many things to think about at the moment, my head is spinning. This business with Briony has upset everything. I think I just don't want to think that anything bad has happened to her. I'm probably 'in denial', as Briony would say if she were here. After work, I jumped in the car and drove straight down to Devon to fetch Mr Catkins. Mrs Parker brought him to the car in his basket carrier as soon as I arrived. I think she couldn't wait to get rid of him.

'There we are, all nice and snuggly…' she said, dumping him on the back seat of my car. Then she noticed all the blood. 'Oh! My goodness! What happened there, then? It looks really nasty…'

'I cut my myself on some glass,' I said, showing her my bandaged hand.

'You should clean that up – it's not hygienic,' she said, looking a bit disgusted.

'I know, I just haven't had time. Have you heard anything about Briony?'

'No. We're all very worried about her, though…I can't move any of her stuff, you know. The police have asked me to leave it all where it is for now.'

'Have you heard of a man called Findlay Connor? She was with him a lot when she was down here.'

'Can't say I have. Sorry.'

'OK, well, thanks very much for looking after Mr Catkins. I'm very grateful.'

I decided to park at the beach front and make some enquiries about Fin Connor since I was here. I'm pretty sure she's going to be with him. Hope Cove is not very big, so it didn't take me long to ask around. A couple of old fishermen called Seth and Brin said they knew him. They looked as if they'd spent a lifetime on the ocean waves. I bought them a pint each to help things along.

'I'm looking for Findlay Connor. Do you know him?'

'Yep, we do…'

'It's my girlfriend who's gone missing and I'm trying to find him…'

'The police 'ave been round 'ere all day,' Seth said, – 'most exciting thing to 'appen down 'ere in a long while!'

'Yes, that's true. We 'aven't seen so many coppers round 'ere since Irene McGill killed 'er mother-in-law with a mattock. Terrible business, that was…'

'Oh yes, terrible… I knew 'er y'know…'

'What, old Mrs McGill?'

'Yep. Nasty old so-and-so…I don't blame 'er daughter-in-law for doing 'er in one bit…'

'Have you seen Fin Connor, though?' I said, repeating myself.

'Well now, I think I seen 'im laaast week. Didn't 'e say 'e was takin' his boat out on Sunday, Seth?'

Seth pulled on his scraggy beard and thought. 'Well, I thought 'e said 'Monday'…'

'No, no, it was Sunday – definitely Sunday…'

'What's his boat called?' I butted in.

Again, Brin wasn't sure. 'I think it's *Sweet Caroline…*'

'No, no, that's Taff's boat. I think Fin's is called *Cleopatra…*'

'No, I don't think that's right,' Brin interjected, – 'I'm sure it's *Jezebel…*'

'Look,' I said, is there anyone else around here who might actually know him?'

'Well, you could ask the barman over there. That's 'is cousin, Jerry…'

I rolled my eyes internally. 'Right – thanks.'

Jerry was more helpful and told me Fin sometimes kept his boat at Salcombe. He told me it was called *Calamity Jane.*

'That's about right,' I said, in response.

Jerry laughed. 'Well. I wouldn't argue with that! Why are you looking for him, if you don't mind me asking?'

'My girlfriend is the girl who's gone missing, and she was with him quite a lot, last time she came down here. I wondered if they might be together.'

'Oh, really! The police were in here today questioning people about her – they gave me this photo to put up…' He got it out and showed me. When I saw it, I realised that Mandy must have given it to the police to hand round. It was one I hadn't seen before. Briony looked so happy and carefree, standing on a clifftop with the wind in her long soft hair and the sun on her smiling face. I suddenly felt a wave of terrible sadness overcoming me. It was all getting too serious now. Jerry noticed and told me to take a seat. He reached up for a bottle and poured me a small glass of whisky. I didn't like to tell him I hate the stuff, but he was being kind, so I accepted it and had to sip it slowly. Even then, I was trying not to cough.

'Look, Alex, my cousin Fin was always a bit of a wild child, and he hasn't really changed. We never know where he is or when he's coming back. We don't know much about his life or his relationships, and he prefers it that way. I've tried to ask him about what he's been doing or where he's been, but he just fobs me off. I've given up asking, to be honest. I haven't seen him since Wednesday, when he came in for a pint. He was on his own, and we just chatted about fixing up his boat.'

Salcombe was still busy as night fell. The orange lights around the harbour twinkled on the rippling water as the warm breeze blew across the seafront. It was a calm evening, and I could taste the salt on the sea air as I walked along by the moorings, trying to find *Calamity Jane* in amongst hundreds of boats of all different sizes and shapes. Jerry had told me it was white with a blue stripe – just like most of the boats I could see. I remembered Fin had said it was 30ft long but knowing him that could easily be an exaggeration. I looked for ages and then had to give up when I suddenly realised that I was starving and made for the Ferry Inn, just in time to order food. Overlooking the harbour from my table, I watched all the boats bobbing about in the twilight and wondered if Briony was out there somewhere, under the silvery moon and stars, sailing away to foreign lands, planning a new 'awesome' adventure with the Wild Man of Hope Cove. My fantasy was broken by a plate of sausages and mash arriving, and I took the opportunity to question the waiter about Findlay and his boat, but the young man didn't know anything. A woman perched at the bar on a high stool overheard our conversation though, and turned to chat while I ate.

'I know Fin Connor,' she said, slurring. 'Slippery as a hagfish, that one!'

'Oh, what do you mean?'

'Well, he's a double-dealing snake is what I mean.'

'Have you seen him recently?'

'No, but if I do, I'll wipe that stupid grin off his face for good.'

'What did he do?'

'It's what he didn't do – that's the problem.'

I looked at this hard-looking woman – mutton dressed as lamb with her leather mini, umpteen jingling bangles and maroon hair, and I wondered whether I could trust what she was saying since she was obviously extremely drunk.

'What do you mean?' I tried again.

'He was supposed to be selling his boat to my partner. Four weeks' ago, my Clive gave that scumbag a holding deposit – *THREE GRAND* he gave him. And now he's nowhere to be seen. He was supposed to be handing the boat over this week. He's done a runner, hasn't he! I'm telling you, he's a crook. He won't get away with it, mind…'

'Have you informed the police?'

The woman cackled, – 'No! My Clive's got other plans that'll be more *effective* if you get my meaning.' She asked the barman for another drink, and I decided to pay my bill and make good my escape.

Chapter 11

I spent all this morning in the police station answering questions about Briony. They asked me some quite odd things too – like, 'how would you describe your relationship?' and: 'Do you consider it to be a healthy one?' When I joked about Briony arm-wrestling me to the floor and banging my head, they didn't see the funny side at all. I even showed them the evidence, which is still a red lump on the side of my head. 'I see you have another lump on the other side,' said one of them. Then, of course, I had to explain about Special Constable Police Training, and I saw them give each other a funny look when I'd finished. I probably shouldn't have told them about the time I nearly blinded Briony when we were playing with her nephew's Nerf guns in the garden, either. 'Does this sort of thing happen often?' They asked. I wish I hadn't said anything, now, as they seemed to be implying that Briony and I spend a lot of time physically attacking each other.

'I'm NOT an aggressive person!' I said, protesting a bit too loudly and possibly sounding like an aggressive person. 'You can ask anyone who knows me!'

'Don't worry, Mr Philpot, we will,' said the female officer, slightly sharply.

They'd seemed friendly at first, but I sensed some hostility emanating from P.C. Flannigan (a steely-looking thin woman with piercing little grey eyes). The other one introduced himself as D.I. Bannister, and had a more amenable disposition, so I addressed my answers in his direction more, hoping that he would recognise a law-abiding citizen when he saw one.

'Why didn't you report your girlfriend missing straight away?' said the steely one.

'Um, well, I know that doesn't look great, but she'd said she wanted some space to think about things…'

'Ah,' said P.C. Flannigan. 'Can you expand on that?'

I exhaled heavily. This wasn't going too well. 'We haven't been getting along very well.' This was greeted with raised eyebrows and questioning looks. 'The usual sort of thing, you know…'

'Like what?'

'Well, um, Briony thought I'd been unfaithful…'

'Right…'

'But I wasn't, and anyway, she was messing around with someone else first…'

'I see,' said D.I. Bannister. 'So, let's get this straight, shall we? Things were looking a bit rocky between you two – is that fair?'

'Well, yes, I suppose so.'

'Let's talk about Findlay Connor now. What was your impression of him?'

'Er, well, to be honest, I don't know him very well. He seemed friendly…'

'So, when you described him to Mandy Vickers…' (P.C. Flannigan checked through her notes), '…as…oh, yes… as a 'parasitic amoeba', was that you just being friendly, Alexander?' P.C. Flannigan had a twisted smile on her face.

I couldn't stop my cheeks flushing red. 'Um, well…OK, so I don't like him, but I don't see what that's got to do with anything…'

'Do you have any idea about where Briony might have gone, Mr Philpot?'

'She was talking about wanting to run away from her boring life in Surbiton – she met Findlay Connor and seemed impressed with him. Maybe she's gone off sailing with him…I mean, his boat seems to be missing…'

'Yes, well, we're looking into that as he seems to be very difficult to pin down. We've had the Coastguard out looking for the boat and checked all the ports and harbours.'

'Apparently it's not unusual for Fin to do a disappearing act,' I said, slightly tersely.

'Yes, well, thank you for your assistance. We'll be in touch.' Both officers smiled – quite artificially, in my opinion, which was disconcerting, and frankly rude, when I'm trying to be helpful.

I went back to work feeling quite disorientated, and pretty cheesed off that Mandy had dobbed me in with the police like that – telling them what I said about Findlay. That made me look a right pillock. If it wasn't for the fact that I need to focus on the business, I wouldn't mind running away myself. It's typical of someone like Findlay Connor to duck out of the responsibilities in life, leaving the rest of us to pick up the pieces. Not only that, but now it looks like he might be a con man too. Maybe I should have mentioned the woman in the Ferry Inn to the police…

'Alex, do you have a minute?' Mr Anderson caught me coming back in through reception. 'I just wondered what your thoughts were about Evangeline's proposals?' I looked at him blankly. 'Mrs Bedlington-Clarke…'

'Oh, right…um, well, I don't know what to say…Steve and I haven't had a chance to discuss it yet…'

'Right…'

'What do you think?' I ventured.

'To be honest, Alexander, I think that statue nonsense is a bloody terrible idea! She's mentioned it on several occasions before, and I've just tried to ignore it. Alfred would turn in his grave if he knew.'

'Oh, right, well, what can we do about it?'

'I don't know. I've tried to dissuade her, but she can be very determined.'

'I'll talk to Gordon – he should know what to do.'

After lunch, Steve and I met up with Gordon for an overview of how things were going, and we took the opportunity to discuss Mrs B.C.'s strange directives.

'There are quite a few things that Mrs Bedlington-Clarke has requested,' said Gordon, pushing his slipping glasses back onto the bridge of his nose. From his briefcase, he took out a piece of paper with what looked like quite a long list of things written on it by hand. 'I'll start at the top and work down,' he said, sighing.

'For God's sake!' said Steve, when Gordon finally finished speaking. 'The woman's being a pain in the backside!'

'Well, professionally speaking,' said Gordon, 'I don't think I've ever come across so many requests when conducting a sale like this.'

'Can she really demand some of these things?' said Steve, – 'I mean, she'll never know if we don't give 10% of our profits to *Fluffy Friends Cat Rescue*, will she?'

'She can check at Companies House, Stephen,' said Gordon.

'Oh, bugger!'

'I'm quite fond of cats,' said Gordon. Steve and I exchanged glances.

'My main concern,' said Steve, – 'is that she's insisting that we sack Pete and Dave. They're our best fitters! There's no way we can agree to that.'

'Or the bit where she says she wants us to stop using our tile suppliers – we've had an excellent relationship for years.'

'This is madness, Gordon,' I said.

'Can we get her certified?' Steve butted in.

'Now, let's calm down,' said Gordon. 'Some of these things can be ignored.'

'And why does she think we would want to buy a company premises that has *no* parking? I mean, why on earth is she proposing to sell the car park?'

'She says she wants to sell the space at the back to her friend who wants to grow geraniums in her retirement,' said Gordon.

Steve rolled his eyes. 'I am seriously thinking that this is a really bad idea, Alex. We might as well just start up somewhere else with a totally new business.'

After our meeting with Gordon, I couldn't wait to get home and switch off. Mr Catkins was actually pleased to see me, which made a change. I suppose cats can transfer loyalty without so much as a by your leave, depending on where the food source comes from. He's missing his mistress, though – he's taken to sleeping on her dressing gown most nights.

This evening the Devon police are putting out a report about Briony and asking if anyone has seen her to come forward. Her parents are going to make a statement to the press as well. They did ask me if I wanted to join them, but I still think she's just run off with Findlay, and I don't want to look like a suspect because I'm not looking upset enough. I've seen how these things can go. One minute you're the grieving relative, and the cameras are zooming in on your watery eyes, and the next minute you're being falsely accused by all and sundry and everyone wants to lynch you. So, I will keep a low profile, thanks very much. Anyway, I can just see the headline now, when they find them:

RUNNAWAY LOVERS FOUND SAFE AND WELL

(Jilted boyfriend gets consolation prize of disgruntled cat and large collection of novelty scatter cushions)

I was just pouring myself a beer and trying to decide what to eat, when the phone rang. It was my mother enquiring after Briony's whereabouts because Josephine Dent, who has a holiday caravan in Slapton, saw the news on Devon local news on the TV and rang my mother immediately to ask what was going on.

'Well, she's gone missing, mother.'

'How long have you known this?'

'Since Tuesday, I suppose.'

'Why didn't you tell me?'

'Because, well…because she might not be missing, exactly…'

'What's that supposed to mean?'

'That she's gone off with someone else.'

'I knew it!' said my mother, almost gleefully.

'Please don't say anything!' I said, suddenly having visions of my mother telling all her friends. 'If she really is missing, then it would be terrible to suggest otherwise.'

'Yes, alright,' she said. 'You know Harry's previous girlfriend, Jemima, is coming to the wedding, don't you? She was such a lovely girl – I don't know why Harry ended that relationship…'

'Mum, I'm not looking for another girlfriend at the moment. I can't believe you're suggesting it right now!'

'Well, the sooner you move on, the better, Alexander. I'm only thinking of you.'

Good grief, my mother is unbelievable! I couldn't possibly consider meeting someone else while Briony is still missing. By the way, Jemima Cobberton-Crew is <u>not</u> a 'lovely girl'. Far from it, to be brutally honest. My mother has absolutely no idea about who would be a suitable match. For a start, Jemima looks like a horse (the poor girl was nicknamed

'Buckaroo' at school). She laughs like a horse as well. Mostly, though, she's not very bright. I mean, who doesn't know the difference between a 'physalis' and 'Syphilis'! Harry's mother, Lauren, was quite taken aback when Jemima asked if she wanted any, because her dad (who is in the fruit and veg business), wanted to 'get rid of it'. The funniest thing of all, though, was when Harry gave Jemima a vibrating egg in her stocking at Christmas and she showed it to everyone at the lunch table, saying what a silly present to give when 'it isn't even <u>Easter'</u>, and he could have given her an 'edible one at <u>least!'</u> Lauren blanched at the sight of it, apparently.

I fired up my laptop to look for the news report from Devon. There they were – Briony's parents and her brother, Tom, standing at the sea front in Hope Cove. They were surrounded by reporters and local people gawping and taking photos – a sea of holidaymakers, scoffing ice-creams and holding onto their dogs and noisy kids, looked on. 'Thank God I'm not there!' I said out loud. As predicted, the cameras zoomed in on Briony's family's' faces. They all looked a bit bewildered. Briony's father read out a short statement. He looked older and thinner than how I remembered him. Briony's mother held onto his arm and was trying to be stoical. After their plea for people to come forward who might know anything, the reporters were heard shouting questions. One of them yelled: 'Where is Alex? Why isn't he here? Is he a suspect?' I switched my laptop off. How could Briony and that idiot put her family through this ordeal. I tried to imagine my own mother in the same position, but I couldn't – she'd probably be saying that it was my own lookout and how selfish I was to go missing like that. On reflection, perhaps there's more of my mother in me than I care to consider. Perhaps I'd better try and be more sympathetic about Briony. I mean, there is the slight possibility that my hypothesis could be wrong.

I rooted around in the fridge for something to eat and realised there was literally nothing remotely edible in there, and the only thing in the food cupboard was a tin of rice pudding and a lone packet of *Salmon Chomp* for cats. Mr Catkins was looking at me hopefully. I decided I'd better go shopping since things were looking pretty dire sustainability-wise. I really detest food-shopping, but Mr Catkins' large sad eyes, and the calamitous lack of beer in the flat, propelled me forwards and up the road to the Co-Op. Whilst perusing the shelves for inspiration, I heard a familiar voice behind me.

'Alex! Hi!' It was Kate. 'Shopping for your tea?' she asked, eyeing up my basket, which embarrassingly only contained beer and wine.

'Oh, yes…I can't decide…'

'Not taking your girlfriend out, then?'

'She's not here…actually, she's gone away, um…probably permanently…'

'Oh, dear! I'm sorry to hear that, Alex.'

'It's been on the cards for a while now, to be honest. It's not really a surprise.'

'Oh, right. Well, I'm on my own this evening, as it happens…' She looked at me expectantly with those shining emerald eyes, and before I knew it, I'd invited her out for dinner.

'I just need to go home and feed the cat…'

'Oh, no problem, Alex. I need to change anyway. See you in an hour?'

I'd suggested Pizza Express, thinking it would be a suitable venue for friends to meet without it being an obvious date. I showered and changed and fed Mr Catkins, and then I walked to the restaurant with a definite spring in my step. I told myself it wasn't a proper date – just a meal with a colleague who happened to be female. A very pretty female non-the-less, with beautiful eyes and a captivating smile…

Chapter 12

I think I found out more about Kate in one night than I've known about Briony in a whole year. Things about her family, her school days, the high points and the disappointments, her myriad of jobs, her friends, and her likes and dislikes. I felt a real connection with her – it was the first time in a long time that someone seemed genuinely interested in my life too. She even wanted to know about the book I'm writing and asked if she could read it. I told her it wasn't fully formed yet, and I would be embarrassed to show it to her. I was also thinking about Briony's reaction to my attempt at becoming an author and I don't really want to repeat that. Kate had some good ideas about Anderson's Kitchens as well – it really cheered me up.

I decided to take a break from police training this weekend. Kate said she'd explain to Jim that I've got a lot on my plate at the moment. She was very understanding about my situation and agreed that there was no need to rush into anything, which was a relief to be honest. I mean, I do really like her, but it's far too complicated right now, and I did feel quite guilty even entertaining the idea of a replacement girlfriend. Jacob, on the other hand, wasn't at all averse to the idea.

'That's great, Alex! Well done, mate,' he said enthusiastically, at the gym the next day.

'She's just a friend,' I said.

'Oh, yeah! Right! You didn't take *Slammer Sharon* out, did you!'

'Well, no, but that's not the point…'

'Come on, Alex – you're not convincing anyone!'

'OK, well, just don't make a big thing of it, please. Things are bad enough as it is.'

'OK,' he said, smiling. 'Any news about Briony and that bloke Fin, then?'

'No, nothing. It's really weird that nobody has seen either of them for nearly a week, now. *Calamity Jane* can't be found either.'

'Who?'

'His boat.'

'Oh, right. Well, that sounds like they've definitely sailed off somewhere, doesn't it?'

'But don't you think the boat would have been spotted?'

'The Atlantic is a big ocean, Alex. Forty-one million square miles, to be precise. It can take weeks to get anywhere. And no one knows where they were headed, do they? So, it would be like finding a needle in a haystack.'

'Maybe something *has* happened, though…'

'Well, obviously that's a possibility, but with modern technology and everything, you'd think that they could have signalled for help somehow, wouldn't you?'

'Well, I suppose so. We'll just have to wait and hope for some good news soon. It's making me ill, though, to be honest. And the police are asking some quite intrusive questions about our life together. It's all getting very unnerving.'

'Well, how about coming back to my house, Alex? Lucy asked if you'd like to come for lunch after we've finished. She's made a fancy fish pie and a raspberry pavlova. My folks are coming over. They'd all love to see you. It'll take your mind of everything for a bit…'

I accepted his invitation graciously, not because I particularly wanted to go but he was right about me needing to be distracted for a while.

'Lucy wants one of those bloody awful *gender reveal* parties,' said Jacob, on the way there.

'What on earth is that, then?'

'It's where you let everyone know if the baby is a girl or a boy.'

'OK. Why do you need a party to do that, then?'

'Exactly! It's the latest trend. Diabolical, isn't it!'

'Can't you just tell Lucy you don't want it?'

He shook his head. 'Absolutely no way!'

'Can't she just have this party with her girlfriends, then?'

'No. She's determined to have all her friends and family.'

'Well, I don't know what to say, Jacob. I guess you'll just have to suck it up!' I was trying really hard not to laugh, because he had a face like a wet weekend. 'Sometimes you just have to let the girls have their way. You have to choose your battles carefully, Jacob!' I said, reminding him what he'd said to me not so long ago, then I couldn't help it and burst out laughing.

Lunch at Jacob and Lucy's was exactly as anticipated. Everyone was on their best behaviour and there was a lot of talk about babies. Jacob is going to have to adapt to a different way of life, to put it mildly. Lucy's got it all planned out for him – especially around his frequent visits to the gym and the rugby club, which will be severely curtailed. She has laid down the law, and with Jacob's parents in complete agreement, his back is well and truly against the wall. I just hope that when the baby comes, he'll step up. He's not looking as happy as he ought to – well, rabbit in the headlights is a better description. I've been trying to imagine how I would feel if it was me, but I suppose you just don't know until it actually happens. Jacob's mum told him that once the baby is born, he will be besotted with it and nothing else will matter. I can't wait to see that! I think Jacob might be regretting inviting me to lunch, now, because his parents told me quite a lot about his childhood. Several times during the meal he tried to shut them up, but it only encouraged them. It's given me some fantastic material to rib him with. I told him afterwards that he was lucky to still have both his parents even if they embarrass him at times, and I think it made him realise that he should be grateful for what he's got.

'Look at me,' I said, as I was leaving his house, – 'things are looking really dodgy, bordering on perilous, right now. And, there's no point in me trying to talk to my mother about any of it – she has about as much empathy as a house brick.'

'Yeah, sorry, Alex – I'm a bit wrapped up in my own stuff. I suppose my problems seem small in comparison…'

'Well, everyone has a cross to bear, don't they! To be honest, a *gender reveal* party does sound quite alarming…'

'Very funny, Alex! By the way – you are invited, you know…Lucy has specifically requested that you be there as a special guest.'

'Now, *you're* being funny!'

'No, I'm being serious…Saturday 8th August 7.30pm – be there or Lucy will hate you forever, and thanks for coming today – you're a really good mate.'

This morning, I was just on my way out when the police turned up unexpectedly at my door. They, very politely but very firmly, invited me to go to the police station for another interview – this time under caution. They also told me they had a warrant to search the flat. I must say, I was quite taken aback by the whole thing.

'Are you arresting me?' I asked them, my throat as dry as a stone.

'No, we just want to ask you further questions at the moment.'

'I think I need a solicitor, don't I?'

'That is your right, Mr Philpot,' said one of them. 'We can sort that out for you. If you'd like one of our duty solicitors, just let us know.'

I'd seen enough crime dramas to know that it was imperative to have a good lawyer present. I rang Uncle Frank straight away. Luckily, he said he could be with me by half past ten and told me to stay calm and not to say anything at all until he'd had a chance to speak to the police himself. Mr Catkins made a very quick exit, abandoning his breakfast, when all the police came marching in through the front door. With hindsight, maybe I should have done the same, then at least I wouldn't have had to put up with the embarrassment of my neighbour witnessing it all. I saw him craning his neck as he leaned across his balcony to see into my flat. I actually thought he might topple over it he was so far over. They went through everything – opening and emptying all the cupboards, looking under all the furniture and Briony's countless cushions, they turned the mattress off the bed and tipped all our clothes out of the wardrobe and the drawers. They even looked inside Mr Catkins' bag of litter. I noticed they drew a line at sieving through his poo tray, but they searched everything else with a fine-tooth comb. They even asked for my car keys in order to search my car.

'What's this?' one of them said, holding up my precious manuscript.

'It's my novel. Please be careful with it!' They ripped opened a plastic zip-bag and unceremoniously dropped it in. 'Why are you taking that?' I asked, perplexed. The policeman didn't respond. I noticed they took quite a few personal items belonging to Briony, like her hairbrush and some photos. They asked about her laptop and diary. 'I think they'll be at the cottage at Hope Cove.' I told them.

One of them found Briony's jewellery case and opened it onto the dressing table. The contents spilled out everywhere.

'Hey, be careful!' I couldn't help saying, picking some of it up off the bedroom carpet. There were quite a few magazine cuttings of rings, I noticed. Could she be dreaming about marrying that cowboy? What a ghastly thought! Surely not!

'Please stand back and let us do our job, Mr Philpot,' he said, sternly.

A small brown envelope had fallen out onto the table. He opened it and tipped out a long leather thong. Dangling from it was a very large, ivory-coloured tooth about half the size of a billiard ball. I recognised it immediately. 'That's Findlay Connor's! He must have given it to Briony.'

'There's a note here,' the policeman said to his colleagues, opening it up and reading it out loud:

'We cannot control the wind, but we can direct the sail. You are my safe harbour – let me be the captain of your heart…'

'Very romantic,' said one of them, – 'looks like a love token, then,' he commented, turning the giant tooth in his hand. 'Is this from you?' he said, pointing at the note.

'No, it certainly isn't,' I said, feeling nettled. 'I wouldn't write something as schmaltzy as that…'

'Oh, right…' The policeman gave the other one a funny look and smiled to himself.

'It's obviously from Findlay,' I said.

'You'd better bag it, then,' he told his colleague.

Towards the end of the search, a policeman came in from searching my car. 'We need to get the vehicle to forensics immediately,' he said.

After they left, I couldn't believe the mess they'd made. I rang Alice and told her I was going to be a bit held up.

'Probably won't get there until the afternoon,' I said, – 'leaking boiler...' I lied.

It took me two hours just to tidy up the kitchen and lounge. Luckily the only thing that got broken was an ugly figurine belonging to Briony, of a louche-looking shepherdess herding some doe-eyed sheep. I think her granny gave it to her. Anyway, I've always detested it, so they've actually done me a favour. Hopefully Briony won't notice. While they were here, they were recording messages from the answer phone, which I'd forgotten to check in the last two days, so I really hope there's nothing rude on there. I mean, Jacob sometimes leaves inappropriate messages, which would be a bit embarrassing if the police heard any of them. The worst thing is the loss of my laptop, which has everything on it. I hope they don't keep it for long. My business stuff is on there and all my emails, and most importantly, my novel and all the research for it. My blood runs cold thinking about the possibility of it all being accidentally deleted by some ham-fisted bozo.

Uncle Frank's face at my door was a huge relief. 'I'm being treated like a criminal!' I complained, as Frank followed me into the still messy kitchen. I moved some things off a chair so he could take a seat. 'It's unbelievable!'

'Make us some coffee, Alex, and tell me what's been going on – I wasn't even aware your girlfriend was missing…I need to take some notes while we talk. I've spoken to the police, so I'll tell you what their position is in a minute.'

'Oh, yes, of course…'

'Right. Start with when Briony left here and went off down to Devon. Take it slowly – I can't write as fast as you're talking.'

Once I'd finished telling Uncle Frank my side of the story, he took his time to let it sink in, and then told me how the police are currently viewing Briony's disappearance.

'I'll explain to you why they are so interested in you, Alex. Please remember, this is *not* my opinion. I'm just playing devil's advocate. So, firstly you've been having relationship problems resulting in physical injuries to yourself, of a worrying nature. ('Don't interrupt,' he said, as I tried to protest.) Secondly, you've shown that you are currently in a particularly jealous and angry state of mind. (He held up his hand to stop me interrupting again.) Thirdly, you took a very long time to agree that Briony is a missing person, and even now you aren't showing that you're convinced or worried. The police know that your car was seen at the Hope Cove address around the time that Briony went missing. They have a witness who has made a statement to say that you were angry with Briony and that you were jealous of a man she'd met called Findlay Connor, and also that you refused to report Briony's disappearance to the police, despite the fact that she'd been missing for three days.'

'Well, none of that proves anything at all!' I said, crossly. 'And, by the way, when I spoke to Mandy, I didn't *refuse* to report her missing, I just thought she was probably with Fin. I can get witnesses for most of the injuries too – they were just stupid accidents…'

'I understand, Alex, but the police are building a case against you. You're going to have to try and remain calm. Is there anything else you can think of that I should know?'

'I don't think so.'

'Are you sure? Because it will be harder for me to help you if you withhold anything that I should know…'

'I can't think of anything.'

'OK, so you have the right to stay silent at this interview – you know you can just say 'no comment'. It's up to you. Just be careful about what you *do* say as they will use it against you if you say anything rash – it's really important to think before you speak.'

'When do we have to go in?'

'This afternoon. Try not to worry. On another note, it's going to be very difficult to avoid news reports about you,

Briony and Findlay, but if you take my advice, you won't read any of it, Alex. The tabloids will be full of speculation and sensationalist nonsense. If you read it, you'll end up blowing a gasket, or getting depressed – neither of which will be good for your mental health.'

'OK, I'll try and ignore it.'

'Good lad.'

We went for some lunch at a nearby café, and Frank tried asking me about the business and how it was all going, to distract me.

'Mrs B.C. is being really difficult,' I told him, – 'some of her demands are ludicrous.'

'It sounds to me like she's feeling very protective of the Business, because of her late husband. I'm sure we can get round most things. She might need a bit of gentle encouragement to get her to be more reasonable.'

'I hope so, because Steve is getting cold feet.'

'I'll talk to Gordon – a strategy meeting is what we need. We'll figure it out. We'll figure all this out, too, I'm sure.'

He gave me a reassuring pat on my shoulder. I didn't feel at all reassured, though. I mean, how could I be calm when the police were accusing me of being involved in Briony's disappearance, or worse…

'Don't second-guess them,' said Frank, as we went up the imposing stone steps and into the police station, – 'just answer their questions as simply as possible. Don't give information they haven't asked for.'

I did honestly try to listen to Frank's advice, but it wasn't easy, I can tell you. My knees were literally knocking. This time the interview was recorded. It was the same two police officers again. The steely-eyed P.C. Flannigan was as unsmiling as before, and D.I. Bannister seemed more serious this time. It was a very nerve-wracking experience. Uncle Frank introduced himself and the interview began.

'Let's begin with Briony leaving the flat on Friday 19th June, and you finding this note…' D.I. Bannister held up Briony's hand-written scrawl for me to identify. 'How did you feel when you saw this, Mr Philpot? It must have been a bit of a shock, wasn't it?'

'Not really. As you know, we weren't getting on very well at that point.'

'Can you remind us why that was the case.'

'Well, like I told you before, Briony thought I'd slept with someone else – a girl called Maggie – while she was away in Devon, which I didn't. Anyway, while *she* was away on holiday, she'd already met Findlay Connor. She sent me lots of photographs of herself taken by him. I think it was because she was annoyed with me for not taking time off work to go to Devon with her. I tried to get the time off, but my boss wouldn't let me. He's not at all flexible. Briony calls him 'the old fossil'. Anyway, she said I should have stood up to him. She sulked all week about it and it really began to get on my nerves. She even refused to come to the theatre with my mother… the tickets had been booked for ages and …' I felt Uncle Frank's hand press the side of my thigh, and I realised I was rattling on which he'd told me not to do, so I stopped speaking.

'On Sunday 14th June, you attended a Special Constable training session, and it was noted that earlier in the week, you had sustained an injury to your head. Can you tell us about that, please.'

'Well, I'd been showing Briony what I'd learned the week before, and she threw me down and I bashed my head on the coffee table. It bloody hurt, too – look, you can still see where it cut the skin…' I tried to show D.I. Bannister, but he wasn't really interested.

'Do you really expect us to believe that your girlfriend, who I believe is, what… 5ft 4 inches and apparently only weighs 9 and a half stone, actually managed to throw you down? I mean, you must be … what… fourteen stone? And a pretty strong young man, I'd say…'

'Well, I know it seems improbable…'

'Yes,' said P.C. Flannigan, staring at me, – 'it certainly does!'

'So, what do you think, then?' I said, getting irritated, – 'that she clobbered me with a frying pan?' Frank's eyes widened and he shoved his fist against my thigh again.

'So, that's what actually happened, is it?'

'No!' I said. 'No, it didn't.'

'Interesting that you told your work colleagues that you fell, isn't it, Mr Philpot!'

I sighed and sat back in my chair. 'I was embarrassed to say that my girlfriend overpowered me…I mean…oh, whatever I say, you'll make something of it, won't you!'

'Let's move on to Maggie Turnbull. You're acquainted with her? Yes?'

'Yes.' I said, catching Frank's eye and remembering I needed to follow his instructions to say as little as possible. 'Well, I only know her as Maggie.'

'Right, well – Miss Turnbull came forward after she saw Briony's parents' appeal on the television, and when she saw your photograph, she recognised you. She thought she should tell us what she knows.'

'Well, I don't see how *she* could possibly have anything useful to say.'

'That's for us to decide, Mr Philpot. We've obtained a mobile phone that was reported as stolen, later identified as belonging to your friend Jacob Samuel.'

'Maggie's the one who stole it!'

'She maintains that she found it in her bag after a night out with you, and couldn't remember how it got there, so she handed it in to the police station thinking it might be useful to our enquiries. I wouldn't go around accusing people like that if I were you…' Frank elbowed me in the ribs.

'Sorry,' I said, begrudgingly.

'This phone has some interesting messages and video footage on it, Mr Philpot.'

'Oh…'

'For instance…now let's get this up on the laptop to show you…'

I could barely look. I mean, our messages are pretty laddish at the best of times. Uncle Frank had a look of wilting despondency on his face.

'See where Jacob says "*Thank goodness she's gone! Let's get smashed…*" and then you say, "*It'll be just like the old days now I'm off the biach's leash…*" and then he responds with, "*Yeah mate, that's brotastic man…*"'

I visibly cringed. 'Look, that's just two mates chatting – it's just banter…'

'That's what you say…' said D.I. Bannister, – 'but it could be interpreted differently, couldn't it? Anyway, there's plenty more where that came from. Now what do you say to this?' P.C. Flannigan flicked a switch and a very blurry image appeared on the screen.

'What's that?' I asked, peering at it.

'Just wait a minute and keep watching.'

The blurry image turned into a bloke dancing badly with a bottle of beer in each hand. Then a blonde girl who looks familiar approaches him and points at the person filming. The faces come into focus, and I realise it's Maggie and me. I am putting my arm round Maggie's waist, and we are dancing around together. I am plainly completely hammered.

'Would you agree that that is you on this film?' P.C. Flannigan said, staring at me in an aggressive manner.

'Well, yes, it is.'

'Would you agree that you were coming on to the girl in question?'

'No, actually, I wouldn't.'

'How so?'

'That's Maggie – we were just larking about. She was actually with Jacob – that's why she came back to stay at my flat that night.'

D.I Bannister and P.C. Flannigan looked at each other with raised eyebrows. I saw Frank sigh and roll his eyes.

'So, when you drove down to Devon on the night of the 26th June, to see your girlfriend, can you tell us what the purpose of that visit was, Mr Philpot?' D.I. Bannister looked searchingly into my eyes.

'To see Briony. I wanted to surprise her.'

'So, it was a romantic gesture, was it?'

'Yes.'

'Did you tell your girlfriend, that Maggie stayed with you on the night of the 19th June – the same night, curiously, that Briony drove down to Devon?'

'No, of course not! Like I said before; Maggie wasn't with me – she was with Jacob!'

'Really? It seems to us Mr Philpot, that your version of events may not be entirely accurate.'

'You can ask Maggie and Jacob. They'll tell you the truth about what happened that night.'

'Let's move on to another of your 'accidents', shall we. Your work colleague, Alice McLean, told us that you appeared at work on three occasions with injuries – one to your head, which she described as 'a massive egg' which you told her you got by falling over, and then a few days later you were limping and wearing a leg brace. Then on another occasion you appeared to have a heavily bandaged hand. She says you refused to say what happened to you.'

'The 'egg' was incurred at police training – you can easily check that, can't you? The leg injury was a bad sprain which I got when I fell off a roof.'

'What were you doing on a roof, Mr Philpot?' P.C. Flannigan was smirking slightly.

'It's a long story…'

'We don't mind,' said P.C. Flannigan. 'Take as long as you like.' Uncle Frank was looking a bit dazed at this point.

'Well, Briony wasn't in when I got there…'

'What day was this?'

'Friday the 26th… when I went to Devon to surprise Briony. As she wasn't there when I turned up, I went to the pub and then, when it shut, I went back, but she still wasn't there. I didn't want to spend the night in my car, and I was over the driving limit, so I decided to climb up and go in through an open window upstairs…'

'You tried ringing her, I presume?'

'Of course I did! I'm not a complete idiot!' They looked at each other in some sort of private acknowledgement that I wasn't privy to. 'Unfortunately, it wasn't the right roof…I got the wrong cottage because her car was parked there, and I thought it was where she was staying…so, anyway, it was raining, and I climbed up, but I slipped on the wet tiles and fell off. I actually thought my leg was broken. It was really painful. Anyway, you can check that as well – I had to go to the hospital in an ambulance.' D.I. Bannister made some notes and then moved on to the next question.

'Your car, Mr Philpot, was seen at Mandy Vickers' holiday home address the weekend Briony went missing…'

'Yes, it was still there from the week before…and then Jacob fetched it for me because of my leg.'

'Do you have any proof of that?' D.I. Bannister said.

'Well, you can just ask Jacob, can't you?'

'We certainly will. Now, shall we take a short break? Would you both like a cup of tea?'

'Can I go now?' I asked, – 'only I've got a ton of work to do…'

'Alex, you need to co-operate with the officers and stay until they have finished interviewing you,' Frank said, – 'because you need to avoid being arrested if possible.' My face drained visibly. 'It's OK, you're doing fine,' he said. I knew he was lying, though. I mean, I saw the look on his face when I told them about Maggie's impromptu sleepover. We all supped our tea in silence, except for the scratching of Frank's pen on his notepad. Then P.C. Flannigan switched the recording machine back on.

'Interview with Alexander Graham Philpot resuming at 2.15pm, Monday 13th July.'

'On the evening of Friday 3rd July, you again travelled down to Devon to retrieve Briony's cat from Mrs Parker, who cleans the cottage belonging to Mandy Vickers. Mrs Parker told us that she was 'horrified' to see the back seat of your car covered in blood. How do you account for that, Mr Philpot?'

'That was from my hand – I cut it on some mirror glass. I've been helping Mr Anderson get rid of stuff from the offices…'

'Did anyone see your injured hand?'

'Well, Mrs Parker saw it…'

'She said she saw you had a bandaged hand, not the injury.' D.I. Bannister, in my opinion, was being unnecessarily obtuse.

'Well, the blood was from *my* hand, I can assure you.'

'We'll obviously be checking that.' P.C. Flannigan was looking very smug.

'Let's get onto the manuscript we discovered in your flat, Mr Philpot. *Rivers of Blood,* it appears to be called. It's a bit of a theme, isn't it!'

'That's a working title.'

'I've had a cursory glance at it and apart from it being a little on the purple prose side, it's a very interesting read.'

'Oh, thank you…'

'I mean, in the way that something very sinister might be interesting.'

'Well, it *is* a murder-mystery novel…'

'To put it plainly, Mr Philpot, we have a possible double murder on our hands here, with the disappearance of two young people, and your manuscript gives a very clear description of a murder. I couldn't have written it better myself!' D.I. Bannister was staring into my eyes with an intensity I found very unnerving.

'You don't think…you don't actually think that I have anything to do with this, do you? Good Lord!'

'You tell us, Mr Philpot,' said P.C. Flannigan, fixing me with her steely glare.

'Why on earth would I want to murder anybody? That's ridiculous!'

'Your choice of the protagonist's name is interesting, isn't it…Axel being an anagram of Alex, plus he seems to bear a very strong resemblance to yourself Mr Philpot. In fact, I'd say he was the spitting image of you. So, my question to you is this: is the protagonist in your novel, you?'

'No! Well, not really – I mean, in the way he looks, I suppose, but in no other way…except perhaps that I tried to imagine what it would feel like to be Axel…' Frank shot me a look to say, 'do not utter another word!'.

'Can you tell us why you chose to murder the victim in your novel by a stabbing followed by drowning? There are plenty of other ways to despatch someone.'

'I…I don't know…I just thought it would be dramatic.'

'Hmm. Did you think it would be an efficient way to dispose of a body – to sink it into a body of water like that?'

'I suppose so…'

'Where are you going with this line of questioning?' said Frank, at last. 'We're veering off the facts here…'

The police officers looked irritated but agreed to stick to the evidence.

'There's some white string cut up into pieces in your flat, Mr Philpot. Can you tell us what that was for?'

'Briony's cat, Mr Catkins. She was making some string toys – you know, bits of paper on the end of a string. Cats like to chase things like that. What's that got to do with anything, though?' They ignored me and asked their next question.

'We also found an item that you say belonged to Mr Connor…' D.I. Bannister pushed a transparent bag across the table for me to see.

'Yes, that's Findlay's – I recognised it at the time.'

'That must have been hard to take, mustn't it – a lover's message and personal gift to Briony from another man?'

'The first time I saw it was when your officers found it.'

'Well, we'll have to take your word for it, won't we.'

'What is it?' asked PC Flannigan, looking at the contents of the bag.

'A megalodon tooth – a fossilized shark's tooth. They're worth quite a lot.' I told her.

'Well, some are,' said D.I. Bannister, – 'but I'm afraid this one is plastic – you can buy them in all the tourist shops in Devon.'

'Really?' I said, – 'so he was spinning her a line… what a reprobate!' I got another look from Frank.

'Do you think you could explain a visit to the town tip on the morning Monday 6th July, when you were seen disposing of several large bin bags from your car?'

'How do you know I was doing that?'

'We have viewed it on CCTV recorded at the tip.'

'Why would you be looking at people going to the tip?'

'Just answer the question, Mr Philpot.'

'That was Mr Anderson's rubbish from work. He asked me to dispose of some things. He's selling the business. He's trying to clear the place before he leaves.'

'What will happen to you, then, Mr Philpot? I take it you will no longer have a job?'

'Well, actually, that's not the case. My partner Stephen Pratt and I are in the process of buying Anderson's Kitchens.'

'Oh, really?' D.I. Bannister looked very surprised. 'Is that so?'

'Yes!'

'That's quite something to take on. You don't earn a very big salary, do you? What is it – around £32,000 per year? You can't have managed to save a lot on that sort of wage at your age…'

'I'm getting some help,' I said. Uncle Frank remained studiously silent.

'Where from?'

'My family are helping me.'

'Is your girlfriend insured, Mr Philpot?'

'Pardon?'

'Is she insured? You know – does she have life insurance?'

'Um, I don't know. I don't think so…'

'We'd better check that,' said P.C. Flannigan, looking briefly at D.I. Bannister, who was looking distinctly pleased with himself.

'Can you tell us anything about Findlay Connor?' she asked.

'Like what?'

'Anything…'

'All I know is that he's a fisherman. He keeps his boat, *Calamity Jane,* at Salcombe occasionally. I met a woman at the Ferry Inn there, the night I picked up Mr Catkins, who told me that Fin had taken a deposit from her husband and done a runner. She said Fin was selling his boat to them, but she reckoned he'd conned them out of their money. That's all I know, except that Briony seemed keen on him. I promise you, that's all I know about him.'

'Well, thank you for your assistance in this matter, Mr Philpot. Before you leave, I've arranged for you to provide a blood sample and we also need to take your fingerprints. Oh, and we need you to let us have your mobile phone too.'

'Oh…'

'Just so we can eliminate you from our enquiries, if that is what we decide to do. Afterwards, you are free to go. Do not leave the area in the meantime. We will probably be asking you to come in again, so do not leave Surbiton while this investigation is ongoing. Do you understand?'

'Yes,' I said, with relief.

Chapter 13

'She was a cold fish,' said Uncle Frank as we got into his car.

'Frozen stiff,' I said, trying to make light of things.

'Well, at least we know what we're dealing with.'

'So, what do you think?' I asked him, nervously.

Frank sucked in his breath before answering, as we drove slowly back to my flat.

'It's a tricky one,' he finally said. 'The trouble is, Alex, that it's not looking too good for you at the moment. I'm sure that once they've established that the blood isn't anyone else's, that Maggie isn't your bit on the side, that your injuries were all either self-inflicted, or foolish accidents, that your debut novel is not a 'How to Murder Someone' manual, and that you have no evil intentions towards Findlay Connor or your girlfriend, then they will have to look elsewhere for an answer.'

When Uncle Frank put it like that, I suddenly felt quite ill.

'What we all want is for the pair of them to rock up unharmed and oblivious to all the fuss they've caused, don't we! The scenario that none of us wants to consider, of course, is that they have been lost at sea. You do realise, don't you, Alex, that that possibility is the most likely one?'

This made me feel even more ill. 'I've been trying not to think about it. to be honest. I'd rather assume she's left me for someone else. At least her parents wouldn't be blaming me for it all.'

'Well let's just take each day as it comes, Alex – the police haven't got anything concrete,' Frank said, as I got out of his car. 'They don't have enough to arrest you at the moment. I'll give you a call when I've had time to digest everything.' He gave me a friendly wave and drove off.

In the flat, I made myself a strong coffee. My head was full of questions. It was too late to go back to work now, but I messaged Steve and told him I was home. God knows what he thinks – maybe he's having second thoughts now. I don't know how I'd feel if my potential business partner was a suspect in a missing person case. This is crazy. Mr Catkins came and sat next to me on the sofa, and I wondered if he was reading my mind. Who, but a cat, would want to associate with a me, now? I saw that the answer phone was flashing on the side-table and sat for a while ignoring it in case it was bad news. I think I might hate Findlay Connor even more than before. Whichever way you look at it, he's taken Briony away, which makes me wonder why the police aren't accusing him. I mean, if they want a suspect, he's the obvious choice, surely! And, he's got form, the cheating ne'er-do-well. I decided I'd better listen to the messages. One was my mother to tell me about her new gardener and asking if I'd decided how I was travelling to Harry's wedding – a veiled attempt at soliciting a lift and my company, no doubt. Then, there was one from Mandy, telling me that she'd asked Briony's parents to go down and collect her stuff from the cottage, now that the police had finished inspecting it all. The last message was from Jacob, complaining that I wasn't answering my mobile. I made myself another coffee and rang him back.

'The police want me to go in and be interviewed, Alex. Why do they want to speak to me?' he said immediately, sounding worried.

'It's just to confirm what I told them, I expect. You don't need to worry. You just need to tell them the truth, that's all. They have your phone – Maggie gave it to them. They also have mine, which is why you couldn't get me on it.'

'Oh.'

'I'm afraid they've seen all the messages between us, and there is some footage of us partying, but there's nothing to worry about.'

'But I don't see why they think I have anything to do with Briony's disappearance…'

They just want you to answer questions about dates of events – like when you collected my car, for instance, and what happened the night Maggie stayed over. You really need to tell them I wasn't with Maggie – OK? They seem to be convinced I was two-timing Briony, and that I didn't care about her.'

'Crikey, Alex – they don't think *you* had something to do with all this, do they? Or me? Do they think I'm involved? Oh my God! Alex! This is getting scary now!'

'Calm down, Jacob. You haven't done anything wrong. I'm the one they suspect. To be honest, I can't blame them. I mean, *I'd* suspect me…How's Lucy?' I asked, changing the subject.

'Oh, well, she's OK, thanks. A bit grumpy. She wants me to start decorating the nursery and sorting out the garden to make a play area. Honestly, Alex, my life isn't my own. She said I have to stop drinking alcohol in the house because *she* can't have any and according to her, it's not fair. She even threw away my bottle opener!'

'Why did she do that?'

'It's the one with a pair of tits – remember? You bought it for my birthday years ago. She said we can't have lewd things in the house when there'll be a child around.'

'Right, well, I suppose you'll just have to go along with it, Jacob.'

'This dad business is going to be tough,' he said, morosely. 'I'm not sure I'm cut out for it…'

'Well, it's a bit late now,' I said, smiling to myself.

'You're enjoying this, aren't you!' he said, sensing my amusement.

'Well, only a bit…'

'You wait until it's your turn, Alex!'

'I'm not planning on becoming a father any time soon, Jacob. In fact, it couldn't be further from my mind. Why don't you come over at the weekend for the football – we can watch it here if you like. I'll get some beer in. By the way, don't forget, you can only get me on the house phone at the moment. The police have mine for analysing, in case I'm a malevolent assassin.'

At coffee break the next day, Steve wanted to catch up about the business buy-out. I must say, I'm struggling to keep focussed on it, and it's stressing me out. He's not daft, either. I've just been hoping that everything will come together, but I feel like I'm between a rock and a hard place right now. On my way to work this morning, I nipped into the local garage for a packet of mints and was shocked to see wall-to-wall papers stacked up in the stands with Briony's windswept face on nearly every single one. There were a couple of front pages with my startled-looking face staring back at me. One of them had a big photo of her parents from the day of the appeal at Hope Cove, declaring ***'PARENTS PAIN FOR BEAUTIFUL BRIONY'***. Another, less erudite and doom-laden headline shouted, ***'VOYAGE TO THE BOTTOM OF THE SEA'***, – it depicted a photoshopped trawler in peril on top of an improbable colossus of a wave in an otherwise flat sea. I scanned across and saw a blurry photo of Fin, obviously retrieved from the dark recesses of some disused grimy wallet. ***'LOVERS' TRYST ENDS IN TORMENT'***, was splashed dramatically across his forehead. ***'THE LADY VANISHES'*** was one of the least offensive. I looked at the two papers that had my gormless face staring out at the world and realised why people had been giving me sideways glances and crossing the road these last two days. One said, ***'INNOCENT UNTIL PROVEN GUILTY!'*** – the inference being pretty unambiguous. Then my eyes landed on the last one which simply said, ***'WHODUNNIT?'*** above my frowning fizzog. I know I should have listened to

Uncle Frank, but I couldn't resist collecting up one from each pile of these vile and reprehensible offerings and reluctantly paying the exorbitant amount of money for them all. Interestingly, the woman behind the counter didn't flinch when she saw me. She obviously didn't recognise me – she didn't even do a double-take. I obviously don't resemble the criminal version of myself, glaring out from these newspaper pages. Still, I resolved to grow a beard pronto.

'The thing is, Alex,' said Steve, putting his cards on the table, – 'I can't risk my money on something that might not work. Don't get me wrong – I know you've got the skills and energy to put into this venture, but you're massively distracted at the moment.'

'I know, Steve, and I'm sorry about what's happened. I really don't know what the hell's going on. I wish Briony would just turn up tomorrow, and we could all just get on with our lives.'

'Well, I suppose it'll take the lawyers a week or two to sort everything out, anyway…'

'Yes, it will. Look, Steve – I promise I'm absolutely committed to doing this. There's no problem with the financial input from my side, and I'm confident we can make a go of it.'

'We should tell the staff what's happening to them, shouldn't we? They're getting jittery.'

'Yes, you're right. Frank says we should hold a strategy meeting with Gordon. How about this Friday? We can get an email out to everyone.'

'What do we do about Alice?'

'I think we should keep her on – she might improve with some incentives. If she's willing to learn, then it could work. For instance, Mr Anderson always used to do all the admin stuff. We don't want to be doing that ourselves, as well as everything else, do we?'

'Well, I suppose it's worth a shot.'

'OK. Well, let's hope Briony is found soon, and that chap, of course – what's his name?'

'Findlay Connor.'

'You know, for some reason, that name sounds familiar to me, but I don't know why.'

Keeping Alice is a bit of a risk. There's the old saying that 'familiarity breeds contempt'. But maybe we can all start afresh. She might cheer up a bit if things are more dynamic and fun around here. I don't suppose it's very inspiring for a young person working for the Andersons. Steve and I will shake things up a bit, that's for sure. Anyway, I've suddenly realised that if we include Alice in some of the decision-making, it might make her feel more valued and that she's making a contribution. Why didn't I think of it before? In fact, that should be extended to the fitters and joiners as well. This is the problem with being so consumed with everything else in my life – I would be coming up with lots of ideas for the business, but I'm spending every waking hour worrying about Briony.

After work I rang Kate to see if she fancied going out. I decided that I can't sit around moping.

'Did you know we've all been interviewed?' she said.

'By the police?'

'Yes. I had mine this morning. They asked a *lot* of questions.'

'Oh, right. What did they say?'

'Well, they asked me what I thought about you, and about the time you banged your head.'

'What did you tell them?'

'That you're accident-prone, and that you're a bit of a klutz, but you wouldn't hurt a fly…'

'OK. Thanks…I think…'

'Well, when I told them that you'd said Briony had gone away *permanently,* I think they decided that it was a sign you'd done something to her, so I realised I needed to recover the situation and tell them what a softie you are.'

'How do you know I'm not a wolf in disguise?' She laughed and said that was a ridiculous idea. 'Well, thanks for the vote of confidence – I must admit, it's very reassuring. Do you want to go out somewhere this evening?'

'I've been waiting for you to ask – I was beginning to think you'd gone into hiding!' Kate suggested a little Italian place she knew called Giovanni's. 'It's good, cheap, cheerful and discreet,' she said. Then she added, – 'this *is* a date, isn't it, Alex?'

'Yes…yes, it is.' *(Well, there's no going back now.)* 'We might have to keep things low-key for a bit though – you know, I've got Briony's family to consider. I don't want to upset them. And if you believe what's in the papers, I'm almost a 'wanted man', so we don't want people staring at us.'

'That's why I thought this place would be a good choice – it's tucked away and a bit old-fashioned, but the food is good.'

It wasn't too busy as it was a Tuesday evening, and relatively early.

'I hope this is OK,' said Kate. 'Shall I order for us?'

'Oh, yes please do…'

'The Tuscan Chicken dish here is to *die for…'* she said. Then she thought she'd better re-phrase it, – 'I mean it's really delicious.'

'Oh, don't worry, – I don't want you treading on eggshells.'

'We missed you at the weekend, Alex.'

'Thanks for explaining to Jim that things are difficult at the moment. I will come this weekend, though. That's if I don't get arrested by then.'

'They should be focussing on looking for the boat…'

'They say they are doing that as well, but I suppose they have to cover all bases. It's a bit weird being their number one suspect. I'm surprised you want to associate with me, to be honest.'

'Well, I did have to consider the possibility that you might be a vicious criminal, but then I looked at your Facebook page and it just made me laugh.'

'What do you mean?' I said, defensively. 'What's wrong with it?'

'I don't know many criminals that are as concerned as you are with the welfare of their pet goldfish, for instance, or who spend their evenings on the sofa with a cat called Mr Catkins, eating a bag of Nik Naks and watching repeat episodes of *Miss Marple.'*

'Oh, I see. Well perhaps I am a bit boring – Briony certainly thinks so…'

'I didn't mean you're boring,' said Kate, laughing, – 'you just like being at home, don't you? You're a homebird.'

'Well, I've got a friend I see for the odd drink – he's called Jacob. Mind you, he's going to be tied up soon looking after his new baby. I'm a bit gutted, actually. Our boys' nights will become a rare thing. I don't envy him, though – he's going to be constantly at the beck and call of his wife and child. His life as he knows it will be over…anyway, it's his choice, isn't it! So, what do you do with your evenings, Kate?'

She thought for a bit, looked me in the eye, and then dropped a massive bombshell – just as our starters arrived.

'I don't have a lot of time to myself,' she said, – 'because I have a little girl to look after. She's five.'

Chapter 14

Last night's revelation sent me into such a spin – I must have made a right pillock of myself. I had to spend the rest of the evening trying to justify my position and persuade Kate that I'm not *against* children per se – it's just that I'm not at that point in my life yet. I don't know what she really thought of me, to be honest. She just smiled and said that sometimes a person doesn't have a choice in the matter. I didn't like to question her about who the father is – I expect she'll tell me at some point, that's if she doesn't dump me before things have even got going. She did ask me if it affected how I felt about seeing her. I told her that 'of course it wouldn't', but to be honest, I haven't had a chance to think it through. One thing I do know, though, is that Jacob will laugh his head off when I tell him. I think I'll save it for later. A *lot* later. I foolishly continued to devour the newspaper articles before bed and stayed up far too late. Some of them are so far-fetched, it makes you question how some of the sort of people who read these rags even manage to boil an egg. Fantasy scenarios abound – absurd notions such as the idea that the *Calamity Jane* was sucked into the Bermuda Triangle leaving no trace, or that aliens have abducted the pair of them, including their five-ton trawler, or (and this really is taking the biscuit), they were kidnapped by the lost citizens of Atlantis and now live as ghosts in the ruins of the city beneath the North Atlantic waves. I finally went to bed with my head full of countless theories and imaginings. None of the articles mentioned the dull but most likely scenario that the boat took on water and simply sank, just like the majority of other boats that don't make it home. As for the hypothesising about my involvement and my relationship with Briony, I could barely bring myself to read their ridiculous speculations. Comments about our living arrangements varied from, '*it was a ménage a trois*' to '*a hotbed of multiple partners and jealous lovers*'. Apparently, Briony and I frequently engage in '*S&M bondage sessions, resulting in profuse lacerations and gruesome contusions*'. I also discovered that my attempt to climb into the cottage upstairs window was '*obviously an attempt to murder Briony in her sleep, only to be thwarted by falling off*'. Police training, according to the Daily Blah, is a cover-up to dupe all the inspector Clouseaus into thinking I'm a respectable clean-living young man, when in reality, I'm a Jekyll and Hyde character – a criminal mastermind with evil intent and an unbridled sexual appetite. Uncle Frank was right – I really shouldn't read this bilge.

Mr Anderson had a long chat with me today about the hand-over. He told me I could talk to him any time if I needed to.

'It would be a pleasure, Alexander,' he said, – 'to give you an old man's advice and guidance – if you need it, of course.'

'Oh, thanks Mr Anderson…'

'Call me Terence now, Alexander – we're going to be friends, and I'm only your employer for one more week. By the way, I'm very pleased to see that you're keeping the staff on after all. Well done!'

'I've been wondering, Mr Anderson…I mean, Terrence, where Declan has gone? None of us has seen him for weeks…'

'Ah, well…that's a bit of a sore point, I'm afraid. He was against me selling the Business. We fell out over it. He'll come round eventually – when he realises it was the right thing to do.'

'Oh, I'm sorry to hear that.'

'He'll be able to set himself up in something of his own when it's all done and dusted, don't you worry.'

'What will you do with yourself?' I ventured.

The old man sighed. 'Well, my wife has been on at me to retire for quite some time, so she's delighted. I expect we'll travel a bit, do the garden, visit relatives – I might take up golf or something. We'll be quite happy…'

'Oh, good.' I got the feeling he didn't really mean it, though. He had a slightly lost look about him. I suppose he's done nothing else his whole life, other than build this Business. I definitely feel an affinity with him – I feel responsible for its welfare and survival now. 'I'm going to do my very best to make Anderson's succeed,' I said to him, – 'and I'll be very grateful for the experience and expertise you have to pass on to me, Mr Anderson…I mean, Terrence…' *(I don't think I'll get used to calling him that – it just doesn't feel right).*

At break time in the afternoon, Alice was cock-a-hoop when she heard she still had a job. She actually thanked me and Steve.

'What do I call you now?' she asked, – 'I mean, I've always called Mr Anderson by his surname…'

'Oh, just carry on as before, Alice,' I said, – 'everyone will be on first name terms.'

'Oh, right,' she grinned.

'There'll be a few changes coming,' I told her. 'My first one will be to get a decent coffee machine.'

'Can we have hot chocolate as well?'

'I expect we can manage that – we might have to charge you, though…' She looked at me, not quite sure if I was kidding or not.

'I'm joking,' I said, – 'it's time this place had a re-vamp, and that means keeping the staff happy.'

'Is there any news about Briony?' Alice asked.

'No, not yet. I will let everyone know if I hear anything. I've been meaning to ask you about Maggie. I still have her bracelet, and since Jacob will get his phone back now, she might as well have it back.'

'OK. I'm seeing her at the weekend, so I can give it to her then. By the way, she told me the police asked her loads of questions – she said they wanted to know what her relationship was with you…'

'Well, I hope she told them the truth, Alice.'

'What she told them was that she wouldn't discuss her private business with anyone. That's what she said to me anyway.'

'Really? She was quite happy to discuss it with you, Alice!'

'Well, that's different, isn't it! She's not a snitch, you know.'

Now I'm slightly regretting re-employing Alice – the company she keeps leaves a lot to be desired. Still, it's not a crime to be unfaithful even if I had been. It's bloody annoying, though, that the police have a false impression of me – like I'm some sort of Lothario character. That's more Jacob's bag.

When I got home in the evening, Uncle Frank had called and left a message:

'Alex I've been investigating this Findlay Connor chap. I think I've found something quite interesting – it might help.'

'Well,' I said to, Mr Catkins, – 'let's hope it does! What do you reckon?'

Mr Catkins cocked his head on one side and looked at me with his usual cool reserve, before yawning and going back to sleep. I poured myself a glass of wine and rang him back.

'How are you?' Frank said.

'I'm OK,' I lied.

'I've been checking out this Fin chap, Alex, and…well, you can have a look yourself. Google *Calamity Jane* – the boat, of course. Type in '2018 boat adrift at sea' – you'll see there's an article about his boat. Have a look and see what you think.'

I fired up my laptop and did as Frank suggested. It was quite a long article describing an incident at sea which left the *Calamity Jane* with a whacking great hole in her hull. The article suggested that the accident occurred due to incompetent or drunk crewmen. It apparently hit an obstacle in the water. The vessel took on water and the crew, who were all named, had to be rescued – one of them was Findlay Connor. There was significant criticism of the crew, saying that they were at best, inexperienced and at worst, reckless. Luckily, they were near the coast and could be rescued fairly easily. The boat was discovered to have had no life raft and only one life jacket on board. I then searched for Findlay Connor's name together with anything to do with the *Calamity Jane.* Intriguingly, I found information about an argument over the ownership of his boat. I wasn't sure how this would help anything, but I rang Frank back anyway.

'I've read the article, Frank, and I found some other information about Fin possibly not being the rightful owner of the *Calamity Jane.*'

'That's very interesting,' said Frank. 'I'll look into it. The main thing is, Findlay seems to have a history of possibly being an incompetent or dangerously reckless individual when it comes to taking a boat out at sea. This is very good news for you, Alex – hopefully it will re-focus the police's investigation and take the pressure off you.'

'That would definitely be a relief.'

'OK. I will inform the police about this and let's hope they double their efforts on search and rescue.'

I must say, in a weird way, this has cheered me up. The flip side, of course, is that Briony has put all her faith in a Walter Mitty character and therefore she didn't realise the dangers. How could she be so foolish, though? She must have been so overcome with desire for a more exhilarating life, that she put her trust in him. I don't know what she was thinking – I mean, she hardly knows him! *I* saw through him straight away. How could she fall for his nonsense? Perhaps she had a sort of psychotic episode or something. Maybe the saying 'love is blind' really is true, but you'd have to be *actually* blind, and deaf as well, to stomach some of the codswallop he comes out with. I can just imagine him trying to baffle her with sailing and fishing jargon – phrases such as, 'my cockpit has ample coaming', or 'look at my impressive foredeck' come immediately to mind. They're probably not lost at all – just swanning around in the Atlantic Ocean living off barbequed mackerel and sautéed squid, while fisherman Fin entertains her with more outlandish seafaring tales. I bet he fancies himself as a bit of a songster – she's probably being subjected to endless appallingly-rendered unaccompanied sea shanties…

I realised I was quite drunk by now, having downed most of the bottle of Sauvignon blanc, and my mind was running wild. I told myself to go to bed and get a much-needed good night's sleep. The trouble with over-doing the alcohol consumption, though, meant that I actually had a terrible night's sleep. In fact, I had a terrifying nightmare. I was convinced that my bed was a boat, and I was having to bail out hundreds of buckets of water. She was sinking fast and I had to save myself and my child, who kept trying to wriggle free – I managed to tie a rope to her to save her from drowning, and then woke up in a cold sweat at 4am, clinging to the mattress and shouting 'mayday, mayday…' Mr Catkins was staring down at me from the upper deck which after a second or two, I realised was the wardrobe, and strangely, the cat seemed to be sporting my dressing gown belt tied roughly around his middle.

'You look ill,' said Alice, when I went into work the next morning.

'Thanks. Actually, you're right, I'm not feeling very good at all.' I had to shield my eyes from her bright yellow blouse and matching headband. 'You're looking bright and cheerful, though…'

'Yes, I'm dead chuffed about my job, Alex. I thought I'd put something sunny on. Do you like it?'

Over the years I've learned to be as diplomatic as possible when it comes to women's clothing choices. 'Um, well it certainly brightens up a dull day, Alice!'

She seemed happy with this response. 'By the way, you've got a meeting today,' she reminded me, – 'it's that strategy thingy.'

Steve was waiting in the design room for me. 'God! You look a bit shit,' he told me.

'Yes, I know.'

'What happened?'

'It's my own fault,' I said, popping a couple of headache pills into my mouth, and swallowing them down with some of our terrible coffee from the polystyrene cup he offered me. 'I don't know what I was thinking. I drank a whole bottle of wine last night, on an empty stomach. Sorry. I promise I won't make a habit of it. I found something out about Findlay Connor.'

'Oh, anything useful?'

'Not sure, but it's starting to look like he's got form – some things in his past seem a bit shady.'

'Hmm, well, I suppose that'll take the pressure off you, won't it?'

'That's what Frank said, too.'

'Right, well we've got this meeting soon, so let's try and discuss some of the problems we've got to sort out – Mrs B.C. in particular. By the way, I saw the fitters this morning and we've lost one of them already, unfortunately, but Pete and Dave are staying and the joiners too – so that's good news at least. Let's get some decent coffee and crack on – I'll get Alice to nip out for some. I tell you what, she's a lot more amenable now – have you noticed?'

'I've certainly noticed her shirt…'

'Hahaha – yes, it's quite an eye-boggler, isn't it!! But this place needs jazzing up a bit. I can't wait to re-paint the walls, and old Anderson's office needs completely gutting…'

'Hold on – I don't want to get rid of everything, especially not his old tub chair – I want to keep it.'

'Are you serious, Alex? That grubby, battered old thing? Really?'

'Yes, really! It's a piece of history – and I quite like it.'

Steve gave me an odd look. 'Well, there's no accounting for taste, but it had better stop there. I mean, we're not keeping all the other tired old-fashioned stuff, are we? Like his ancient desk? And the filing cabinet? Or that ugly, dusty old lamp?'

When Gordon arrived later in the day, Steve and I had gone over most things and generally agreed on them, except for Mr Anderson's office furniture, of course. I suppose I could always take it home with me.

'So, let's talk about Mrs B.C.'s requests,' said Gordon. The three of us sat down in the main office to try and work out what to do about her demands. 'One of her requests is actually quite do-able. Charitable donations are tax-deductible. I suggest we don't specify exactly which charity – we can word it so that we don't have to stick to rescued cats.'

'It would be good to donate to something a bit more appropriate to our business, wouldn't it?' said Steve.

'Yes, but you will have to decide what that would be. Anyway, the next thing is her demand to get rid of the fitters, which in this case is actually against the law, so we are home and dry on that score. When it comes to your suppliers, we can argue that alternative sources of your products are not available – I don't know…perhaps they are the only company that can supply top quality black marble from Rhodes in Greece – I'll leave that to you to work out.'

'He's good, isn't he!' said Steve to me.

Gordon smiled, – 'we're not finished yet.'

'Now, the car park area that she wants to sell to her friend to grow plants…'

'Utterly ridiculous…' I interjected.

'Well, this is what I discovered in my searches. The land around this immediate area is not suitable for growing plants. In fact it's contaminated soil due to industrial use – there used to be a pesticides factory here.'

'Oh, YES!' Steve shouted. We high-fived. 'That's brilliant news!'

'Well, not for the plants…' said Gordon, dryly.

'What will you say to her?' I asked.

'As nicely as I can, I'll explain that it would be an unmitigated disaster for anyone to contemplate growing anything anywhere within a mile of this site.'

'So, what do we still have to sort out?'

'Her plan to have a statue made of her late husband.'

Steve groaned. 'I can't believe we have to agree to such a ridiculous idea…'

'Well, I'm not sure she has actually looked at the cost of such a thing. It's thousands. You pay at least £1,000 for something the size of an egg.'

'So, what are we going to do?'

'What would you say if I could persuade her to compromise – let's say I suggest that she gets a nice bust of him…'

'I still find the whole idea ludicrous,' Steve sighed.

'We could put a big plant in front of it, couldn't we?' I suggested, – 'then no one would really notice it.'

'I suppose so…or, what about this idea – we display one of our nice big fancy kitchen cupboards in the foyer, and put him inside it? And then, if you open the doors, there he is!'

'That's funny! I like it,' I said, laughing.

'Well, let's try and persuade her that a bust is a much better plan,' said Gordon.

'You're not going to tell her it'll be stuck in a cupboard?'

'No, I will be economic with the truth, as they say. My aim is to get this thing done as smoothly as possible. One more thing – this request to stamp her husband's name on everything. I suggest you agree to it…'

'No! We can't possibly do that!' said Steve, jumping in. 'That really is a step too far!'

'You stamp the backs and not the fronts,' said Gordon.

'Ah, yes – why didn't we think of that! Gordon, you're a genius!' Steve said, delighted.

Back at the flat, I was toying with the idea of contacting Kate. The weekend was looming and so far, I had nothing planned except for training on Sunday. Mr Catkins was steering clear of me since I tried to lasso him in the night and was giving me nervous glances from his perch on top of the fish tank.

'I am really sorry,' I said to him, – 'but if you hadn't been sleeping on my leg, it wouldn't have happened. You've got a perfectly good cat bed in the kitchen…' For reasons only known to himself, he refuses to go into his ridiculously expensive, purpose-made fluffy sleeping pod and prefers just about anywhere else that takes his fancy. They're such contrary creatures, cats. You never know where you are with them. The fish, on the other hand require very little interaction. I noticed, though, that the bulge is getting bigger. I really should look that up. Jacob rang me while I was googling '*unsightly lumps on fish*'.

'It was torturous!' he said, – 'I thought they'd never let me go home!'

'What was?'

'The interview – with the police…'

'Oh right, yes – I'm afraid they can be pretty long. So, what did they ask you?'

'Endless questions about you and your relationship with Briony, and they wanted to know about me picking your car up. They wanted proof, but I don't really have any. They asked about Maggie…'

'So, what did you say?'

'The truth, of course – that I couldn't remember. Sorry, but I honestly don't remember anything about that night, except in the morning when you said she was in your bed…'

'Is that what you told the police?'

'Well, yes…I mean, I wasn't going to lie, was I?'

I put my head in my hands and sighed. 'Thanks a bunch, mate.'

'Well, I'm sorry, but what else was I supposed to say?'

'Did they say anything about the messages on your phone?'

'Yeah – they described them as 'adolescent drivel' – a bit embarrassing to be honest. They gave me it back. I told them that the messages don't mean anything – it's just chat. They asked me if you ever exhibited any sign of evil intention towards anyone.'

'And…?'

'I told them the only time I witnessed anything along those lines was when you pushed me into the fountain in Trafalgar Square on New Year's Eve.'

'You pushed me first!'

'Well, whatever…' Jacob sniggered.

'You didn't tell them about the time I accidentally strangled you with that washing line, then?'

'No, I forgot about that. I'd better call them back…'

'You'd better not!'

'Only kidding! That *was* funny though, apart from the being strangled bit, which wasn't really very funny – not at the time anyway.'

'Oh my God! If you'd told them about that, I'd be rotting in a prison cell right now, marking time for eternity!'

It was a sunny day in July five years ago. Jacob, me and a couple of friends drove down to the Dorset coast for a day on the beach. We had a dinghy that just about took all four of us, but it was pretty unstable. Anyway, we had a washing line as a tow rope. When we were pulling the boat into the sea, the rope came undone and started floating off. Jacob swam to get it and stupidly put it round his neck so it didn't get swept away. I didn't see him do this as I was on the other side of the boat. I saw the end of the line in the water and grabbed it to pull it back. When it didn't come easily, I pulled even harder. Suffice to say, Jacob wasn't best pleased about having a purple ring around his neck, ruining both his tan, and his dating prospects that evening. Still, he was alive, which was the main thing.

'They seem to be quite obsessed with that book you're writing, Alex. I didn't really know what to say about it – I mean, I don't really know anything about it.'

'No – well, it's a murder mystery. That's all you need to know at the moment. It'll only complicate things if I tell you any more.'

'Well, as long as it isn't autobiographical,' said Jacob. 'They took some blood from me and fingerprints while I was there…'

'That's probably to check my car to see if you actually drove it or not. I forgot to tell you, but there was blood on the back seat of the car – it happened after you drove it back for me.'

'What do you mean, 'blood'? How?' He sounded alarmed.

'It's OK. It was from a cut on my hand, Jacob. Don't panic.'

'They want to talk to Lucy as well.'

'Why?'

'To verify that I went to fetch your car, and what time that day, I suppose. I'm bricking it Alex, because they'll probably bring up the subject of Maggie, and my phone going missing. They were asking if we made a habit of covering for each other. I think they have a suspicion that we are in this thing together.'

'They're clutching at straws, Jacob. Listen, I've found out some stuff about Fin – the police ought to be concentrating on that, not wasting time harassing us. Are you still coming over tomorrow to watch the football?'

'Yeah, sure. We can talk more then.'

I decided I might call Kate up and see if she fancied a drink at the pub, but she didn't respond, so I resigned myself to a night in with Mr Catkins for company and a cheese toastie. I've found myself avoiding crime dramas on the TV at the moment – it's too close to home. My writing has ground to a halt as well. Not surprising really. I think it's best to put it on the back burner for a bit. Anyway, the police still have my manuscript and my laptop. I watched some old episodes of *Country File* instead – suitably innocuous, I thought, should the police be monitoring my programme choices or bugging my flat. Mr Catkins seems to have forgiven me now – he curled up next to me on the sofa this evening, which was comforting in a small way.

Chapter 15

'I'm very concerned about you,' my mother said, on the phone the next day. 'Your Uncle Frank tells me you had to be interviewed by the police.'

'Yes, Mother, but you don't need to concern yourself with it – it's nothing to worry about.'

'I think perhaps I should come down there and stay with you for a bit, Alexander…'

'Oh, no, Mum – really, there's no need. I'm fine.'

'Your Uncle says it's *not* fine – he says it's quite serious.' *(Damn it! Why did he have to tell her?)*

'It won't help if you come, Mum…and, well…' I searched around frantically for an excuse, – '…the cat's got fleas, and, um, terrible diarrhoea,' I said, in desperation.

'Really? That's disgraceful! Honestly, Briony never looked after that poor cat properly – no wonder it's ill. You'd better take it to the vets as soon as possible, do you hear?'

'Oh, yes, of course I will.'

Phew, that was a close call. My mother coming to stay would be the last straw. I can't even bear to contemplate it. She treats me like a five-year old and spends the whole time, interfering. Last time she visited the flat, she re-arranged all the kitchen drawers and disposed of Briony's favourite houseplant. 'It was on its last legs,' said my mother, flatly refusing to accept that, even if it was, it wasn't for her to chop it up into pieces and shove it in the food bin. Briony had had that plant since university days and was very attached to it, sentimentally (something that my mother has little truck with). 'How can you mourn for a tatty, dead plant?' she'd said when Briony discovered the crime of the century and called my mother a 'plant murderer'.

'Anyway,' she continued, – 'haven't they found that boat yet?'

'No.'

'Well, I suppose that's a good sign, isn't it?'

'Not really, Mum. It could've capsized.'

'Oh, dear. There are a lot of sharks in the Atlantic Ocean, aren't there? Only the other day, I saw a programme on the telly about them. There's an enormous one called Iron-something-or-other – it's nearly 12 feet long, apparently.'

'That's not really helping, Mum – I don't want to think about the worst scenario. I think they're still alive. It's a huge ocean and people can drift for weeks without being found.'

'But what would they eat?'

'Well, Fin is a fisherman, Mum…and I've heard of people eating sea birds if they can catch them.'

'Really? That's horrible…'

'You can drink their blood to survive if you run out of water.'

'Alexander! That's revolting! I'm going to go now, but I'll give you a call later in the week.' The quickest way to get rid of my mother is to tell her something shocking. I've had a lot of fun with it over the years.

She takes the biscuit, though. I hate to say it, but I think she'd actually be secretly pleased if a massive shark had eaten Briony. At least she wouldn't be worrying about being upstaged at Harry's wedding.

I went out and got some beer in for the afternoon. I was looking forward to not having to think about lost boats, or people being mauled by giant sea creatures, or about being stuck in a 6ft by 8ft cell for the rest of my life. I just wanted to have a good shout at the game with Jacob and forget everything else for a few hours.

When Jacob turned up at 3pm, he was carrying a large holdall and a sleeping bag. This did not bode well.

'Where are you off to, then?' I asked.

'Yours,' he said.

'Pardon?'

'Your flat.'

'What on earth has happened?'

'Guess.'

'Have the police already spoken to her, then?'

'No, but I thought it would be better coming from me.' He plonked his bag down in the hall and I went and got us both a beer.

'I'm sorry, Jacob. What did she say?'

'That I'm an idiot, a cheat, a thoughtless moron, an inconsiderate selfish git – I could go on…'

'But didn't she believe that you didn't do anything?'

'Not really. I don't blame her, though. I have been all those things, and worse, in the past.'

'So she threw you out?'

'Yep.'

'For how long?'

'For good, she says.'

'Oh, no! This is terrible, Jacob. What are you going to do?'

'Stay here, if you don't mind, until I get myself sorted with something else. I hope that's OK?'

'Of course. But do you want me to talk to her?'

'No, mate. She's decided you're as bad, to be honest.'

'She'll come around, Jacob. She always does.'

'Well, I'm not sure about that. It's not looking too good. She said she's changing the locks tonight, and she's already blocked my number on her phone.'

'Crikey! Well, I suppose there's nothing we can do at the moment. Let's just watch the footy and drown our sorrows, eh?'

I left Jacob sleeping soundly on the sofa, as I let myself out the next morning to go to police training. It was another sunny day, and I decided to walk through the park, which takes longer but on a day like this it was nice to smell the warm grass and the scent from the flower borders. It gave me time to think about Jacob's predicament too. It sounds like Lucy has really lost it with him this time. I wish I could help in some way, but she obviously isn't going to listen to me. The baby party was supposed to be next weekend, as well – I'm guessing that's not happening now. What a mess! That girl, Maggie, has had a huge impact on both our lives – it's like the *Butterfly Effect.* We're now suffering the consequences of one foolish decision – *Chaos Theory* in motion. I wish we could rewind to that night and change what we did. If we could have anticipated what would happen, that split second, when Jacob invited her back to the flat, I would have called her a taxi, and it would have been a totally different outcome, and maybe none of these things would have happened. It's so strange to think that one ill-considered moment can change your life completely, and in both our cases, totally ruin it. I was just getting near to the kids' play area when a familiar voice called my name. Kate was standing by the swings, pushing a little girl with brown curly hair and a spotty, yellow dress. The child was laughing and shouting to go higher.

'Hi, Alex,' said Kate, smiling, – 'this is Polly.'

I've never conversed with a small child before, and it showed. 'Hello,' I said, – 'how are you?' She looked at me with a highly suspicious expression.

'Do you like rabbits?' she said, finally, climbing down off the swing.

'Well, I've never had one, so I'm not sure, but I've got a cat…'

'I don't like cats,' she said, firmly. 'Cats eat rabbits.'

'Well, my cat would never eat a rabbit, especially not your rabbit.'

'That's OK, then,' she said, seemingly satisfied.

'My Mum's just coming,' said Kate. 'She looks after Polly while I'm at the training session.'

'Are you going to catch bad people?' asked Polly.

'Um, not yet. We've got a lot to learn still.'

'I'm learning to skip – can I show you?'

'Oh, yes, that would be great.'

'Here comes Grandma,' said Kate, – 'it'll have to wait until next time, Polly.' Kate's mum was an older version of Kate; slim, blonde, petite, a little more guarded than her daughter, but friendly enough.

'She's so good,' said Kate, when they'd both gone. 'It's such a relief to know my mother can step in like this. What's your mum like?' she ventured, as we walked towards the exit gates of the park.

'Well…not like yours,' I said, cryptically. Kate gave me a questioning look, expecting more.

'She's not very maternal, I'm afraid. She's a lot older than your mother, and, well…she's from a different era…'

'You're making her sound like an antiquity!'

'She sort of is. She was quite old when she had me, and then I was sent to boarding school at eleven. She's a bit spikey…Briony calls her the *Munster-in-Law*…'

'Oh, right…she sounds a bit scary!' I instantly regretted telling her this. I mean, it's a sure-fire way to scare off a girlfriend. I tried to backtrack a bit.

'Her bark is worse than her bite – she doesn't mean to upset people.'

'I can't wait to meet her!' laughed Kate.

Training was an interesting experience. Jim decided to do some de-escalation techniques with us, which turned into quite an intense session. We were given scripts and roles to play, but some people just couldn't stick to their particular lines.

'Slow down your speech and use a calm voice – intonation is all-important here. You need to lower the pitch of your voice when trying to calm a suspect down. Think of it like this; waves breaking gently on the shore, or the warm summer breeze blowing softly on your face, or perhaps the pitter-patter sound of evening rain on leaves in the garden…'

I think he got a bit carried away to be honest. Leo fell asleep while he was in full flow, and we had to wake him up. I did try to do as Jim suggested, but somehow it was just too difficult. Rick was really good at being an aggressive and incredibly annoying criminal – he really got under my skin, and I lost it with him.

'This isn't going as planned, is it?' Jim told me. 'How will you cope with a real-life situation if you can't get it together during role-play? Remember what I said about keeping your voice low and soft? You sounded like a foghorn going off. Maybe you should swap roles – you might be better at being the offender today.'

I think Jim might have regretted suggesting I take the bad guy role, because I was a little too enthusiastic about that as well. Rick said he nearly cried at one point, I upset him so much.

'Fancy stopping at the pub on the way home?' said Kate, at the end of the day. 'I could do with a break before I go back to the house.'

I didn't need any encouragement. 'Yes, great idea.'

'You were really getting into your part there, weren't you!' said Kate, when we sat down with our drinks. 'I thought you were going to headbutt Rick at one stage!'

'Oh, yes, I did go overboard a bit. Maybe I should go to boxing or something and get rid of the pent-up stress that way. It might be a more socially acceptable way to off-load.'

'You've got a lot to cope with right now. I understand,' she said.

'Well, I'd say you have a fair amount to deal with yourself – working, having a child to care for and training as well. That's quite a heavy responsibility.'

'It's not so bad, really. Mum is very supportive, and since we all live in the same house, it works quite well. By the way,' she said, smiling at me, – 'you were very good with Polly – I think she liked you.'

'Oh, well, I don't know – I mean, I haven't had much to do with children before. Actually, I've been a bit worried that I was a bit thoughtless the other evening when we went out for supper. I'm sorry if I came across as being negative about kids. When you didn't respond to my phone call on Friday, I wondered if perhaps you'd decided not to see me again. Briony always says I've got two left feet where women are concerned…'

Kate laughed and told me I was over-thinking things. 'Let's just see where it takes us,' she said, 'we don't know what might happen next, do we?'

When I got home, Jacob was watching the TV, surrounded by dirty plates, a half-eaten pizza, several cups and glasses, and at least ten empty beer bottles.

'I hope you're not going to revert to student laziness while you're here,' I said, picking some of it up and taking it into the kitchen.

'Sorry, mate – I'll tidy up in a bit…'

'Any news from Lucy?' I enquired, hoping for something positive.

'No. She won't take my calls. By the way, this sofa's pretty uncomfortable, so I got my pal from work to lend me a fold-up bed.'

'Oh, right…'

'Well, I could be here for some time, couldn't I?'

'Um, yes, I guess you could…' (*Oh dear! This wasn't what I had in mind. Living with Briony was one thing, but Jacob is a lazy slob at the best of times, and pretty selfish to boot. He'll drive me nuts if he's here for long. This could seriously damage our friendship. I need to think of a solution, and quickly.*)

The next morning, I had to bite my tongue to keep the peace. As I anticipated, Jacob nipped into the shower just as I was hoping to, and then spent an aeon in there. Afterwards, he finished all the *Crunchy Nut* cornflakes in the box and left hardly any milk for me, before disappearing off to work with barely a nod. Even Briony would have acknowledged my existence and said, 'have a good day', or some such platitude. Honestly, Jacob has probably got what he deserves if this is how he behaves at home. I noticed with deep displeasure, the pizza and bottles still in the lounge, along with dirty clothes strewn across the carpet. To make matters worse, the police rang me to request another interview. With a heavy heart, I called Frank to let him know.

'This is old Mr Anderson's last week, isn't it?' said Alice, this morning. 'We should do something for him leaving…'

'Oh, yes, of course. You're quite right, Alice. Thank you. What do you suggest?'

'A leaving party on Friday after work. We could just hold it here.'

'We'd better get the invites out quickly,' said Steve. 'Invite all the regular clients, local suppliers, and all the workforce – can you think of anyone else?'

'Mrs B.C.,' Alice and I said at once.

'Oh, yes, well, we can't leave her out of it, can we!'

'We'd better make sure Gordon has sorted everything out first.'

'Alice, please can you email the invitations – say 6pm to 8pm here – wine and nibbles.'

'We need to give him a gift, don't we?' Steve said, as we walked away from the reception desk.

'Yes, something for his long service and dedication to the industry. I'll speak to Gordon. I can't afford to buy anything right now, myself. Briony hasn't been here to contribute to any bills – I'm a bit strapped, to be honest, until all the financial stuff gets sorted next week.'

'I can't either,' said Steve, – 'as you know, I've had to borrow the money for this buy-out and I don't have anything spare at the moment.'

'Mrs B.C. should buy him something, shouldn't she?'

'Well, I guess so, but we don't know whether they are on speaking terms or not, do we? Last time she was here, they weren't exactly getting on.'

'Hm, I'll do some sleuthing. Gordon might be able to suggest it to her.'

'I wonder what she would come up with?' Steve laughed. 'By the way, we need to advertise for another fitter.'

'OK – I'll get Alice onto that as well.'

'I meant to tell you, Alex – that kitchen you designed, the one with the green doors and no handles…'

'Yes?'

'The client loves it. Dave told me on Friday. He's just finishing the tiling off.'

'Oh, that's great to hear. We should get some photos for the new brochure.'

'Definitely, but we can't carry on using Geoff Peacock – he's about to fall off his perch…'

'Did you actually mean to say that?' I said, smirking.

'No, but it's funny! Let's get a new photographer in – I'll check it out. Start as we mean to go on, eh?'

Chapter 16

Uncle Frank knocked on my door at 8.30am and walked in to find Jacob and me arguing over who left the freezer door open all night.

'Sorry, Alex, but I have to go. See you later,' Jacob said, neatly exiting past the small lake that had formed on the kitchen floor. I threw some towels down and shut the freezer.

'Oh, dear!' said Frank.

'He's a bloody menace,' I said.

'Who was that?'

'Jacob – he's staying with me at the moment. His wife threw him out.'

'Is that because of the girl, Maggie?'

'Pretty much, but I think it's probably not the only reason.'

'No…' said Frank, eying the home-made tsunami creeping across the lino. 'You might be right. Are you ready to go?'

'Just give me a couple of minutes.'

When we arrived at the station, Frank told me again to stay calm. 'We don't want you getting locked up,' he said, – 'they'll try to provoke you like last time, and that's when people say stupid things. Keep your answers short.'

I took a deep breath in preparation for another grilling.

'We've had a chance to take a good look at your phone and laptop, Mr Philpot,' said P.C. Flannigan, her penetrating grey eyes searching my face for a reaction. 'It's, how shall I say – troubling?' She turned to D.I. Bannister.

He looked me straight in the eye. 'Let's start with the phone messages, shall we?' He began to read a series of text messages between Briony and me which were less than edifying:

Alex: *'Do you think Mr Catkins could be homed elsewhere? I found four cat hairs in the butter this morning!'*

Briony: *'Don't be so anal, Alex.'*

Alex: *'I'm not being anal, nobody wants a furry crumpet…'*

Briony: *'If Mr Catkins goes, I go.'*

Alex: *'Well, what if I accidentally ran him over, couldn't you get one of those bald ones instead? I could organise that, you know…'*

Briony: *'Now you're being mean and nasty.'*

Alex: *'And you're being utterly self-centred.'*

This next set of messages was just as bad. D.I. Bannister was really enjoying himself. He continued:

Briony: *'Your mother is a f*****g pain in the ass, Alex.'*

Alex: *'Why? What's happened?'*

Briony: *'Did you see what she sent me for my birthday this morning?'*

Alex: *'No…'*

Briony: *'A stupid book on family relationships. It's called 'Kindness Costs Nothing'.'*

Alex: *'What's wrong with that?'*

Briony: *'Are you serious? She's being passive aggressive AGAIN! She's suggesting that I'm not kind to her, you idiot!'*

Alex: *'I don't see it like that, and I'm not an idiot.* **You** *buy books for me!'*

Briony: *'To help you, Alex.* **Not** *to criticise you!'*

Alex: *'So 'Cut the Crap and Get Shit Done' was supposed to help me, was it?'*

Briony: *'Yes!'*

Alex: *'Well, it didn't. I just wanted to kill the author,* **and** *the person who gave it to me…'*

Briony: *'I rest my case!'*

He finished speaking and waited for a response from me.

'Well, all couples fight,' I said, lamely. 'Everyone says things they don't mean, don't they?'

'Hmm.' said D.I. Bannister, – 'let's talk about the laptop now. Tell us, Mr Philpot, why you were researching things like *'50 ways to Kill Your Lover'*, *'how much blood is in the human body', and 'why do dead bodies float to the surface after drowning?'* You seem to strongly favour a site called *'Cadavers R us'*, and another one called *'Getting Away With it'.'*

'I'm a writer.'

'That's a very convenient cover, isn't it? Anyone can say they're a writer, can't they? You haven't had any publishing success yet, have you?'

'No, but as you can see, I've written several chapters, and quite a comprehensive synopsis.'

'A very good way to redeem yourself…'

'This is ridiculous,' I said, getting irritated. I felt Frank's eyes on me.

'We don't think so, Mr Philpot. We think it's highly plausible for a person to plan a murder and then try to cover it up with a flimsy excuse that they're writing a literary masterpiece…' D.I. Bannister smirked.

I didn't rise to it, and Frank's relief was palpable.

'We also found a few emails that were significant, Mr Philpot. One that you sent to *'We Buy Any Old Car'* was of particular interest.'

'Really?'

'Yes. We are interested in why you suddenly wanted to sell your car. Why was that?'

'Because it's old and crappy…'

'Nothing to do with the fact that the back seat is covered in blood, then? Or that there may be other evidence inside it to link you to a possible crime?'

'No. I told you the blood was mine. Anyway, I'm not sure that even that company would have bought it.' D.I. Bannister gave a small smile at this point.

'I'd like to ask you about the string you used to tie the body up with,' P.C. Flannigan took over.

'Pardon?'

'The body – in your book, of course.' P.C. Flannigan showed me some white string in a bag.

'This string,' she said.

'It's just string…'

'Interesting, isn't it, Mr Philpot, that we found a lot of it in your car, along with some black plastic binbags, and this…' She held up another transparent bag containing the brass letter-opening knife.

'That's an old-fashioned letter-opener – I saved it from going to the tip. Mr Anderson was throwing it out.'

'And the string?'

'My passenger door is bust. The string was holding it shut…and the binbags were spare ones for the office. I told you I was helping to get rid of stuff. You can ask Mr Anderson.'

'In your book you talk about using white string and binbags to wrap up the body – a bit of a coincidence, isn't it?'

'Not really – it's just what I used to tie up rubbish from the office for the tip. It just seemed obvious. It's what writers do – they write what they know. You draw on your own experiences…' I fell hook line and sinker, and instantly felt a complete fool. Frank sighed a deep sigh, and I knew I was in trouble.

He stepped in. 'Look, you've questioned Mr Philpot several times now, and unless you have something compelling, it doesn't look like you can hold him here. There's no evidence that a crime has been committed. My client is entitled to leave now, if you have no further questions.'

'That was getting a bit hairy,' I said, as we climbed back into Frank's car.

'Well, they're barking up the wrong tree. The main thing is, they still have nothing to connect you to any crime, so unless something comes to light, that's how it will stay. They haven't found the slightest bit of evidence to incriminate you, Alex. It's all circumstantial. They have forensically examined your car, your home, your possessions, and Briony's too, and found nothing useful. The blood on the car seat has turned out to be yours, as you told them, and the only evidence of anything untoward on your phone and laptop is either related to research, or the usual sort of bickering with your partner, which to my mind is perfectly normal.'

'Thanks Uncle Frank. I don't know what I would do without you.'

'It's the least I could do,' he said, giving me a friendly pat.

'When will I get my things back, and my car?'

'I don't know – I imagine it'll be once they find Briony and Findlay. I think you might have to buy a new laptop and phone, Alex. By the way, I've been trying to locate the disputed owner of the *Calamity Jane.* It's someone called Jason Coleridge. Apparently, he lives somewhere near Southampton. I think I might have found him on Facebook. He was the only Jason Coleridge who seems to have an interest in boats. Might be worth tracking him down…'

'Yes, thanks for that. Aren't the police interested?'

'I think they're just focussed on the *Calamity Jane* and, since it appears to be registered in Findlay's name, they aren't particularly bothered about pursuing it.'

'Well, it's worth talking to this guy – he might know something.'

'That's what I thought. Anyway, I'd better go – your aunt needs me to go and help choose Harry and Julia's Wedding present. I don't really know why she needs me, though. She'll get what she wants anyway!' He dropped me at work, waved and swiftly drove off down the road.

'Nice car!' said Alice, who was standing outside the entrance.

'Why are you out here, Alice?'

'I'm going out for lunch,' she said, – 'I'm waiting for my boyfriend.'

'Oh, I see. That's nice.'

It hadn't even occurred to me that Alice might have a boyfriend. I ought to pay more attention to what's going on around me. The fact that even Alice has someone to go out with suddenly made me feel a bit envious, and a bit sorry for myself if I'm being honest. It's all very well going on the odd date with Kate, but I'm in a weird sort of limbo, and I can't just do it with gay abandon. I would be a pariah in everyone's eyes. When Briony finally resurfaces I don't know what the situation will be. Will she want to come back to me or will she have made up her mind that I'm a pathetic no-hoper and go on her way with that dodgy chancer, Findlay Connor, by her side. And then there's the possibility that they remain missing for weeks, months, even years – what then? At what point is it acceptable to get on with your life and move on? And then there are other people's opinions and remarks to cope with if I make it public that I'm with someone else. I can just imagine some people will have a field day. I don't even want to think about that – Briony's parents will be merciless. I really am between a rock and a hard place right now. I hope she's got a bloody good excuse for absenting herself like this.

Life has a funny way of suddenly turning everything on its head, doesn't it! I was making myself a cup of tea and looking for the packet of biscuits I'd tried to hide from Jacob, when the landline phone rang. I'm scared to pick it up these days, since it's usually the police. I took a deep breath and answered it.

'Is that Alexander Philpot? This is Karen Long from Interpol. We want to let you know the Coast Guard Investigative Service has just informed us that the *Calamity Jane* has been found abandoned on rocks near one of the Westman Islands off the south coast of Iceland.'

'Iceland!'

'Yes, Iceland.'

'Have any people been found?' I asked, shakily.

'No, they haven't. I'm sorry. The coast guard search and rescue team are currently searching the area. We'll let you know as soon as there's any news.'

'Do the families know?'

'Yes – we have informed them.'

'What are the chances…'

'The weather is currently quite warm, so if they managed to get onto dry land there's a good chance that they will be alive. The boat is badly damaged, though – the mast has snapped off at some point, cutting off communications.'

When I put the phone down, I realised I was shaking. I felt conflicted and a little nauseous. It wasn't sounding good. If the boat was damaged and had run aground on rocks, there was obviously loss of control…I looked up the islands on the internet and discovered there are fifteen of them – a string of bare, craggy peaks scattered along the coastline. They looked bleak and inhospitable. The only saving grace was that it's summertime at the moment, so if they did manage to get onto land, they would hopefully survive. I rang my mother to tell her the latest news, before she found out from anyone else.

'Is that where they were going, then?' she said.

'I don't know. There are lots of puffins there – maybe they were going on a nature tour…'

'Briony never struck me as someone who had an interest in wildlife, Alexander.'

'No, well, I have no idea why they ended up there. Hopefully they'll be found soon.'

'Mm,' said my mother, – 'if the mast is broken, that could mean they were in a nasty storm. That doesn't bode well…' *(Trust my mother to be the relentless harbinger of doom.)*

'Well, we'll have to hope for the best, won't we?'

'Of course!' said my mother, totally unconvincingly, if you ask me.

Chapter 17

On Thursday, I asked Kate if she would be free for supper – same place, same time.

'This is getting to be a habit,' she joked, sarcastically.

'I know I haven't been around much,' I said, – 'but there's been a lot going on.'

'I know. It's fine. So, any more news?'

'No, they're still searching. It's not looking good – I mean, what would they eat? And there's hardly any fresh water there.'

'They might be more resourceful than you know…'

'I hope so. Anyway, I've been thinking about it all week and my brain hurts. There's nothing I can do to help, so I just have to keep going. Let's order some food and wine. I can tell you all about the exciting plans afoot for Anderson's Kitchens!'

'Ooooh, I can't wait! You're going to be CEO of your own company – it's very impressive.'

'I can't really believe it myself. How's your job going?'

'I'm leaving, Alex. It's so boring. I've decided to join the police force.'

'Oh, that's great! So, you took Jim's advice, then?'

'I guess so.'

'Does that mean you won't be training with us any more?'

'I think I have to continue with it, and then I'll join another set of training courses, so you'll still see me for a while. I hope we can still see each other, anyway,' she said, taking my hand in hers. Her skin felt warm and soft, and I couldn't help thinking about how much I'd missed the physical touch of another human being. She was holding my gaze, waiting for an affirmation of some kind.

'I'd like to, Kate – in fact there's nothing I'd like more…'

It was only the fact my flat contained a displaced and extremely annoying homeless idiot, that prevented us from going there after the meal, which was probably a good thing in hindsight.

'Thanks for a lovely evening,' said Kate, after we kissed, out on the street in the cool night air.

'Sorry about my flatmate…' I said, dismally.

Kate laughed as I took her arm, and we walked back to her house. 'I'll be worth waiting for,' she said, when we got to her gate. I kissed her again, but it didn't feel right, and I couldn't shake off that nagging guilt nipping at my heels.

Jacob wasn't in when I got back to the flat. He's obviously been and gone out again. I don't know how much longer I can stand it. Mr Catkins has taken to the streets since this trespassing invader has encroached on his territory, and I feel like doing the same. I decided then and there to go and see Lucy the next day and plead his case. Surely, if she knew the truth about Maggie's overnight stay, she'd forgive Jacob and take him back. It's not as if he was even capable of being unfaithful to her that night. Anyway, I have to preserve my own sanity. If Jacob stays here much longer, I won't be responsible for my actions. When I came back tonight, the flat looked almost as bad as when the police did a search and sling. I checked the phone messages and saw that I had a couple. One was from Harry to say I should keep my chin up and not to forget his stag night next weekend, which I had. The other one was Claire from my author's group asking if I'll be able to make it on Tuesday evening. I'm really not in the mood to go to my author's group at the moment. I've had the wind taken out of my sails big time, and anyway, I need to concentrate on Anderson's Kitchens.

God knows what time Jacob came home last night, but he didn't make it to his camp bed. In the morning I found him lying prostrate on the lounge rug, fully clothed and still wearing his shoes. I poked him to make sure he was still alive and made myself some toast and coffee. Even the cat jumping on him didn't wake him. He was a sorry sight, but

I didn't have time to administer any TLC. Besides, I'm not feeling particularly sympathetic towards him, to be honest – especially when I discovered he's used up all my shaving foam, and borrowed my best work shirt, which I'd ironed especially for Mr Anderson's leaving do. I dread to think what condition it will be in when I get it back. Don't get me wrong, I'm very fond of my friend Jacob, as long as he keeps his distance and doesn't impinge on my personal space too much. Unfortunately for him, my tolerance levels have been tested to the limit. I made a promise to myself last night, that I'd visit Lucy tomorrow afternoon, before the party, and try to talk to her.

Since the police impounded my car, I've been having to walk to work every day, which in some ways is a good thing. Briony would certainly be pleased to see how much weight I've lost. She'd also be quite impressed with my improved dress sense, I think. Since Jacob had a go at me, I have been making more of an effort in that department. CEO's have to look like they're serious people, out to make a mark in the world, don't they? It hasn't gone unnoticed to me, that if you present yourself as a scruffy ne'er do well, that's how people treat you, unless you're clever enough to pull off 'shambolic chic'. But obviously I'm not going to get away with that. My mother would have something to say about it without a doubt.

As soon as I got into work, I rang Gordon to find out if Mrs B.C. was coming to the party.

'She's agreed to come and honour his achievements and long service, but I don't know what she's going to give him as a leaving gift. She wouldn't tell me. She said it would be a surprise.'

'That makes me quite nervous, Gordon.'

'Well, I can't deny I feel the same. Perhaps we could have a back-up gift just in case….'

'I reckon,' said Steve, at break time, 'that we should give him and his wife a new kitchen.'

'That's a really good idea, Steve…I bet they haven't had a new one for years. You know how stingy he is! It's a bit sad, isn't it – the old man going – I'm going to miss him.'

'I won't miss this coffee!' said Steve, chucking half a cup of it down the sink. By the way, I got Alice to ask the local press to come over this evening. It's a momentous occasion for the Company and an exciting new beginning – I thought it would help us to get noticed a bit…'

'Good job I put a decent shirt and tie on, then.'

'You know, people don't really wear ties any more, Alex…'

'That's right,' piped up Alice, – 'it's all loose collars and no socks now.'

'Right – well, I'll ditch the tie, but there's no way I'm going sockless.'

At the end of the day, I girded up my loins to go and see Lucy. I wasn't really sure what I'd say to her, but 'necessity is the mother of invention', as the saying goes, and there was definitely a large amount of necessity in this particular situation.

'Come in,' she said, lumbering down the hall.

'Wow! You've got bigger since I saw you last,' I said, somewhat tactlessly.

'That's what happens when a woman allows a man to impregnate her with his sperm – it's an unfortunate consequence of an ill thought-out and impulsive collaboration.' Lucy was clearly in a fighting mood.

'Shall I make us a cup of tea?' I said, watching her ease herself carefully into an armchair.

'Yes please, Alex – that's very thoughtful, unlike Jacob.' *(Oh dear! This isn't going to be easy.)*

'Do you want to know how he's doing?' I asked, tentatively.

'Not really, but you might as well tell me anyway.'

'He's a mess, Lucy,' I said, laying it on thick. 'Seriously – he can't cope on his own.'

'Well, I know that – he can barely work the washing machine and he thinks food miraculously appears in cupboards by magic, similar to money growing on trees and fairies doing washing up.'

'I don't mean his less than desirable attitude to domestic chores (and I totally sympathise) – I mean he's lost without you – he doesn't know what to do with himself.'

'You mean, he's spending his evenings in the pub drinking…'

'Well, yes, a bit, but he's really missing you, Lucy…'

'Hmm.' She sipped her tea.

'I actually think he's really scared about becoming a dad.'

'He's got a funny way of showing it.'

'He wasn't with Maggie that night, you know. She was with me the whole time.'

'That's not what she says, apparently.'

'What do you mean?'

'She refused to tell the police what she was doing at your flat.'

'Look, Lucy, he definitely wasn't with her – she was in my bed for heaven's sake, so I should know.'

She thought for a minute. 'Well, even if she was, his behaviour leaves a lot to be desired, and yours too…'

'Give him a chance to repair things between you, Lucy – please? Once the baby comes, he'll be a changed man. That's what happens to lots of us – we see the light! Honestly, you'll probably see a change in him for the better, I'm sure of it…'

By the time I left, she'd come round a little. Now I needed to go back and work on Jacob. There was not time now, though. I needed to be at work for Mr Anderson's big send-off.

Thank goodness we kept Alice on – she really did a great job organising food and wine and keeping everything hidden from Mr Anderson until the last minute. He really had no idea – even when people started turning up at close of business.

'Why are all these people coming in just when we're about to close?' he said, irritated by a man holding a large camera seemingly just meandering around aimlessly. 'Do you think he's from Craftisan, Alex?' Mr Anderson whispered, – 'he seems to be taking photographs of the showroom – he might be a spy…'

'I don't think so. Oh, look, here's Mrs Bedlington Clarke coming in…' I said, distracting him. Soon the place was filling up and it became impossible not to say something. I grabbed a spoon and banged it on the table to get everyone's attention:

'Thank you for coming here tonight, everyone – as you know, you've all been invited to celebrate a special person's long service and brilliant contribution to the kitchen design industry. Terrence Anderson – where are you?' Mr Anderson appeared and came to stand by me, looking a bit embarrassed and slightly bewildered. 'You may not be aware, but Terrence here, has won several awards in his illustrious career as a highly skilled designer of beautifully hand-crafted kitchens for clients all over the UK. Tonight, we are very sad to be saying goodbye to Terrence who has carried the torch alone for high quality design since his business partner and close friend, Alfred Bedlington Clarke, sadly passed away ten years ago. Happily, his late wife, Evangeline is here this evening to honour the memory of her late husband and to join us all in wishing Terrence a long and happy retirement. We also want to say 'thank you' – Terrence, for your impressive and admirable contribution to the world of hand-crafted kitchens.' I held my glass aloft to toast him. 'To Terrence Anderson, Master Craftsman!' Mrs B.C. stepped forward, shook his hand and gave him a shoebox sized wooden box. He smiled and thanked her but didn't open it.

'What do you think it is?' whispered Steve, intrigued.

'No idea. He seems happy enough, though.'

'Jolly good speech,' said Gordon coming towards us.

'Yes, it was impressive, Alex – without notes as well!' Steve slapped me on the back.

'Well, I knew what I wanted to say, I suppose.'

'Well, the old man's legacy will be hard to match, but we're going to try, aren't we Alex!'

'Can I just get a photo of you all together?' the photographer butted in. 'Thanks, that's great.'

I didn't manage to avoid talking to Evangeline Bedlington Clarke, unfortunately. She made a beeline for me as soon as there was a gap in the crowd.

'Alexander, there you are! I want to speak to you – it's very important.' Steve scooted off to avoid her and left me with the old dragon, defenceless. 'Now, I know my lawyers have come to an agreement on most things, but I'd like to make a personal request, Alexander. I feel very nervous about handing Anderson's Kitchens over to a couple of inexperienced novices, but in the absence of any other sensible buyers, I've had to capitulate. It's not been an easy decision, as you can probably imagine. Anyhow, I've got a special favour to ask of you. You will be aware of my involvement with the charity, *Fluffy Friends Cat Rescue?'*

'Yes, of course…' My heart sank.

'Well, for the last twenty years, I have been patron of this marvellous charity, but I feel it's time to hand it over to someone younger and more energetic.'

'Oh, yes – well, I'm sure you'll find someone…' I wasn't sure where she was going with this.

'I'd like to nominate you, Alexander. It would be fitting that the Company continues with the good work that I've spent many years doing, dedicating myself to the valuable cause of helping these poor creatures. Alice tells me you have a cat of your own, so I thought you would be a sympathetic supporter.' She was looking at me with the determined gaze of a vulture circling its dying prey. 'Don't forget, I haven't signed *all* the papers yet…' She smiled at me. A nicotine-stained grin with one gold tooth glinting in the glare of the office strip lights.

'Um, well, I'll have to give it some thought,' I said, hesitantly.

'Well, don't take too long, Alexander – I have to inform the trustees on Monday. I know you'll be the ideal choice,' she said, putting on her jacket to leave. 'I'll just go and say 'goodbye' to Terrence.'

'Oh God!' I said to Steve, once she'd gone. 'You'll never guess what she wants me to do…'

'Jump through more hoops, I imagine.'

When I told him, he roared with laughter.

'How can I get out of it, Steve?'

'Say you're allergic to cats…'

'I can't. Alice stupidly told her I've got a cat!'

'What does it entail, anyway?'

'Promote the charity, I suppose – help raise funds for it…'

'Well, you can probably step down after five years…'

'FIVE YEARS!'

'Some of these jobs are longer, so it could be worse! Anyway, you should be flattered – it's not as if you're a 'somebody', is it!' Steve laughed again.

We stayed behind to clear up after the guests had gone and switched everything off.

'This time next week, this'll be ours,' said Steve. 'Can you believe it!'

'No, it's going to take a bit of getting used to.'

Mr Anderson was getting his coat form the office and taking a last look round. In his hand he held the little box firmly in his grasp.

'Do you mind me asking, Terrence – I'm intrigued – what's in the box?' Steve asked him.

Mr Anderson was silent for a minute and then gave us a slow smile. 'Something very special,' he said, – 'I didn't think she would return it to me, but she has, and now I can go home happy. I've done my apprenticeship! Goodbye lads, and don't forget you can call me any time.' And with that, he was gone.

'Well, I wonder what that was all about, Alex?'

'We'll probably never know.'

Chapter 18

Walking back to the flat, I was thinking about what to say to Jacob. A selection of possible approaches presented themselves to me, ranging from extremely blunt to completely chickening out. '*Get out of my flat you lazy scumbag,'* whilst being almost irresistible, would be a tad mean. Alternatively, I could say, '*you're welcome to stay as long as you like, since you are my best and only friend, but wouldn't it be a good idea for you and Lucy to consider going down the route of reconciliation?*' Probably too wordy and woolly, and since he has the concentration span of a goldfish, he'd lose the thread. I plumped for something simple but inoffensive.

'Jacob,' I said, making us both a cup of tea, – 'I think you should talk to Lucy…'

'I've tried, Alex. She won't take my calls.'

'Well, how about a romantic gesture.'

'Like what? The last time I suggested that to you, it was a total disaster!'

'I know, but this is different. It's not as if there's anyone else involved.'

'That's not what Lucy thinks.'

'She's had time to think about it now and she's probably calmed down a lot.'

'Well, what do you suggest?'

'How about making something for the baby? You know, you could make a wooden crib or a toybox, or something…'

'You are kidding? I'm crap at carpentry – I can't even put an Ikea bookcase together without losing half the screws.'

'OK, well, you could buy something special – what about one of those posh hand-made rocking horses?'

'Have you any idea how much they are, Alex? I'd have to take out a second mortgage!'

'I tell you what, I'll ask Kate – she's got a child. She might have an idea…' Oh dear! It was out of my mouth before I had time to think about it.

'You what? A child? Really?' Hahahaha! Alex, you kept *that* quiet!'

'She's not mine, Jacob!'

'Well, obviously – but you have to admit, that is quite funny…'

'I knew I shouldn't have told you. Anyway, it's not a serious relationship.'

'Not yet,' said Jacob, smirking.

My mother saved me from further ribbing by ringing me just at the right moment.

'Alex, is that you?'

'Of course…'

'Well, it could have been that foolish friend of yours…'

'How do you know about Jacob?'

'Walls have ears,' she said, cryptically.

'Oh, you mean Uncle Frank told you,' I guessed.

'Well, he did mention your friend was currently homeless. I hope he doesn't get too comfortable there.'

'It's just temporary,' I said, mentally crossing my fingers. 'Anyway, how are you?'

'Terrible,' she said, launching into a tirade. 'My so-called friend, Meredith Postlethwaite, has been calling me up and asking about Briony, insinuating all sorts of things. She told me the police have a suspect and then asked if you'd been arrested yet.'

'Mother, as far as I know, they don't have a suspect, and they don't have evidence to arrest anyone. It's all supposition. Just ignore her – it's all nonsense.'

'Well, I told Meredith that you couldn't possibly have murdered anyone because you're training to be a policeman.'

'I'm not sure that would completely rule me out – it's not mutually exclusive, you know…'

'I also told her that you were a very well-behaved boy at school. In fact, you always got the most house-points in class for politeness and thoughtfulness…'

'So did Harold Shipman…'

'You shouldn't joke about this, Alex!'

'Sorry. Thanks for the vote of confidence, Mum,' I said, feeling a bit sad that she felt she had to defend me against her busybody 'friends'. 'Don't worry – I'm not going to get locked up yet. Shall I come over tomorrow and take you out somewhere? We could go to Fortnum & Maison for afternoon tea.'

'Oh, yes, that would be nice – as long as they don't skimp on the butter. Felicity Crachet said that last time she went there, they only provided enough for *one* scone!'

'Why didn't she just ask for more?'

'Oh no, Alex – that's terribly unseemly. One can't be seen to appear gluttonous. What would people think!'

My poor mother must be suffering particularly badly at the moment, always being so concerned about what people think. She and the other old crones she hangs out with seem to have nothing better to do than speculate endlessly about other people's private lives. God knows what she tells them about me. At least she'll soon be able to boast about her son being the CEO of his own company, unless of course it all goes tits up at the last minute. Mrs B.C. could have a sudden change of heart. I don't know how I'm going to get out of being a patron for her cat charity – the old bat has well and truly got her claws into me.

Kate told me off when I called her to see if she was free.

'I can't just drop everything, you know,' she said. 'I have to organise a babysitter, so I need more notice. You could come here, though…'

'Won't I be intruding on family time?'

'Not really. Polly goes to bed at 7pm. Mum and Dad are out tonight, and my brother and sister are at a party, so we'll have the place to ourselves.'

When I said 'yes' to her invitation, I knew what it could mean, and I felt the warm glow of anticipation growing exponentially inside me.

'Are you going out?' Jacob asked.

'Yes – to Kate's. I'll ask her opinion about how best to try and patch things up between you and Lucy. By the way, if you stay here, do you think you could clear up after yourself?'

'You're just like Lucy, mate! You're turning into an old nag.' He could see my hackles rising and decided to change his tune. 'OK, OK, I'll do it!'

To my disappointment and utter frustration, the evening didn't go quite as I'd hoped it would, and I was back home by 9pm.

'Did her dad come home and chase you out?' said Jacob, laughing. 'What happened?' I traipsed back into the flat, my unopened bottle of wine in hand.

'Polly is what happened. She had a temperature and a sore throat and kept waking up. In the end I said to Kate that it would be better if we left it for another time.'

'Oh, right, so no action for you two lovebirds tonight, then!'

'You don't have to be so crude, Jacob…'

'Sorry, but just saying…'

'Well, don't.' Jacob tried to look apologetic, but it never really comes off – he's naturally unapologetic, which is another of his problems.

'Shall we go down the pub?'

'Yeah, might as well.'

Harry called me up this morning to make sure I hadn't forgotten where we were meeting up this evening. He told me one of his friends had dropped out at the last minute, so I asked if Jacob could come instead.

'You haven't forgotten you have to wear an animal onesie, have you? I've earmarked a donkey for you, and Jacob can have Ian's Pink Panther one. It's going to be awesome!'

'Yes, Harry, I'm sure it will be!' I tried to sound enthusiastic.

'We're going to go on the London Eye first – I've booked us a private pod.'

'Great!'

'Then we're going on the tube to Soho.'

'How many of us will be there?'

'Fifteen.'

'Fifteen! Wow! That's really great!'

Why am I dreading it? It'll be a brilliant night out, and I could really do with just letting my hair down. Maybe I'm just 'in the doldrums' as Steve says. I'll have to pull myself together for Harry's sake – I mean you only have one stag night, don't you! It's a good job I told Mum that I'll take her out today and not tomorrow. God knows what state we'll be in after tonight.

'Why are we getting a taxi?' said my mother as we waited for it on the pavement outside her house.

'Because the police still have my car, Mum.'

'Oh, goodness me! What on earth do they want that old thing for?'

'Well, you might ask…it's in case I stashed a body in it.'

'Alexander, I've said before – I wish you wouldn't joke about it.'

'It's my way of coping with it. Anyway, it's much easier for us to get a taxi, and probably cost the same.'

'Well, I'll pay – I don't suppose you get much at that company you work for. You really ought to consider going elsewhere. Your Uncle Frank would advise you…'

'I promise you I will be getting on with it very shortly – just as soon as everything calms down.'

'Frank told me they've found the boat – in Iceland of all places. You can't survive for long in those temperatures…'

'Ah, here it is…' I opened the door so she could climb in and shut it quickly before she could carry on.

'Where to?' asked the driver.

'Alexander, do you mind if we don't go to Fortnum and Mason's? I'm a bit worried there might be people we know there…'

'Oh, right. OK, well, let's just go to Covent Garden, then.'

'Perfect,' said my mother, breathing a sigh of relief.

'Who are you trying to avoid?' I asked, somewhat put out.

'Well, Meredith Postlethwaite's sister, Portia, shops there at the weekend. I'd rather she didn't see you.' My mother was behaving very oddly.

'I don't really see why that matters, Mum.'

'I've told them you're abroad…they keep asking questions, you see. It's easier if I just say I haven't seen you…'

'Right. Shall I just put a bag on my head, then?'

'Don't be ridiculous, Alexander!' She began rummaging in her bag. 'I've brought this, though – I thought you could put it on while we're out and about,' she said, producing my late father's brown, felt fedora, which looked decidedly crushed from being crammed into her handbag. I capitulated, however, knowing that it would be easier just to go along with wearing it. Anyway, I've always quite liked myself in it – fancying the idea of being a bit of an Indiana Jones character. Ridiculous, really, as I'm quite the opposite. The fact that my mother kept telling me to pull it down over my eyes more, probably drew more attention to me than less, defeating the purpose, but she wouldn't be dissuaded.

Of course, things never go as one would hope, do they! Best laid plans and all that…

'Philippa!' The unmistakable voice of Jemima's mother, Lara Cobberton-Crew, rang out like a foghorn across the crowded plaza. We could not hide as we had already sat ourselves down in what we thought was a discreet corner behind a pillar, waiting for our order of tea and cakes.

'Oh, hello, Lara,' my mother was forced to respond, as the woman strode purposefully towards us.

'And who is this with you, Phil?' said Lara, peering beneath the brim of my hat.

'It's…Alexander,' she said, defeated.

'Ah, it's nice to meet you finally! I thought you were away until October, though…' she said, confused. 'You only just left last week, didn't you?'

'He got sunstroke,' said my mother. 'It's terribly hot in the Outback…'

'Really? Even in winter?' Lara looked even more confused.

'Climate change,' I said quickly. 'It's everywhere.'

'What did you think of Oz, then, Alex?' I looked to my mother for guidance, but none came.

'Er, well, it was very dry…the Koalas were nice…'

'I saw your picture in the papers, Alex,' she said, her face changing from bewildered to sympathetic verging on pity. 'I never believe what they say in these rags. I hope they find her soon. Fancy her going off with a scruffy deadbeat like him when she's got a nice man waiting at home for her!'

'Thanks, Lara. It's very kind of you to say so.'

'You know, Jemima's back from Switzerland next week. She's been on an intensive health and weight loss retreat. One of those fancy places where they do yoga and chronic infiltration, or something. You should give her a call…' She winked at me and waved as she walked off.

'Why on earth did you tell people I was Down Under, Mum? What else did you say? I need to be forewarned!'

'Just that you were there visiting a cousin in Wellington…'

'You do know that's in New Zealand, don't you?'

The rest of the afternoon was spent fending off my mother's pressing suggestions about taking Jemima out for dinner. I could see the dollar signs in her eyes positively glowing with excitement at the prospect.

'There's no way I'm taking her out – wild horses wouldn't drag me there!'

'Meredith tells me she's had a nose-job…'

'I don't care how much surgical intervention she has, they can't reconfigure her brain.'

'Well, you're not getting any younger, Alexander.'

'Actually, I think I am – every day that I spend away from nagging women is lengthening my life by a week; it's a scientific fact.'

She sighed and prodded at her Victoria sponge. 'I only want what's best for you,' she said for the umpteenth time.

Chapter 19

Suffice to say, I did not make it to police training today. Jacob and I were dead to the world until mid-afternoon, and even then we were the walking dead, so not much of an improvement.

'Pass me a crisp,' said Jacob, in a whisper, as we sat on the sofa nursing our hangovers. 'I can't lean…' The bowl of carbohydrates lay tantalisingly on the coffee table before us, but the effort of reaching over was too much for him to contemplate.

'I need a drink of water,' I said, making a gargantuan effort to prise myself from the comfort of the sofa and shuffle to the kitchen. Mr Catkins was sitting by his empty bowl, looking forlorn. He meowed loudly when I opened the food cupboard.

'I'd better feed you, hadn't I?' I said, reaching for a food pouch with the speed of a tortoise. He meowed impatiently. Bending down and depositing the stinky contents into his bowl, I retched uncontrollably. Luckily for me, the sink was within vomiting distance.

'You OK?' groaned Jacob from beneath Briony's borrowed blanket.

'No, but I'll live – mostly…'

What were we thinking last night? Trying to keep up with a bunch of twenty-somethings. I'd lost count by ten o'clock, how many shots we'd downed. Luckily the trip on the Eye was before anyone got completely hammered, although

Harry and Jack had obviously had a few beforehand. The donkey costume got mislaid somewhere between Edgeware Road and Turkey Street and I was forced to improvise. Harry's flatmate rummaged around in her closet and found me a Wonder Woman outfit, which I stupidly agreed to wear. If only I'd had a crystal ball. Thank goodness the night was warm. Getting all fifteen of us across town at once proved harder than you'd imagine. Escalators aren't built to withstand several T-rex's, three giant inflatable hamburgers, two Homer Simpsons and a Miss Piggy crammed onto the stairs in one go. There was nearly a nasty accident involving a cascading tray of doughnuts and a shocking pink feather boa. Luckily, someone had the foresight to bring a penknife. We filled a whole carriage on the tube at Waterloo, which got a bit too hot and one of the T-Rex's fainted. We had to relieve him of his costume to cool him down, which would have been OK, except he hadn't bothered with any underpants. Someone else lost their shoe down the gap, and the Pink Panther got his tail caught in the sliding doors. By the time we got to Piccadilly Circus, that tail looked very sorry for itself. We lost Miss Piggy along the way – he told us later that he'd been signing autographs down by Pret a Manger. The inflatables didn't last very long – it was too tempting for other drunk idiots to stick a burning fag butt into the plastic and watch them deflate to wrinkly unidentifiable heaps. One by one the T-Rex's succumbed to the overbearing heat in the bars we trawled round and had to ditch their costumes, but not before we collected a following of raucous women out on a hen night. Gradually though, our fan base slipped away into the night and most of us went home too, except for Harry, Jack and Patrick, who were still going strong at 3am. I don't know how we managed to get a taxi to agree to take us home, but someone must have felt sorry for us. I have no recollection of the latter half of the evening, but my bank account appears to be £300 down. I've no idea why I spent fifty quid in Ann Summers. I didn't even know they opened that late.

'I'm ready to lead a life of abstinence now,' said Jacob. I don't think my liver can take any more.'

'I bet the others have been awake for hours,' I said, sipping my water and trying not to gag.

'Yeah, it's time, Alex. Time to let go of our irresponsible selves. Let's make a pact…'

'Well, if you like…'

'No more binge drinking!' he said, clanking his Alka Seltzer against my flask of water. 'I've decided to go round to my own house this evening.'

'OK, well you'd better get cleaned up. What are you going to say to Lucy?'

'I had an idea. You're good with words, aren't you?'

'Er, well…'

'I thought you could write her a letter.'

'What – you mean, like a love letter?'

'I know it's a bit of a cliché…'

'Have you *seen* Cyrano de Bergerac?'

'What? No! What's that? Sounds like some kind of cocktail…'

I rolled my eyes. 'Ugly bloke writes love letters to beautiful woman he fancies but pretends they're from a handsome young soldier who she admires. Woman falls for the poetic and seductive writing, thinking it's from handsome soldier. Handsome soldier is actually an uneducated nitwit. It doesn't end well…'

'I don't care – please Alex – you can rough it up a bit, so she doesn't suspect anything…'

Once I felt more human, I gave in to his relentless pestering and got out some paper and a pen.

'This is such a bad idea, Jacob…'

'No, it isn't. It could work…'

'Or we could be strung up.'

'It can't get much worse for me, can it?' said Jacob, looking slightly teary-eyed.

'So, what do you want to say?'

'I don't know, you're the writer.'

'I know, but I need something to go on. What about *'can't live without you,* etc…Something along the lines of, *'I'll wither and die alone*'.'

'Well, that's a bit over the top – I don't think she'll go for it…'

'I'm kidding.'

'Oh, right.'

'Let's start off with something about you missing her.'

'Yeah, that's good,' he said, his eyes drifting back to the TV.

I decided I needed to go to my bedroom for peace and quiet and tried to write my first love letter to someone I barely even like. Then I realised I needed to write it to someone I actually do love, a lot.

When I'd finally finished, I handed it to Jacob.

'Man, that's brilliant,' he said, chuffed to bits.

'I roughed it up like you suggested. There are a few spelling mistakes and bad grammar in there.'

'I can't tell…'

'Exactly.'

'Thanks, Alex. I owe you one! I'm going to go now. Wish me luck! I'll call you and let you know how it goes with Lucy.'

I fell asleep for a while on the sofa, until the intercom buzzed suddenly, waking me up, and Harry's cheeky face appeared at my door.

'How do you feel today?' Harry said, smirking.

'Bloody awful!'

'But what a night, Alex! We had the best time, didn't we!'

'I'm not sure,' I said, laughing.

'I've got some cracking photos to show you.'

'Do I really want to see them?'

'You should. The ones of you are hilarious!'

My heart sank slightly. I made us some coffee and we hooked Harry's phone up to the TV so we could see them in all their outrageous and inappropriate glory. It was an excruciating experience – mostly I felt sorry for the passers-by and the long-suffering bartenders having to put up with a marauding bunch of larger louts.

'Oh, my God!' I said, when Harry paused the photos at an image of one of the T-Rex's dangling a hamburger over the side of Lambeth Bridge.

'It's OK, we tied your tights round him.'

'Jesus! I wondered what happened to them.'

There were lots of photos of us climbing up things and, of course, it was inevitable that we would attempt to scale the lions in Trafalgar Square. Not very easy, however, if you're wearing a slippery plastic costume. Only a few of us managed it, but there was plenty of hilarity and high jinks in the process. It was also irresistible for the inflatables to ignore the tremendous photo opportunity of floating around in the fountain. The Pink Panther didn't fare too well, though – his fabric costume soaked up water like a sponge and there was a photo to prove it, of Jacob desperately wringing it out by hand. The Homer Simpsons had a race down the steps of the National Gallery and ended up mostly rolling – incredibly, neither of them sustained any injuries. Miss Piggy's wig ended up on one of the dolphin's heads, and there was a particularly good picture of me riding a triton. Then we came to the last few photos, the photos of shame, I'd call them.

'You can't keep those!' I said with alarm.

'Aw, it's just larking about – no one cares…'

'I do! What if our parents see them?'

'I'm not going to let them see those ones…'

'I bloody hope not! I had no idea we were even in there until I saw my bank balance this morning. I don't remember anything about it.'

'We got thrown out, anyway…'

'I'm not remotely surprised,' I said, staring incredulously at the set of embarrassing photos of the boys messing about with all the sex toys in the shop and trying on some of the gear.

'That's a great one of you!' Harry laughed.

'Thank God you can't tell!' I cringed when I saw my head encased in a slave hood complete with muzzle. Miss Piggy appeared to be whipping me ferociously with a cat o' nine tails.

'So that's why I've got a sore backside…What did I spend £50 on, Harry?'

'Oh, yeah, well – when we were in the shop, you broke one of their electric penis pumps trying to use it on the Pink Panther's tail and, 'cos it was wet, it shorted out and they made you pay for it.'

Oh, good grief! Where is it now?'

'You gave it to the policeman who came to evict us…'

'Oh, really?'

'Yeah, you told him he could stick his truncation in it…'

When I got into work on Monday morning, there was an odd atmosphere which I couldn't put my finger on. Alice was smiling at me in a strange way, like she knew something I didn't.

'What's so funny?' I said, eventually, getting irritated.

'This!' she said, holding up the *London Evening Standard.* 'Sorry, Alex, but it's pretty funny, isn't it!'

'What is?'

'Haven't you seen it?'

'No…'

She left me to digest the frontpage news article, which was accompanied by a shocking photo of someone clinging onto the Eros statue in the middle of Piccadilly Circus. Entitled '*Stupid Cupid',* the idiot who'd scaled the eleven-metre-high centrepiece, was plainly off their head on booze and possibly not the full shilling. On closer inspection, I realised the man was wearing a blue skirt, a red bustier, and brandishing a golden sword. When I turned the page, there was a fuzzy blow-up photo of Wonder Woman's face, and there was no doubt about who it was. The article described the chaos which the reveller caused by climbing up the statue and dancing on the top, in front of crowds of people who'd gathered below to watch. Twelve policemen, two fire engines, an ambulance, and a cherry-picker were apparently brought to the scene at around 2am, but the man climbed back down and escaped arrest by fleeing the area. He was last seen legging it down Shaftesbury Avenue with a Pink Panther in pursuit. Finally, it said that the police have several witnesses who could identify the person responsible, and an arrest will be likely to follow shortly.

'How on earth did I manage that? I can't even climb a tree these days!'

'Fuelled by drink and high spirits,' said Steve, – 'it's pretty impressive!'

'I have absolutely no recollection of it…'

'Unfortunately, the police do, and you should probably go down and hand yourself in before they turn up here.'

'Do you think I'll be arrested?'

'No idea. They can't do you for being drunk and disorderly because they can't prove it now.'

'The tabloids are going to love this, aren't they! I might as well just turn to a life of crime at this rate.'

I decided to follow Steve's advice and take myself down to the station.'

Expecting to be arrested, I rang Uncle Frank to tell him.

'I'll be down shortly,' he said, – 'I know about this already – Harry showed me the paper this morning. He feels responsible since it was his stag night.'

'I take full responsibility, Frank – no one forced me to drink gazillions of shots.'

'We've all been there, Alex. I was a bit of a party animal myself at your age.'

'Really?'

'Yes, I know – hard to believe now, isn't it! You were just letting your hair down, and who can blame you, it's been a tough time. Let's hope the police are lenient.'

Luckily for me (or so I thought), they let me off with a caution. Not before they had a laugh at my expense, though. P.C. Flannigan was immensely pleased with herself to have me by the short and curlies.

'Well, well Mr Philpot, here again so soon! You're becoming somewhat of a celebrity, aren't you! Your mother will be proud…'

By the time I got out of there it was lunch time. Frank suggested we went for a pub lunch, so we sat down for an hour and mulled things over.

'There's still no news, is there?' he said.

'Not a thing…I know they towed the boat back to harbour. Apparently, it's badly damaged but they don't know how it happened.'

'There's something fishy about that boat,' said Frank.

'You're not saying!' I laughed.

'Joking aside, something's not right – I want to try and get to the bottom of it. The other strange thing is that there's been very little mention in the papers of anything to do with Findlay's family and friends – haven't you noticed?'

'Yes, I have, but I thought maybe he doesn't really have any…'

'His cousin at the pub was mentioned once or twice, but why has no one else missed him? It's a bit odd, isn't it?'

'Well, his cousin did say he's a loner…'

'That's suspicious too – what's he got to hide, do you think? There's something fishy about the whole thing.'

'Hahaha, you're probably right. I mean, he's definitely a cod – I mean 'con' merchant, isn't he!'

'We need to find more out about him. Briony got herself mixed up in something dodgy, I think.'

Chapter 20

It looks like Jacob and Lucy might have made up. When he didn't come back to the flat last night, I guessed that was the case. My literary efforts must have done the trick. I can't say I feel good about it, though, having been achieved under false pretences. These things have a nasty habit of biting you on the bum. I've got more pressing things to contend with at the moment, though. The damn tabloids have got hold of some photos of my night on the town. I don't know how they got hold of them, but they've poured more fuel on the fire, that's for sure. Now that I've been photographed in an uncompromising position, wearing bondage gear and getting a whipping from a muppet, the hacks have been having plenty of fun and games, feasting on this juicy material like rabid piranhas.

'ALEX JUST CAN'T GET ENOUGH', screamed one headline, in the Sunday Stunner. Another appalling one claimed, ***'ALEX PHILS HIS POT'*** (*how do these people sleep* *at night!).* The worst one said, ***'SEX-STARVED ALEX GETS DOMINATRIXED'*** Thank God my mother and her posh friends don't read these rags. The same can't be said for other people, unfortunately – particularly the staff at Anderson's Kitchens, who've been lapping it up vociferously. Steve says it will all blow over, but this is going to follow me around for years, like a bad penny it'll show up at the wrong moment and be impossible to shake off. And what on earth will Briony think, if she ever comes back? She'll think I've gone loopy in her absence. Maybe that's partly true – I think I have definitely lost my way without her to keep me grounded.

The one thing that is going to plan is the business, thank goodness. We've got new brochures, a new layout, and a new approach. The coffee machine came today, much to everyone's delight. The painters are busy making the place a brighter more joyful place to be. We've ordered new lighting and decent furniture. Alice will have her own office too. The look on her face was very gratifying. We've promoted her to the role of secretary and decided to employ a new receptionist. Steve and I have a new set-up with better and more up to date equipment, and we've managed to attract two new clients in the last week already. I decided to speak to the staff about what they've seen in the papers – Steve thought that it might help to get them on side. It wasn't an easy thing to do, though. I nearly bottled it, but my new grown-up alter ego won over, and I had to bite the bullet. I decided to try and make light of it and make them realise I'm just a victim of circumstances. The truth is, that if Briony wasn't missing, they wouldn't have had any interest in my alcohol-fuelled antics on a night out in the city.

'Take us with you next time!' said Pete. 'I could do with a laugh!'

'I think it'll be a long time before I get over that one,' I said. 'Let's just say that I'm lucky to be alive, to be honest, and come out of it in one piece. I don't recommend that anyone attempts to climb up a huge edifice like that in a drunken state – I could be dead now.'

'Yeah, you should keep away from 'huge edifices'…' said Dave, guffawing. 'That Miss Whiplash looked bloody scary!' The men roared with laughter until I banged on the table to shut them up.

'I just want to say thanks for being understanding, and let's just get on with making Anderson's the best it can be.' I got a clap at the end, and they all went off home, hopefully with a better impression of their new boss, although I'm not expecting miracles.

I rang Kate when I got home and asked how Polly was.

'OK, thanks, Alex. How are you?' It was a loaded question. Had she seen the papers? I had to assume she had and I couldn't lie.

'Well, it's been a rollercoaster of a few days, actually. Did you see the Standard?'

'Um, well, yes, I did. I can't believe you did such a crazy thing, Alex!'

'Even worse is that I don't remember anything about it…'

'That's quite worrying…'

'Things got a bit out of control – it was my cousin's stag night on Saturday, and we all drank way too much. I just lost control for a bit.'

'My colleagues at work showed me some other things too…'

'Oh, God! Right, well, we were just larking about in a sex shop – it wasn't serious…'

'That's not how it looks in the photos.'

'Honestly, Kate, we were just messing about…'

'I think it would be good to cool things off for a bit, if you don't mind, Alex. I've got stuff going on myself – my ex has reappeared and…'

'Oh, right…well, I'm really sorry if I've messed things up…'

'It's not just that…let's just leave it for now.'

Talk about a punch in the stomach. Now I feel like a total prat. I've messed up royally and now I'm suffering the consequences. I refrained from taking solace in a bottle of wine and rang Jacob to see if he was free.

'You didn't call me,' I said to him. 'How is everything?'

'Good, Alex. Really good. Thanks for all your help, mate. It worked a treat.'

'Really? She fell for it, then?'

'Not exactly.'

'What does that mean?'

'She said there was no way that I would have written it.'

'Oh.'

'But she forgave me anyway and said it was a nice gesture.'

'So, it was still worth the effort, then?'

'Yes. I didn't tell her it was you, though. She's not very happy with you right now, especially with all the stuff in the papers.'

'Well, she's not the only one. I'm currently a social outcast. Did you see the *Standard,* by the way?'

'What about it?'

'The front page, dummy!'

'I did see it… I didn't really bother reading it, though. Some pissed up idiot climbed up a statue…Hang on, was that you? FUCKING HELL! Jesus, Alex! That's mad!'

'It was, and you were with me.'

'I don't remember you climbing on that thing. That's crazy! I mean, you could have died!'

'I know, but I didn't. I almost wish I had…'

'Mate, you don't mean that.'

'Everyone hates me, even my own mother.'

'Well, no offence, but that's normal for you, isn't it?'

'Fair.'

'How's it going with what's-her-name?'

'Kate? It's not.'

'Oh, sorry to hear that. Look I've got to go. Let's catch up on Saturday, yeah?'

Feeling very sorry for myself, I rummaged in the cupboard for something to eat. All I could find to make a meal with was a tin of tuna and some frozen onion rings. I shoved the rings in the oven, despite the fact that I suspected they were the same ones that Briony produced to clamp to my bruised head several weeks ago, and then got put back to re-freeze. Oh, well, I was passed caring. Who cares if I die from food poisoning? Mind you, there are probably enough preservatives injected into those things to survive a nuclear blast. It was, as predicted, a particularly revolting tea, illustrating how miserable my life has become. I switched on the TV, whilst digging into the last scrapings from a tub of ancient ice-cream – the flavour of which was indeterminable, not helped by the fact that it was so old the label had perished. At this point I also remembered that Jacob had left the freezer door open all night on more than one occasion, so the likelihood of my imminent death was creeping ever closer. I still didn't care.

I flicked through the TV channels trying to find something undemanding to watch. Suddenly, and to my utter astonishment, a newsflash tagline popped up announcing something: '***Breaking news*** *(it said)*– ***runaway lovers found safe and well***'. There was some fuzzy footage of a dinghy on choppy water by some rocks. Then I saw Briony and Fin being helped onto it by rescue people in orange waterproof gear. I could hardly believe what I was seeing. The camera zoomed in on their startled faces. There was no mistaking them. Then my phone began to ring and before long I could hear people starting to gather outside on the street. I picked up the house phone, cutting off the caller, and rang my mother.

'Are you sure?' she said.

'Turn on the news…it's on practically every channel.'

'I can't, Alexander – I'm with Felicity Crachet. We're just deadheading her petunias. There are rather a lot of them. I'll call you later.'

I called Uncle Frank to give him the good news, and he was delighted, unlike my mother.

'Thank God for that, Alex. That's fantastic news. Now we can all get back to normal and get on with our lives. Keep me updated, won't you!'

I left the phone off the hook and sat down. What was 'normal' going to look like? Would Briony come home now, or stay with Findlay? Would she despise me now, anyway? I haven't exactly behaved very well. Neither has she. Would I be able to forgive her? Maybe I don't want to forgive her. Perhaps she won't want me to forgive her. Maybe she doesn't love me any more? She might be perfectly happy to carry on as she is, with the hateful Findlay by her side. Her parents probably don't approve of me at all now, either. How can I redeem myself in people's eyes? I'm a pariah, a walking disaster, a drunken, moronic, fool. Who in their right mind would want to be associated with me now? My thoughts were spinning like a pinwheel. I looked outside – the crowd had already grown. A camera pointed up at my window and I quickly shut the curtains. I looked for more information on the news channels and discovered that they'd been sheltering in a cave on one of the smaller islands, and that they were now being taken to Reykjavik to be seen by doctors and given the usual health checks. On the film they'd looked remarkably well, but definitely a lot thinner. Mr Catkins came and laid himself down on Briony's dressing gown, and incredibly, started to purr.

'At least you'll be happy now, won't you?' I said, stroking his soft stripey fur.

Chapter 21

I decided that there would be no more news until tomorrow and went to bed with some of Briony's earplugs stuffed in my ears. They mostly worked except that someone managed to get let into the lobby during the night by a neighbour, and then banged on my door for fifteen minutes. These bloody reporters! Don't they ever give up? I didn't sleep well, though – a combination of anxiety, nervous anticipation and a dicky stomach was probably to blame.

When I checked the street outside in the morning, I could see quite a few cameras and people milling about. I put the phone back, but it instantly rang like crazy, so I took it off again. I called Steve to give him the news.

'That's incredible! Fantastic! Best news ever!' Then he thought about it and told me to stay away from Anderson's. 'You'd better not come in, Alex. They'll be all over you like a rash if you turn up here. We don't need that kind of publicity.'

'Yes, you're right. Maybe I'll go to my uncle's house. I'll call him now.'

'Have you contacted Interpol, or the police yet?' Frank said.

'No, I wasn't sure about it – Briony's parents will know what's going on, won't they?'

'Why don't you ring them, Alex, and find out?'

'It's um, well, it's quite awkward – I'm not exactly flavour of the month, you know. They think it's my fault she ran off…and then everything that's gone on since then hasn't helped…'

'I see. Well, I'm happy to speak to them if you give me their number.'

'I'm sorry, Frank – my head is spinning, and I just don't know the best way to deal with it all.'

'I'm sending a taxi for you, Alex. Be ready in twenty minutes, OK? When you leave the flat, just smile and wave. Got it?'

'Yes.'

'Don't speak to any of them. There'll be plenty of time for that later.'

The whole situation felt surreal. I had to tell myself what to do next: *Feed the cat, feed the fish, take a shower, shave, get dressed, make coffee, have breakfast…no, not hungry, check the post, brush teeth, check pockets for keys and wallet…* I felt like an automaton. Once I'd gone through my usual morning routine, I looked down from my window and saw the taxi pulling up outside. The paparazzi readied themselves, jostling for position. *Right, deep breath, don't need to rush, take your time, you're in control, everything's fine…*

Lauren rushed out and gave me a massive hug when I arrived, and ushered me inside.

'Did you call your mother?' she asked, switching the kettle on.

'Yes. She's disappointed.'

'Surely not!'

'Well, obviously she wasn't hoping they'd actually died (*I honestly couldn't be sure of that statement*) – probably just that they'd found themselves an island to live on, hopefully forever…'

'Well, they certainly found an island!'

'I imagine that wasn't quite what Briony had in mind.'

'What does your mother have against her, anyway?'

'Mostly that she's not Jemima Cobberton-Crew, or some other wealthy heiress…'

'I'll let you into a secret, Alex; when your mother met your father, he wasn't particularly well-off, but she ignored her own father's wishes herself. In the end it worked out very well for her, as you know. She doesn't have a leg to stand on, so just ignore it. You decide for yourself – no one can tell you who to fall in love with.'

'Thanks, Lauren. I wish Dad was here now.'

'We're here instead, Alex, and we'll always have your back. How do you feel about her coming back?' Lauren said, handing me a mug of tea.

'I don't know. She might not want to come back to me.'

'But what if she did…what then?'

I couldn't answer her. I've spent such a lot of time hating Fin and being annoyed with Briony, that I think I've lost any ability to feel anything any more.

'I've just got off the phone to Briony's parents, Alex,' said Frank, coming into the kitchen. 'They didn't have much time to chat for long, but they said Briony would be travelling back alone tomorrow and getting into Heathrow some time in the afternoon. Apparently, she's OK health-wise, but quite shaken up after her gruelling experience at sea. They don't know anything else, except Findlay is being held back for questioning by the police in Iceland.'

'Did they mention me at all?'

'Only that you would have to wait for her to contact you herself.'

'Oh, right.' (*Another kick in the stomach.*)

'We'd better get on and retrieve your mobile phone and all your stuff from the station.'

So now, I was going to be in limbo for hours, wondering what she's thinking. I mooched around in the lounge while Frank sorted some things out. I spotted the Evening Standard lying on the coffee table and picked it up, absentmindedly flicking through the pages. It occurred to me that whoever gave the photos to the tabloid papers taken in Ann Summers' basement, must have been with us. But who? One of Harry's friends was obviously a conspirator, or an opportunist. I looked again at the photo of me on the front page and considered the possibility that maybe I *actually* thought I *was* Wonder Woman that night. Good God! I might have been so intoxicated that I believed I could fly! Maybe someone spiked my drink? To have a sudden and unprecedented burst of super-strength needs a serious dose of adrenalin-fuelled substance of some kind. Someone was out to exploit me, and they certainly got their money's worth. Slowly it began to dawn on me that it wasn't such a daft idea. There I was, swaying from the top of Eros with my cape flying in the wind, like a bird of paradise on acid. What a nutter! How on earth was I capable of such a thing? I still can't believe it. I mean, the bravest thing I've ever done physically was borrow someone's skateboard and attempt a rail trick, and that didn't end well, I can tell you. It was only two feet off the ground as well. Briony has always called me a wimp when it comes to stuff like that. Mind you, she's going to be amazed when she sees this. Maybe it'll boost my image in her eyes. She might realise I have hidden depths, like Atticus in *To Kill a Mockingbird,* she could suddenly gain renewed respect for me. Obviously climbing illegally up a public monument and endangering my own life and possibly others as well, isn't the same as getting out a gun and shooting a rabid dog to save the town, but still, she might see me a bit differently now.

P.C. Flannigan looked less than pleased to see me. You'd think she would have been happy to discover that I'm an innocent man, wouldn't you?

'I believe this belongs to you, as well, Mr Philpot,' she said, stony-faced. She held up a torn red cape and a very bent toy sword with *Wonder Woman* emblazoned along its shiny gold blade.

'I've been lost without it!' I said, regaining some confidence. Frank gave me a sideways look, basically warning me not to push my luck. Finally, I had all my things returned to me and I was free to go.

'Do you think she was born like that?' I said to Frank as we went down the steps of the station and outside into the sunshine.

'You're a disappointment, Alex,' said Frank, – 'they were hoping to discover a body or two and gain a bit of notoriety to boot. It makes their job more exciting than just dealing with a Drunk and Disorderly.'

'Well, they got two for the price of one with me, then!'

I climbed into my car which smelt so appalling I nearly passed out. My next job was a no-brainer – I needed to get it to the valeting place down the road urgently. I drove there double-quick with all the windows wide open and the fans on full blast.

Two of the workmen were standing idle when I arrived and wandered over to assess the car.

‘Oi,’ said the one with a big moustache and bald head, – ‘your face looks familiar.’

‘I know,’ said the clean-shaven one wearing a baseball cap, – ‘it’s that bloke what climbed the big fairy in Piccadilly Circus. Would you Adam and Eve it!’

‘I think you’ve got me confused with someone else…’ I lied.

‘Nah, I’m sure it’s you. Anyway, if it isn’t, why ’ave you got a big gold sword on the front seat, what says on it…’

‘It’s fucking Wonder Woman!’ butted in his mate.

‘Ah, Jesus, that was the funniest thing I’ve seen in ages. I nearly died laughing! ’Ere – where’s your dress, then?’

‘I only wear it at the weekends,’ I said, giving in, – ‘but it’s a bit worse for wear…’

‘Like you was!’ They both fell about laughing. ‘Fair play, mate, you looked a right radio rental with your Alan Whickers on show!’

‘OK, joke’s over. Can you look at my car, please?’

‘Blimey mate,’ they said, when they spotted the back seat. Looks like a murder’s been committed…’

‘Well, you’re not the first to say so.’

‘It’s going to need a lot of cleaning – it’s going to cost…’

‘Well, just do the best you can, please.’ As I walked away, I saw the pair of them reeling from the smell when they opened the back doors. I couldn’t help but smile wryly.

Being a local celebrity, though irksome in most respects, does seem to have an upside. I discovered, as I scrolled through the many messages on my phone, that I've been getting calls and messages from a publishing house called 'Black Deed Publishing' – a woman called Stacey Armstrong had left several voice messages which I listened to with growing interest. Basically, they seemed very keen to publish me, even though they haven't even seen my novel yet. A bit bizarre, but the world of publishing really is a foreign country to me. I decided to give her a call while I waited for Bill and Ben to spruce up my car.

'Hi, Stacey – this is Alex, Alex Philpot…'

'Alex? Oh…yes, just a minute…oh, yes, Alex! (I could hear papers being rustled) Good of you to call back…'

'I'm sorry it wasn't sooner, only my phone was taken by the police and I've only just got it back.'

'Oh, yes, we're very keen to hear all about your experience, Alex. I'd love to talk to you about an exciting proposal we have for you. When are you free? Tomorrow's good for me…how about lunch at Padella's in Shoreditch, say 1pm? I'll book it – you'll be my guest, by the way. See you then?'

'Oh, yes, righto…'

God, I sounded like an imbecile – I mean, who says 'righto' any more? Jesus! Oh, well, she probably wasn't really listening. She certainly sounded very busy – I could hardly get a word in!

I went back to fetch my car, which on inspection, looked a lot better. The smell still lingered, though. I made a mental note to buy one of those dangling pine trees. I reluctantly paid their whopping cleaning bill of £60 and drove home. There were a few paparazzi hanging around waiting for my return.

'Hey, Alex, how do you feel? It must have been terrible to be falsely accused – is that why you went on a bender?' one of them shouted.

'Are you embarrassed, Alex? Is that why she left you? Was it because of the cross-dressing, Alex?'

I did as Frank told me and waved and smiled, although I had the sword in my hand, so I'm not sure how that'll look in the papers. I was glad to get back home. It was nice of Frank and Lauren to invite me to stay with them, but I just wanted to be in my own place. There were a couple of messages on the house phone which I listened to while I made a cup of tea.

'Alex dear, it's your mother here…I've had a number of phone calls today about someone called Wonder Woman. I've no idea what they're talking about. Unless you've suddenly joined the Magic Circle, they must be hoax calls. Your uncle tells me you're no longer under investigation, so that's a relief. I was getting very tired of Meredith Postlethwaite's insinuations….'

There were plenty of other messages from various reporters and radio people, and even one from the Breakfast Television Studios.

'I think I might need an agent at this rate,' I said to Mr Catkins, who was lying comatose on top of the fish tank. I noticed that the bulge on Xander's side was even bigger. I googled what to do about it and decided to follow the instructions for fish dropsy, since that seemed the most likely affliction. I put him in a separate tank with some Epsom salts and some plants to hide behind. Well, even fish don't like being stared at, do they? I surmised that if he didn't improve, I might be forced to euthanise him – not something I really relish doing, but needs must. Wonder Woman wouldn't shy away from doing what's right, would she? I don't know why I feel so attached to my fish – perhaps because I've had them a long time, and weirdly, they're the only consistent thing in my life right now, so it seems imperative to keep them alive. I turned on the TV and phoned for a Chinese takeaway. Luckily, the beer supply hadn't been completely decimated by Jacob, so I opened one and sat down. Maybe by tomorrow the press will have lost interest and leave me alone.

Chapter 22

I called Steve this morning to tell him I need to take another day away from work. There are still one or two people hanging around on the street outside, and with Briony flying home today, there'll probably be more press activity. Anyway, it gives me breathing space to think about this meeting with Stacey. It hasn't really sunk in that someone is actually interested in my novel! Wow! If ever I needed motivation to finish it, this is it! I suppose I *should* get an agent – I know that much. If Briony was here, she'd tell me what to do – PR and media stuff really is her area of expertise. Amongst all the reclaimed possessions I got back from the police, I found my manuscript and looked at it with fresh eyes. I felt a renewed sense of purpose and excitement about it now – it's somehow achieved an elevated status, an acknowledgement of value to the world out there, someone was interested, enthusiastic, even. I removed it from the grubby plastic bag it had been deposited in and placed it back on my desk along with my laptop.

Thank goodness for Jacob making me buy some decent clothing, I thought, as I wound my way through the hip, happening streets of Shoreditch to my lunchtime rendezvous.

'Alex!' A woman roughly in her forties, with a black page-cut hair style, red lipstick and a large, beaded necklace, was waving from across the room. I made my way around the tables and shook her outstretched hand. She flashed a big white smile at me and asked what I'd like to drink.

'Have whatever you'd like to eat, Alex. I always eat salad at lunch time, but you lads need more than that to sustain you, don't you? Now let's get down to business – I've got an hour, tops.'

'OK, great! I've brought my manuscript along, although it's quite a long way from being completed…'

Stacey looked slightly confused. 'Oh…right – I didn't know you had actually written anything yourself.' She sucked sedately on the straw of her iced lime and strawberry mocktail.

Now it was my turn to look confused. 'I thought that was why you'd invited me here?' I felt suddenly thrown off balance. 'Wasn't that the reason?'

'Um, no, Alex, not really. Let me explain what we can offer you. We specialise in memoir and real-life stories –

particularly exciting, dramatic tales of life-affirming experiences…' She could see I was not quite getting it. 'Like your story, Alex! Your own personal journey – the highs and lows, the good and the bad, life and death…'

'Oh, well my life isn't really terribly interesting you know…'

'Well, maybe it wasn't, until now – until that fateful day when your beautiful girlfriend was snatched away from you, and your world turned into a living nightmare. That's what we are interested in, Alex. We want to hear about your own heart-rending emotional roller-coaster of a journey from that terrible day, through the ordeal of becoming a number one murder suspect until the incredible and mind-blowing news of the discovery that Briony was still alive and coming home at last!' She leaned across and touched my hand for emphasis.

'Oh, I see.'

'It's a wonderful story, Alex. Our readers are absolutely going to love it!'

'I'm not sure I can write something like that…my novel is in the genre of crime fiction – that's what I really enjoy doing.'

'Oh, you don't need to worry your head about that. We have a whole team of people to write it for you.'

'Oh, really? So, what do I do, exactly?'

'You tell us your story, in every detail – names, places, events, conversations, how you felt…EVERYTHING! Once that's done, you sit back and let us do the rest. How does that sound, Alex?'

'Well, it's not what I was expecting…I don't know, I mean, I'd have to think about it.'

'This might help to galvanise those thoughts, Alex.' She pushed a napkin towards me, her bright red nails glinting in the shaft of sunlight that fell across our table. I looked down at what she'd written. I had to look twice. Scrawled on the thin paper was a five-figure sum. I looked at it in disbelief. 'I've brought along some paperwork for you to sign to get things moving.' She plonked a thick wad of papers in front of me which looked like a load of legal documents. 'Just sign where I've marked with a cross.'

'Um, I don't think I'll sign anything until my lawyer has taken a look at it, Stacey, if you don't mind.'

'Well, don't take too long, Alex. My brief is to get this done and dusted by 4pm Friday.' She smiled again and patted my arm. 'Funny old world, isn't it!' She handed me her business card. 'Email me your response as soon as you can. I'll be waiting!'

Before we went our separate ways, Stacey called someone over who'd been sitting nearby. 'Mervyn's just going to take a publicity shot,' she said, – 'I've got a good feeling about this, Alex. I think we'll work very well together, don't you?'

Wandering around the streets for a while afterwards, I tried to make sense of what just happened. I felt like I'd been hit by a freight train. Part of me hated the idea, but that was a *lot* of money to turn down. How was my story worth that much? And then there was the disappointment, the horrible realisation that she wasn't remotely interested in my own work. Of course not. How could I have been such a fool to think so. No publisher worth their salt would say they were interested in a novel without even laying eyes on it. I must have looked a right twit. So then, I'm thinking, what's the catch? It all seems too easy. I wished Briony was here to talk to. Oh, well, at least I'd have a few days to mull it over. Frank will look over any contracts, I suppose, so at least he'll have my back. With all that money I could pay back the business loan and have plenty left over. I'd be able to buy my own flat as well…I found myself standing in front of a travel shop, perusing all the exotic holiday destinations for the coming winter. *'Come to the Sunny Canary Islands'* a vibrant poster coaxed, with its boundless white sands, luminous sky-blue water, and swaying palm trees. *'Beautiful Brisbane Awaits'* said another. Pictures of paradise islands, and smiling people in straw hats drinking ice-cold cocktails, languishing on sun-loungers in their Ray-Bans, looking smug, made me feel suddenly hungry for the good life. My two-week holiday planned for August is dead in the water (no pun intended) because, obviously, my holiday partner legged it. I haven't spoken to Steve about what I want to do about it. I guess I'll just carry on working for now. Anyway, it's not as if Briony and I were planning on anything exotic, since our funds are quite tight. But just imagine, if I agreed to Stacey's offer, we'd be able to have the most fantastic holiday, anywhere in the world. I stood there for quite a while daydreaming about safaris in Samburu, skiing in Chamonix, basking in Bali, living it up in LA…

While I was contemplating a parallel universe where my life would be trouble-free and money was no object, I received a phone call which jolted me out of it.

'Alex, I've been trying to call you. I can't get through on the house phone and your mobile's been off the whole time…'

'Oh my God! Briony! It's you! Where are you?'

'At my parent's house. I just got back. We really need to talk. I'm sorry Alex, about everything. I can't talk on the phone – there's too much to say. I'm coming back tonight.'

'Back at the flat, I raced round tidying up, trying to make up for several weeks of no proper cleaning. Mr Catkins beat a hasty retreat when I unleashed the hoover on the lounge carpet which was harbouring several days' worth of detritus from Jacob's refusal to use a plate. Off came the sofa cushions – brave and risky thing to do, I can tell you. The stuff you find in sofa crevices doesn't bear thinking about. I hoovered, dusted, washed and disinfected until the place was gleaming with cleanliness. I put new sheets on the bed and plugged in one of Briony's room fresheners, which I actually detest, but I can put up with the pungent smell of 'patchouli and grapefruit bouquet' for one evening, since I knew it would please her. Once the flat looked as good as it could with only a couple of hours to turn it round from being neglected and stale to acceptable, I flew down the road to get some wine and Briony's favourite snacks and a cake. If I'd had more time, I could have made one, but on second thoughts, cakes aren't my strong suit. The last one I baked ended up on the bird feeder and stayed there for months. I paced the flat, waiting for her to come in, feeling agitated and restless. I looked out onto the street and saw only one lone paparazzi loitering about. What a weird life that must be, and so boring. I almost felt sorry enough to invite the bloke up for a drink. I could certainly do with one, but I needed to keep a clear head. Then, around 9pm, the buzzer went, and I heard her voice for the first time in six weeks.

'I lost my keys along with everything else,' she said. 'Alex, I've had the most horrendous time…I can't tell you… it's been a nightmare.' Tears filled her eyes as I reached out to embrace her and I knew at that moment, that it wasn't just Briony who'd been adrift for weeks, we'd both lost our way for a while. I suddenly knew that this was the real deal. Holding her again in my arms, after so long apart, made me realise that perhaps we might actually find each other again, despite everything.

'Do you have to go to work this morning?' Briony asked, when we woke the next day.

'Only for a short time. I'll be back to take you out for lunch.'

'That old fossil still has you under the thumb, Alex! Today of all days, you should have had the day off.'

'Well, I know, but there's an important meeting which I can't miss. I'll tell you all about it when I get back.'

'OK.'

'Get some more sleep. You need to recuperate.'

I did feel bad, leaving her, but today was our big day at work – the transferring of the business officially to me and Steve. A watershed moment, which I should have been feeling very excited about, but I've been swamped by so many other things, that I really haven't given it my full attention. Anyway, today's the day. A new turning point in Alexander Philpot's life.

When I walked into the office, Alice had put balloons up and a 'Congratulations' streamer. She was wearing a sage green trouser suit to match our new colour scheme.

'Is that for me?' I pointed at the streamer.

'Well, it's a double celebration, isn't it! Isn't it amazing that they've been found! What an ordeal they've been through! I saw it all on the TV last night. They looked exhausted. Where is Briony, at the moment?' she asked me, looking innocent.

'In our flat, sleeping. Don't tell anyone though – the papers don't know yet. She managed to sneak in last night – the guy waiting outside missed his opportunity. He must have dozed off.'

'Did you make up?' I smiled at her lack of discretion. I have zero chance of her keeping schtum about Briony's whereabouts. 'Yes, we did, thanks for asking. But we have a lot to discuss. There was no time to talk much last night, so I can't tell you anything about what happened to her. She was very tired.' Alice seemed satisfied and moved on.

'Gordon's coming at 10am, Alex. Shall I get some pastries in or something?'

'Very good idea, Alice. Please do.' I gave her £20 to go and get some.

'Alex!' Congratulations!' said Steve.

'And to you!'

'Well, I think you've obviously got a lot more to be pleased about.'

'It's early days, Steve. We're both shattered, to be honest.'

'I was thinking about that, Alex. I've had my holiday this year – what would you think about taking your leave soon? I can manage things here for a couple of weeks. We've already done most of the re-fit.'

'That's very generous, Steve. It's what Briony and I both need. Some time away would be most appreciated.'

'Good, that's settled then. Just say the word.'

It's amazing how many things there are to sign in these situations. A never-ending pile of forms, declarations and statements, clarifications and ratifications. Anyway, we got through it all and suddenly it was over.

'Right lads,' said Gordon, – 'that's all the paperwork sorted now. You're good to go!' We shook on it, smiling broadly, like two Cheshire cats.

'We need to do this properly, you know – to mark the occasion…'

'I've already thought of that,' said Steve. 'The photographer will be here any minute. We can pose outside in front of our new signage. I've lined the staff up to come and stand behind us. If the photographer gets the image across to the local paper in time, we can make the Business section tomorrow.'

'I hope you don't mind, Steve, but I'm taking Briony out for lunch…'

'Just take the rest of the day, Alex – it's not every day that you find out your girlfriend is alive and well!'

'Yes, it's all a bit weird, isn't it!'

'Oh, I wouldn't worry – everything will go back to being dull and uneventful in no time!'

'Believe it or not, I'm looking forward to that!' I laughed.

Briony was up and dressed when I got home, curled up on the sofa with Mr Catkins, who was looking exceptionally pleased with himself.

'I've been looking at these,' she said, pointing to the large pile of newspapers on the table.

'Oh, yes, those…' My face reddened. 'It was…a bit of a disastrous few weeks,' I said.

'You're not kidding!' she said, – 'and there was I thinking that it was me who was having the worst time ever!'

'It was a terrible time for both of us, Briony. I think that the insanity of Harry's stag night was the culmination of everything that went wrong for me. It was like a sort of exorcism. I lost the plot for a bit.'

'What are you talking about?'

'Oh, you haven't seen that yet?'

'No, I've been reading about the police enquiries into you…'

'To call it 'enquiries' is an understatement. More like the Spanish Inquisition.'

'You poor, poor thing!' she said. 'I can't believe they actually thought you'd be capable of murdering anyone. It's ridiculous! Anyway, what's this about Harry's stag night?'

'Well, I'm surprised your parents didn't tell you.'

'They told me to have nothing more to do with you. When I asked 'why?', they said that I'd find out soon enough.'

'Oh, that's pretty unfair!'

'They said I'd had enough to cope with, without your 'transgressions' to deal with on top of everything else…'

'I don't know why they didn't just tell you that I'd become a… (I picked up one of the rags and quoted), – "a sex-crazed deviant with a fetish for cross-dressing as a Super Heroine", or … (I picked up another), "a serial lady-killer in drag", or this… "Blunder Woman".

'Oh, no! Why did they write horrible stuff like that? And what do they mean by 'Blunder Woman'? – who are they talking about?'

I dug out the *Evening Standard* and the *Sunday Stunner* and showed her the worst offenders.

'OH MY GOD! ALEX! WHAT THE HELL?'

'I know it looks bad from these photos, but honestly, it's not what it looks like, I can assure you.'

'Isn't it?' Who is that?' she said, pointing at Miss Piggy's blurry face.

'It's one of the lads on the stag night – honestly, just ask Harry!'

'What were you doing in a sex dungeon in Soho, Alex?'

'We were in Ann Summers just messing around – like I said, it's not what it looks like.'

'Hmm, well, what about this?' She flapped the Evening Standard's front page in my face. 'What in God's name were you doing?'

'I don't know. I think someone spiked my drink, Briony. I honestly don't have any recollection of climbing anything or being so utterly reckless.'

'You could've died doing that, Alex!'

'Well, I don't think I cared much at that moment.'

Briony looked at me in disbelief. 'I feel as if I've gone away and come back to an entirely different person. This isn't the Alex I know, at all!'

'Well, people can change, Briony. Maybe you aren't quite the same person after what's happened to you…'

'Maybe.'

'Tell me about Findlay – I'm not going to be angry any more, I just want to know.'

'There's not much to tell, Alex. What the papers were saying – it's not true. Nothing actually happened between us, if that's what you're asking. We weren't 'runaway lovers' – that was all nonsense.'

'Why did you go with him, then?'

'You're probably not going to believe this, but we were only supposed to be going to St Ives. I don't know, I just wanted to do something more interesting than yet another boring weekend in Surbiton. I thought he was fun and interesting, but there was no chance of romance – he's childish and too much of a dreamer.'

'Really?'

'Yes, really!'

'So, what happened, then?'

'His GPS broke down, so we didn't know where we were.'

'Didn't he have back-up, or spares or something?'

'No.'

'Didn't he have any other means of navigation?'

'No.'

'Good grief.'

'He didn't even have a compass.'

'Good lord!'

'And then we got into a bad storm in the night. It was really scary, Alex. I thought we were going to capsize.'

'How did you survive all that time at sea? What did you eat? How did you have enough to drink?'

'He had about fifty cans of Fanta and some beer on board, and some boxes of crisps and nuts.'

'You can't have lived off that for six weeks!'

'No, we did catch fish for a while, but we had a few days when we ran out of fuel and had no electricity to cook. Fin made a make-shift fire in a wok which we cooked some fish on, but we ran out of things to burn.'

'It must have been awful…'

'Let's just say, I never want to see another can of Fanta again, and fish is definitely off the menu, especially mackerel.'

'Well, I suppose that was healthy…'

'It was a really frightening experience, Alex. Any boats we saw were miles away. When we ran out of fuel and power, we thought that was it, and we'd never survive. I wrote a goodbye letter to my parents and to you, and some of my friends. We really didn't think we'd make it home.'

'So how did you end up on the Icelandic coast?'

'I don't know. We were caught in a storm and taken there, I guess. The most terrifying thing that happened that night was when the mast snapped off and a massive wave came right over the boat – we thought that was the end for us. I couldn't believe it when we were still afloat in the morning and right next to land. We managed to jump out onto rocks and found the cave.'

'It was ages before they found you, though. How did you survive? I mean, I looked on Google Maps and it's just bare rocks!'

'You have to promise not to be shocked.'

'OK…'

'Puffins – we ate puffins.'

'Really? Those incredible birds with beautiful colourful beaks?'

'Yes, those.'

'Wow!'

'Well, you would too, if you were starving, OK? Anyway, Icelandic people eat them all the time. They're not endangered, you know.'

'Blimey. What did they taste like?'

'Sort of like salty, fishy brisket…'

'Sounds pretty unpalatable.'

'Well, I'd like to see you turning it down when you haven't eaten for two days. Anyway, it rained for several nights in a row, so we managed to catch some water in a bowl. That made a nice change from Fanta.'

'So, how did you cook the puffins?'

'We had a cigarette lighter, and we found some driftwood. You can eat puffin's hearts raw, though. Did you know that?'

'No, I didn't. That's revolting.'

'Well, it's amazing what you'll do when it's a life and death situation, Alex.'

'I suppose Findlay the 'Sea Sage', told you that…'

Briony smiled. 'No, he didn't. I actually knew that already. I had an Icelandic boyfriend once.'

'You never told me about him!'

'You don't know everything about me.'

'So, there was no romantic relationship with Fin, then?'

'No, Alex. There wasn't. He's a bit of a dickhead, to be quite honest. He kept prattling on about his conquests and how ingenious and knowledgeable he is.'

'Sounds ghastly. How did you stand it?'

'I just said, 'compass', whenever he started up.

'Hahaha! Did it work?'

'Not enough.'

'So, are you going to keep in touch with him? I mean, there's probably no need, is there?'

Briony grinned. 'Don't worry, Alex, nothing on God's earth would interest me less than the idea of Fin as my significant other. To be fair to him, he'd probably say the same about me. He did call me a miserable cow a few times.'

'All this talk of food is making me hungry,' I said, – 'let's go and have lunch. Somewhere that doesn't serve fish or puffins.'

'Or seaweed stew.'

Chapter 23

The next couple of days were a crazy, chaotic time full of phone calls and requests for interviews and information. I finally told Briony I'd bought Anderson's while she was lost at sea, which blew her mind a little.

'How? I mean, why? Are you mad?' She just couldn't get her head round it. 'Why would you buy that tired old Company, Alex. It doesn't make sense.'

'It makes perfect sense,' I told her. When I explained it all to her, I think she realised Steve and I do know what we're doing. Although, I can't deny that I do suffer from *Imposter Syndrome* from time to time, and sometimes I have to pinch myself. It's been a strange couple of days, getting used to her being here again. We've talked about going away and she said she'd just like to go somewhere very simple and quiet. Maybe next time we could go somewhere more exciting. I don't really mind – just to escape the phone ringing all the time would be nice. My mother left another message yesterday. She doesn't know that Briony is here with me yet, and it's a good job I listened to it out of Briony's hearing.

'Alexander…I want to discuss the Briony situation. From what you've told me, it's over, and I think that's for the best. I hope you won't be having second thoughts now that she's back. I hear she's at her parent's house. It's the perfect opportunity for you to pack up her things and send them there, and then you can move on from this whole sorry episode. Do call me soon…'

Oh, dear! My mother is going to get a bit of a surprise when I tell her about Briony coming home. At least she'll stop trying to foist her friends' unmarried daughters onto me every five minutes. I haven't told her about buying Anderson's either. I have to admit I have been avoiding talking to her since we went out for lunch, possibly because

I'm worried her health might suffer if I'm forced to tell her the truth about everything. She is getting quite frail these days. On the other hand, she'll be really angry if she hears it all from someone else. I need to 'man up', as Briony would say, and face the music.

Zenith have told Briony to take it easy and go back to work when she's ready. It's quite nice for me because she's enjoying being home again, and because of having to live on sea flotsam and stale crisps, she's cooking for us. I must say, it's not a lot of fun eating on your own all the time, and I have really missed that. She says she'll never take food for granted ever again, which I fully appreciate after what she's told me. I'm surprised she didn't collapse with malnutrition on that boat. Tonight, when I got home from work, she'd made this amazing beef curry and coconut rice dish. It was the best thing I've had for weeks.

'That was amazing!' I told her, after I couldn't eat one more mouthful.

'Thanks! I know I didn't cook much before, but I think I could really get into it now.'

'Well, I won't be stopping you! That was lovely.'

'What did you eat when I wasn't here, Alex?'

'I was lazy. When there's only one of you, it's so much effort. I mostly lived on noodle pots and toasties, and when Jacob came, he was even more lazy, so we got takeaways a lot.'

'Why was Jacob here?'

'Oh, well, Lucy chucked him out.'

'Let me guess…he strayed?'

'Um, sort of…'

'Was it because of that girl, Maggie, by any chance?'

'Yes.'

'So, he's back with Lucy now, I take it?'

'Yes, only just, though.'

'I wondered why I found a plate with a half-eaten pizza shoved under the sofa.'

'Oh, no! He's terrible! He drove me mad when he was here.'

'What? More than I did?'

'Definitely more than you. To be honest, Briony, it helped me put things into perspective a bit. Jacob was the worst flatmate ever and he hasn't changed at all. I don't know why Lucy puts up with him.'

'Because she loves him, Alex.'

'I guess so…'

'That's how it works – living together…' Briony smiled. 'You'll have to learn to chill more about untidiness, and I'll have to try and ignore your anal attitude towards it.'

'OK, deal! By the way, I've been meaning to tell you about something that happened while you were waiting to fly back from Iceland. This woman rang me up – from a publisher, and we met for lunch. She wants to publish my story, and she's offered me £60,000 for it. Can you believe it? I've got to give her an answer by tomorrow afternoon.' I poured us both a glass of wine. 'Let's go in the lounge and talk it through. I've been waiting to ask you about it.'

'So, which publisher is it?'

'They're called 'Black Deeds'…'

'Oh…'

'What do you mean by 'oh'?'

'Tell me more and I'll explain.'

'OK, so the woman was called Stacey Armstrong, and…'

'STACEY ARMSTRONG! OH MY GOD, NO!'

'What do you mean? What's the matter?'

'She's an absolute shark. I'm amazed she didn't try to get you to sign on the dotted line there and then!'

'She did, but I said I needed time to consider and have my lawyer check it out.'

'Phew, thank God for that, Alex. She's notorious for being utterly ruthless. She takes what she needs and spits out the rest. She'll make mincemeat of you. What did she want from you?'

'Well, she said she just wants me to tell them all about my experience of being under suspicion for murder and what it was like to suffer the misery of you having been 'snatched away' and then presumed dead…'

'I wasn't 'snatched', Alex. That's what I mean about her. Have you read any of her articles in the tabloids? She's the Stunner's number one journalist. Let's have a look, since you've got all these papers here. Oh, here you go, Alex.

These pieces about you with the terrible photos, which by the way, I cannot get out of my head now. They were written by her – look! She uses a pseudonym: *Len Harper*. She's actually created the worst stories about you, and then has the cheek to try and dupe you into selling her more personal information which, no doubt, she will embellish like crazy and then pimp it out to all the other rag newspapers once she's squeezed every last drop of juicy exposé from you.'

'Oh my God! That's awful. What sort of person does that?'

'Her.'

'What should I do, Briony?'

'Just say 'no', Alex.'

'Oh, but all that money, Briony! Just think what we could do with it. We could buy our own flat, I could pay off a chunk of my business loan…it's life-changing!'

'I'll tell you what's life-changing, Alex, and that's allowing a duplicitous cretin like her into your life. She's done enough damage already, don't you think?'

'Yes, I suppose you're right.'

'Listen, our story *is* worth a lot of money, but that figure she gave you is not an honest one. It would get whittled down – they hook you in and then before you know it, there's fees for this and fees for that, and it's halved within weeks of signing your life away. I can get us a good deal with a reputable publisher, Alex, if you'll let me handle it.'

I thank my lucky stars I didn't fall for Stacey Armstrong's false charm. I knew there was something naggingly superficial about her. If it wasn't for Briony's good sense, I'd have been fed to the lions and God knows where I'd be – probably rocking back and forth in a secure unit for the criminally insane. I should just stick to what I know from now on and stay out of trouble.

I went to see my mother on Friday after work and told her the news she was not going to take well, and then the news she was definitely not going to take well, and then the news she would never take well, no matter how long we all live.

'You'd better sit down, Mum,' I said, as I walked down her hallway, trying to look business like.

'Why?'

'Because I have something to tell you. Well, a few things, actually.'

'Oh, goodness – we'd better make a cup of tea.'

'So,' I said, as we sat in her sunny conservatory, – 'the first thing is, the papers have been full of nonsense about me and Briony, as you know. None of it is true. I am not a callous murderer or a sex-mad lunatic in a dress.'

'Well, of course you're not, Alexander. Everyone knows that.'

'Well, thank you, Mum. And…Briony did not run off with a pirate on the high seas…' My mother remained silent. 'They were only supposed to be sailing to St Ives.' Still silence. 'Whatever you've read about that, it's incorrect.' Still nothing. I sighed and continued. 'Anyway, Briony is safely home, thank goodness, and I for one am very happy about it.' My mother shifted in her wicker chair, cradling her cup of tea and looking pensive. 'The second thing is, well…I'm now a CEO!'

'How on earth did that happen?' she said, incredulously.

'Uncle Frank helped me buy Anderson's Kitchens.'

'Good grief, Alexander – why didn't you tell me about it? You're not remotely equipped to run a company of your own. Have you gone mad?'

'No mother, I haven't. And contrary to what you might think, I am perfectly capable, thank you very much.' She looked like someone had clobbered her with a brick. 'I think you should put your tea down, while I tell you the next thing.'

'I'm not sure I can take any more shocks like that, Alexander.'

'Well, Mum, usually, the next thing I'm going to tell you is met with joyous excitement and heart-felt congratulations.'

As predicted, my mother's response to the news that I intend to ask Briony to marry me was verging on unprintable and possibly defamatory.

'You've taken leave of your senses, Alexander! My God, your father would be turning in his grave. I've always known she was an attention-seeking temptress, and she's proved herself to be exactly that – swanning off to God knows where with some flashy ne'er do well, and when that didn't work out, she's come straight back to you, Alexander.

She's just using you until someone else more exciting comes along. Mark my words.'

'Well, I'm sorry you feel like that, Mum, but you're wrong about her, and I'm going to marry her whether you like it or not. And please don't mention Jemima horse-face to me ever again.'

I left, trying not to slam the door on my way out.

'How was your mother?' asked Briony, when I got home.

'As expected…'

'Oh, right.'

'She'll have to start getting used to the fact that I'm my own boss these days, I'm afraid.'

'Wasn't she pleased about you becoming CEO of your own company? I mean, that's pretty cool!'

'No, not a bit of it. She threw cold water all over it.'

'Well, I think it's brilliant! You're going to be amazing!'

'With you by my side, I will be. I think we make a pretty good team, don't we?'

'You know, I went away seeking excitement and something new, and all the time it was right here at home, Alex. Isn't that funny!'

Chapter 24

'There's something else I forgot to tell you…' I said to Briony when we woke up this morning.

'What? Was it that you've won loads of money on the lottery? Or you're taking me out to a very expensive restaurant tonight, or maybe your mother's getting a personality transplant…'

'None of the above. You'll never guess.'

'Well, don't keep me in suspense, then…'

'Jacob and Lucy are having a baby!'

'No! Wow!'

'And this evening you will not be going to a fancy restaurant, because we are invited to their house for a special celebration…'

'OK.'

'Have you heard of 'gender reveal' parties?'

'Er, yes. They're not having one of those, are they?'

'They are. Sorry. Anyway, we *have* to go.'

'Well, *you* do!'

'Oh, come on Briony, I can't go alone…I need you.'

'Hahaha! Oh, well…will there be champagne?'

'I doubt it. Because Lucy is pregnant, she's not drinking, and Jacob isn't allowed to either. It'll be as dry as an Arab's flipflop.'

'I can't imagine Jacob being a dad, can you?'

'Not really, but neither can he!'

'Crikey, I missed so much while I was away. What other surprises have you got up your sleeve?'

'Hopefully, none.'

The papers seem to have finally lost interest in us. When I looked out through the window today, there was no one hanging around. It's a relief to get back to a normal routine. Briony is back to leaving her stuff everywhere: i.e., not putting the top back on the toothpaste, or the marmalade back in the cupboard, or shoes in the shoe holder I bought last year as a Christmas present, but she refuses to use it and I spend my time tripping over her large collection of footwear, scattered around the front door. I can't pretend it's not still annoying, but she says I might as well get used to it, because she's not going anywhere else any time soon. I think she was probably mad at me at the time, for buying it instead of something frivolous. I don't really see the point in buying things that aren't useful, though. We'll probably *never* agree on that one.

'Have you got any plans today?'

'Not really…'

'Fancy a road trip?'

'Depends…'

'I want to go in search of a man called Jason Coleridge. He might be able to shed some light on Findlay's activities.'

'What do you want to know about him for?'

'Well, do you know why the police are holding Fin in Iceland?'

'Not really – something to do with ownership – Fin said it was a misunderstanding.'

'Hmm. Frank and I would like to know what he's been up to, and this bloke might know.'

'Where are we going?'

'Portsmouth. We could visit the Mary Rose!'

After searching the Electoral Roll on my laptop, I discovered two Jason Coleridges in the city.

'We might be wasting our time,' said Briony.

'Yes, but you never know, do you? It could be the key to unlock the mystery, the missing piece of puzzle, the answer to all our prayers…'

'Alright, Detective Inspector Philpot!'

'That's got a nice ring to it, don't you think?'

The first address was a flat in a retirement complex.

'Did you check the date of birth, Alex?'

'Er, no…'

'When we knocked on the door, an old woman answered and wasn't particularly pleased that we'd interrupted her evening viewing of *Strictly Come Dancing*.

'Yes?'

'Are you Jason Coleridge?'

'What do you think?'

'Well, I'm sorry but I just wondered if I've got the right person – you never know these days…'

'Well, you haven't. I'm a Joy. Now bugger off.'

'Did you check the gender on the Electoral Roll?'

'No.'

The second address was obviously the one we were banking on. It was a modern semi in a cul-de-sac with kid's bikes and toys outside.

'This looks more promising,' I said, hopefully.

'What are we going to say to him?'

'I don't know…I'll just be direct.'

It took an age for someone to answer. Finally, a frazzled-looking woman opened the door.

'Yes?'

'We're looking for Jason Coleridge – is he in?'

'He's gone out – probably down the pub. You'll likely find him down at the Ship Inn with his mates. What do you want from him?' she suddenly asked.

'We're looking for him in connection with Findlay Connor.'

'Are you the police, then?'

'No. We're just interested in any information to do with the *Calamity Jane.*'

'It was me who went missing recently and got cast adrift in the Atlantic.' said Briony. 'He was the skipper.'

'Skipper, eh? If you could call 'im that, the dozy idiot! I thought you looked familiar. You look a bit familiar too…' she said, peering at me.

'Can you tell us anything?'

'Only that he's a rogue, that one – you ask Jason, he'll fill you in.'

The Ship Inn was only a short distance away. We got a couple of beers and looked around for the likely candidate. The barmaid pointed him out, sitting with a crowd of men in their fifties telling jokes and generally being quite raucous. We approached him – a stout, broad-shouldered man with thinning curly hair and tattooed, thick brown, fisherman's arms.

'Jason Coleridge?'

'Yeah, that's me,' he said.

'We're trying to find out information about Findlay Connor. He's being held in Iceland at the moment. His boat, the *Calamity Jane,* was wrecked on the Westman Islands a couple of weeks ago. This is Briony – she was with him at the time.'

Jason stood up and indicated he would speak to us in private at another table.

'Well, I'm happy to tell you what I know.'

He proceeded to explain that he and Fin had shared ownership of the boat until the disaster that wrecked her hull. The insurers excess charge was big, and Fin couldn't afford his share, so they agreed that Jason would pay for it and Fin would sell his share of the boat back to Jason. Fin disappeared with the boat, and this didn't get resolved, so he still owed Jason. What's worse is that, according to Jason, Fin must have forged Jason's signature and put the whole boat in his name, so it looked like he owned it.

'He's a terrible sailor as well,' said Jason. 'He's reckless and takes risks. That's probably why he ended up adrift with you for so long. My guess is that he didn't have any back up equipment…'

'Yep, that's true,' said Briony.

'Well, in my opinion, he endangered your life as well as being an outright crook. Anyway, the authorities have caught hold of him now. He won't find it so easy to wriggle out of it. I got a good lawyer. It's a good little boat, though – you are lucky to be alive.'

'Well, I suppose we know the whole story now, don't we!'

'What a bullshitter!' said Briony, as we drove towards the dockyard. 'He told me he owned several boats and that he'd been all over the world.'

'Well, he might have – running away from the law!'

'I doubt it! I bet he's only been as far as the Isle of White before now!'

'Hahaha! You could be right, but he's getting his comeuppance now, isn't he? I mean, he could go to prison.'

'I don't feel too sorry for him. He's lied to me about so much stuff, and he tried to blame me for things going wrong. He laughed at me when we were desperate for food and ended up eating horrible things like winkles to survive. I had to hold my nose, they were so disgusting. He showed off a lot too – a couple of times he bit the heads off a raw herring. He said it was a rite of passage thing that a true sailor has to do to prove himself. He actually tried to make me do it, can you believe it!'

'Yes, I can.'

'He told me that I would need to toughen up if we were going to survive and that he couldn't be expected to put up with a feeble woman who needed help all the time. He turned into quite an unpleasant human being out there. I was even scared he might kill me if we didn't find enough food!'

'What a nasty piece of work!'

'He wasn't very complimentary about you either.'

'Right…'

'He said you were a stuffed shirt…and a pompous ass…'

'And what did you say to that?'

'That you are a little bit, but it isn't intentional…' She smiled.

'Thanks! Well, I don't care what he thinks, anyway – he's the loser in this scenario, and a tosser, to boot. The police found that plastic shark's tooth in your box of stuff, by the way, and the schmaltzy note. Why did he send you that, by the way, if there was nothing going on between you?'

'Oh, no! That wasn't from him, you knucklehead! I got it in the shop. I was going to give it to you as bit of a joke present. They come with the message attached. The shops sell them to all the tourists – they're very popular.'

'Oh.'

'You silly ass!'

Later, at the gender reveal party, Jacob had a face like a slapped arse most of the evening. I sneaked in some vodka and coke for us to drink, to cheer him up and numb the pain of having all those relatives cooing over Lucy and the bump, and giving him home-spun advice in bucket-loads. I did have to check I was still Godfather to be, just in case Lucy had realised the lunacy of her decision and thought better of it. When she entered the party, Briony was greeted with huge cheers and squeals of delight by everyone in the room.

'Wow, Lucy – look at you!' said Briony. 'I hope you'll be letting us babysit for you when the time comes. I can't wait!'

Cripes, I hadn't thought of that. We'll be expected to actually be involved with the baby. It suddenly occurred to me that I'd have to start being responsible as well. I'd be even less equipped than Jacob to care for a small infant. I mean, at least he would have had lots of practice. I took him to one side and asked him if it would be possible to rethink the Godfather thing.

'No way, Alex – you've already agreed. There's no going back now!' he sniggered. Then Lucy opened a box of blue and pink balloons and let them out one by one, until the last one which she revealed as being a pink one, with a big flourish.

'It's a girl!' shouted her mother, clapping her hands.

'Let's go home, open a bottle of wine and slob on the sofa,' said Briony, – 'I'm quite tired now.'

'Good plan,' I said, relieved she didn't want to stay late.

The answer phone messages back at the flat were mostly from radio people and reporters again. Stacey Armstrong was amongst them:

'Hi there, Alex! I didn't hear from you yesterday, so I'm just calling to let you know you've got an extra couple of days to decide. It's the best offer you'll get, daaarling! Call me ASAP!'

'Ooooooh, Alex daaaaarling,' Briony teased, – 'you'd better jump to it!'

'I will call her on Monday to ask her where she got those photos from.'

'She won't tell you, Alex.'

'Well, I know, but I'm going to have a go.'

We chilled out and watched a documentary about Africa, and Briony fell asleep half way through. I decided to go and write a bit of my novel, since I'm in the mood for it again. Now I have a new muse: Stacey Armstrong. A duplicitous, immoral, shameless phony. Maybe I should change my cadaver to a woman…

'He'd covered his tracks well and was confident no one would suspect him. All he had to do now was patiently wait for the police to do their duty. Each day, he quietly checked their progress. The description of the dead man in the news seemed so slight, so ordinary, that he almost wondered if he had actually committed a crime at all. (Man found stabbed in ally-way near Stanton Hill. No witnesses. No clues, No leads. No fuss…). He knew they'd come knocking soon, once it was established the old bastard had children. His sister would look at him with eyes as black as coal. Her words would be barely audible, and she would know. She would know her brother would not let it lie. And she would know he did it for her.'

I went to bed feeling happy that I'd made some progress with my book. I have no idea whether anyone will ever be interested in publishing it, but somehow, I don't really mind. Sometimes you just have to do things for yourself.

'Why is Xander in a different tank?' Asked Briony this morning.

'I think he's got a bad case of dropsy.'

'What's that?'

'Fluid retention.'

'That's a weird thing for a fish to get.'

'I think he might be dying.'

'Oh no!'

'I think I'll put him back with Xavier – I don't want him to die alone…'

'You're such a big softie, Alex, I don't know how you can write about bloodthirsty murderers and dead people.'

'Maybe I need the contrast!'

I suppose it is a bit strange to want to write about evil things, but no one wants to read about happy uncomplicated lives, do they? We all need some drama to escape the mundanity of our true existence. Mind you, I'm not short of drama in my own life – there's bags of it. The Sunday paper this morning carried a huge double spread all about Briony's miraculous survival:

'Brave Briony Battles Near-Starvation', it said. *'We were desperately hungry all the time. I can't believe I survived.' said Briony, fighting back the tears. 'It was the most horrific experience – the only thing that kept me going was my boyfriend, Alex. I never stopped thinking about him and it was my love for him that kept me alive. I truly believe that.'*

'Is that true? Did you actually say that?' I asked her. You never told me…'

'Of course it's true,' she said matter-of-factly. 'You were my only reason to live, Alex. Apart from Mr Catkins, of course,' she said, ruffling his fur and tickling his tummy. 'Until you're in that situation you just have no idea how you cling onto something for dear life. It was your face in my mind's eye every day that made life worth striving for. I mean it, Alex, it really was.'

I've never heard Briony say anything like that before – it's as if she's had a sort of revelation, a paradigm shift in her opinion of me…I'm not entirely sure it can be trusted. Extreme stress can alter your brain function. I've heard that chronic stress can have a shrinking effect on the prefrontal cortex. Maybe Briony is experiencing the effects of that? I will have to keep a close eye on her.

'Do you mind if I go to police training today?' I asked Briony. 'It's just that I've missed some over the last few weeks, and I don't want Jim to think I've given up.'

'No, that's fine, Alex. I'm just going to read my new book. I just got it in the post yesterday. It's called '*Don't Throw the Baby Out…*'

'Right…'

'It's basically about appreciating what you've got – you know you can make changes without changing everything, to have a better life.'

'I see. Well, that sounds like an interesting book.' To be honest, I don't really see why Briony needs to read a book to tell her what's already staring her in the face, but I'm not going to say so.

'Great to see you!' said Jim, when I walked in.

'I've missed you all,' I said. I noticed that Kate wasn't there.

'She's joined another training session now she's training to be a fully trained officer,' said Jim.

'You missed a good session last week,' said Rick. 'We were working with the Police Dog Squad.'

'It was brilliant,' said Sharon. 'They're so well-trained – they can pee on demand!'

'What, the men or the dogs?'

'Hahaha,' Alex. We've missed your jokes!'

'What are we doing this week, then?'

'Well, we've only got you, Sharon, Rick and Leo. Theo got a nasty bite on his rear end last week and is currently recuperating.' Jim was trying not to smirk.

'Oh no! What happened?'

'Well, the dog, who was called Rambo, started off being pretty well-behaved and followed his handler's instructions perfectly, until the chap went for a lavatory break. Up until that point, he'd been showing us how Rambo could ignore a sausage placed on a plate in the middle of the room and wait ten minutes for the command to be allowed to go and eat it. Theo decided to put one of the sausages in his back pocket for his own dog later on.'

'Oh, cripes! Is he going to be OK?'

'Rambo only sustained minor injuries!' joked Jim. 'But Theo will be a bit sore for a week or so. He'll be fine, though.'

'It's his own fault for snaffling a sausage,' said Leo.

'Anyway, let's do some revision on crimes,' said Jim. 'What are the most common crimes perpetrated on a typical night out on the streets of London?'

'Drunk and Disorderly,' said Rick.

'Criminal Damage,' said Sharon.

'GBH,' said Leo.

'Resisting Arrest,' I said.

'So,' said Jim, getting out a large cutting from a newspaper, – 'let's contemplate this…'

'Look! It's the photo of you, Alex!' Rick guffawed.

'Why are we using this as an example?' I said, embarrassed.

'I thought it would be entertaining,' said Jim, laughing. 'So, here we have Wonder Woman climbing on a public monument. Can we arrest her?'

'Yes,' said Rick.

'Why?'

'Criminal Damage?'

'Apparently there wasn't any in this case.'

'OK, well, what about endangering others?'

'Good, yes that's a possibility…'

'Trespass?' said Sharon.

'Yes if it's also considered a 'nuisance'.'

'How, if it's just a statue?'

'For putting the fear of God into passers-by, that's how.'

'Did she resist arrest?' asked Leo.

'No, she scarpered before they could catch her, apparently. I'm afraid that she really doesn't remember anything about it.' I said.

'Why didn't they get her for being drunk and disorderly?' asked Leo.

'Because she ran away before they could get hold of her,' I said. 'She was a very fast runner, Leo. I did hand myself in you know, as soon as I could. They let me off with a caution.'

'Why did you fess up to a crime you didn't commit?' said Leo, confused. 'That woman was the one who did it…' Everyone looked at him in amazement. 'What?' he protested.

'It's Alex, you numpty.' said Rick, not one to mince his words.

'Anyway,' said Jim, – 'you were lucky to get off with a caution, but joking aside, you could be barred from becoming a Special Constable, now.'

'Oh, that hadn't occurred to me…'

'I'm afraid it's on your records. You can still come to the training sessions, of course.'

'I think my dreams of being a part-time policeman are over, Briony,' I told her when I went home.

'Oh, why?'

'Because I'm a criminal.'

'What?'

'The caution – it still goes on your records.'

'But you weren't responsible! That's not fair! Someone drugged you!'

'I can't prove it.'

'We'll see about that. We're not going to let that woman get away with this, Alex.'

Chapter 25

On the way to work, something occurred to me that put an extra spring in my step. If I have a caution on my records, surely it bans me from becoming a patron of a charity? Oh, my goodness! There *is* a God! Even if the caution gets expunged from my records, I will have been rejected already by *Fluffy Friends Cat Rescue*! Brilliant! I couldn't wait to tell Steve. Of course, Evangeline will be really annoyed with me, but it lets me off the hook.

'I got us both office chairs,' said Steve, when I arrived. 'Ta daaaa!' he said, his arms outstretched and indicating the two matching swivel chairs by the reception desk. 'Look!' he said, jumping into one and spinning round. On the back, it said 'BOSS'.

'What does mine say?'

'NO, I AM!'

'Hahahaha, very good, Steve!'

'Let's get to work, then!' It was a very busy morning, being our first proper 'going it alone' day. I managed to give Stacey a call mid-morning.

'I won't divulge my sources,' she said, predictably.

'What if I agree to give you an interview? We could do an exchange of information…'

'No. I would never betray him – he'd never work for me again.'

'You could get another undercover photographer – they must be ten-a-penny…'

'Nice try, Alex. The answer's 'no'. Good luck with trying to get any other offers, by the way – tomorrow's chip paper etc.!'

At lunch time, I decided to go over to Soho and visit the shop. I had an idea and was hoping I was right.

'We do have CCTV in the basement, but I'll have to speak to Head Office,' said the young assistant.

'Can I give you my number?'

'Sure.'

'Are you able to view it yourself?'

'Not really, not without permission.'

'Well, just to let you know, what I'm looking for is the person who took this photo…' I showed her the least embarrassing one from the tabloids on my phone. 'It was Saturday night, around 10.30pm…'

'OK, I'll see what I can do.' She smiled at the clipping.

'You're *Wonder Woman*, aren't you?'

'Yes, I'm afraid so.'

'We've got some great female super-hero costumes over here on the rail by the window. We just had a lovely new order in of *Black Widow* outfits…they're real leather and super-tight…'

'Oh, no, it's OK, thanks – I don't usually…it's not normally…I mean, it was just that one time… The thing is – someone invaded my privacy…' I looked at her nametag, – 'um, Jane… and they've damaged my career prospects. My girlfriend is really upset about it too. Some scumbag tabloid photographer has made a lot of money out of my distress, and he's laughing all the way to the bank.'

Jane looked very sympathetic and agreed with me that whoever did this was indeed a 'total scumbag' and beyond the pale. Then she suddenly said, 'Look, don't tell anyone, but I can show you if you like. Come with me.' She led me into a small dingy back office where three monitors were up and running. She searched for the date. 'Did you say 10.30pm?'

'Yep.'

'OK…so here it is…there were quite a lot of idiots in the shop that night – a stag night, I expect. They just mess about and never buy anything…Ah, look, there you are…'

I squinted at the small screen and saw myself with Miss Piggy brandishing the whip. Then, Bingo! There he was, in exactly the right position to take the compromising shots of me.

'Got him!' I said, – 'thank you Jane, you're an absolute star!'

'But how do you know who it is?'

'I know enough.'

Briony was impressed with my sleuthing skills. I have to say, I am shocked at my own chutzpah.

'So now we know who it was, how do we prove he spiked your drinks?' she asked.

'Ah, well, firstly, he wasn't the only hamburger, so I've got to speak to Harry and ask him which of the three is most likely to be our man, then I don't know where we'll go from there.'

'This is fun, Alex, isn't it! I haven't enjoyed myself so much in ages.'

'Maybe you should consider a change of career, Briony. You've often said you're bored of the corporate advertising world.'

'I'm not going to jump ship yet…'

'Oh, very good! You must be feeling a bit better if you can joke about it.'

'Maybe. Anyway, you need to call Harry.'

My cousin was not massively helpful. He said that one of the hamburgers was a friend from Uni and the other one was a childhood school friend who he'd lost touch with but invited at the last minute. Harry didn't seem to know what either of them did for a living. The third one was his brother, Patrick, so we can be fairly sure to rule him out. I checked out their names on the internet, but neither of the two suspects had much of a presence on there, so that was a bit frustrating. I thought I'd give Lauren a call, since mothers are much better at remembering details about friends. My own mother is no exception. She often brings up the subject of Charles Higginthrope who was my best friend in year four in prep school. She remembers every minute detail about him – his parents, where they lived, where they worked, where they bought their furniture, what their dog was called, what Charlie's maths scores were in class, even which snacks he brought to school every day. She still asks me today if I'm in touch with him. Anyway, my instincts were right, and Lauren did possess a useful piece of information.

'One of those boys is his old school friend, Robert McClegg. He got in touch with Harry recently – he'd heard that Harry was getting married. Harry invited him on his stag night for old time's sake – I mean, it's a long time since they'd seen each other; it was probably fifteen years ago. He said he didn't even recognise him! What's the reason for asking about him, Alex?'

It might have been him who took the photos, Lauren – the ones in the *Stunner…*'

'Oh, really? That's terrible! I never liked him much, to tell you the truth. He was quite a nosey lad, and always asking for things. I found him in Frank's office once, looking in a drawer. He said he was looking for batteries. I suppose what I'm trying to say is that I didn't trust him, so it wouldn't surprise me if it turns out to be Robert.'

'I've got something to tell you,' Briony said, when I came off the phone.

'Oh,' I said, feeling slightly worried.

'I've got us an agent to deal with all the press stuff and to try and get us a good publishing deal. She's really experienced – my boss at work recommended her.'

'Oh, right,' I said, relieved. 'I thought you were going to announce something bad. I've got something to tell you as well. Lauren says she thinks our culprit could be Harry's old school friend, Robert. She thinks it's a bit suspicious that he suddenly wanted to come to Harry's stag do when they haven't seen each other for years.'

'That is a bit weird, isn't it? But how would he have known you were going to be there? It doesn't make sense.'

'Well, he could easily have seen Harry's Facebook page – he's probably a friend on there, and then he would have seen photos of me as well; we took some at the dreaded kilt fitting. I mean, we're both Philpots as well, so he would know we were related and that I was likely to be going on the stag night. These people are ruthless, Briony. They'd sell their own mother to get a good story.'

'So, what do we do now?'

'Not sure. The trouble is, I don't have time at the moment to follow it up.'

'Well, you could let me try – I don't have to go back to work yet, so I've got time on my hands. By the way, I've been reading your novel. I actually think it's pretty good, Alex.'

'Do you?'

'Yeah – I think you should try and find a publisher for it. Maybe our agent can help with that.'

'It's not really ready to show to anyone yet…'

'People get publishing deals based on a lot less than that, Alex, believe me…'

'But I'm not famous or anything, am I? Stacey Armstrong said she'd get a load of ghost writers to write my life-story, and she wasn't interested in my own novel at all…'

'That's not her bag, Alex. She only prints things with a shelf life of an overripe banana. She wouldn't recognise quality if it bit her on the arse... Why are you laughing, Alex?'

'You just reminded me of something that happened at police training, that's all.'

'Well, anyway – you just need the right person to see it and believe in you.'

Briony seems to have changed since she came back. I don't know what it is that's made her less distant than before and happier in herself, but I'm not complaining.

'Your mother rang today, by the way.' *(That's another thing – Briony has stopped calling her the Munster-in-Law.)*

'What did she say?'

'She just asked me to tell you, that's all. She asked me how I was, though.'

'Well, that's progress, isn't it!'

Perhaps my mother is finally relenting now that she can see that her efforts to dissuade me from making a life with Briony, are futile. I haven't had the will to contact her since our altercation the other day. She was probably quite surprised by my vigorous defence of Briony in the face of her shrewish hostility. She's seen a fair number of girlfriends off in the past. Not many could stay the course. I remember one in particular; Susan Olive – a sweet-natured girl who was quiet and, on the whole, not given to contradicting the older generation. 'That girl doesn't say 'boo' to a goose,' said my mother after their first meeting, – 'I was wondering if she is selectively mute?' I told my mother that she was just shy. Of course, that was a red rag to a bull. My mother couldn't leave her alone and commanded the poor girl to speak up and voice her opinions. Susan began to dread seeing her, and our relationship died an inevitable death, but not before Susan had a sudden outburst and threw a spoon at my mother, shouting that she would never set foot in her house ever again. 'I told you she was unstable,' said my mother. 'She's obviously volatile – not a nice trait in a woman, Alex.' And then there was Georgina, or 'George', as she preferred to be called. Again, this was leapt on by my mother, – 'Goodness, what a funny thing it is to want to be called that,' she said to her, – 'you'll be growing a moustache and smoking a pipe next.' George had a bit more spunk than my mother bargained for and told her she could 'stuff her coq au vin where the sun didn't shine, lit a fag and blew smoke everywhere on her way out. 'I told you not to trust a woman who smokes, Alex. They'll walk all over you.' After these early disastrous attempts at introducing girls to my mother, I kept the rest away from her. I told them she lived in Mustique. I had no idea where that was, but it sounded exotic, and a very, very long way away. Then Briony came along, and because she moved in, it wasn't really possible to keep my mother at a distance. When she finally met Briony, it wasn't any better than with the previous girls, but the difference was that Briony was able to 'compartmentalise' my mother. When I asked her to explain, she just said that she puts her in a box, mentally, and shuts the lid. Like you do with an unpleasantly large electric bill, or leftovers that you don't really want to eat, but can't quite throw away, or an unwanted gift you can't stand, but because a good friend gave it to you, you can't dispose of it. To be honest I don't really get it, but if it works for her, then as far as I'm concerned, that's great! It doesn't stop her complaining, though, so obviously the lid on that box isn't very airtight.

'Shall we get a takeaway this evening?' I suggested to Briony. 'It's been a long day. I'll just go and get it now, if you like.' Korma Sutra is just up the road from the flat and very handy. Probably a bit too handy, in fact. Jacob and I have frequented that establishment far too often in the past. These days I'm much better at making an effort in the kitchen, and therefore, my bank balance has improved significantly. Anyway, I was waiting in the foyer flicking through this week's *Sunday Stunner,* when I saw another very distressing photograph. The blood drained from my face instantaneously. It was a picture of me with Kate, the night I took her out for dinner, when I walked her home. That bastard photographer must have been stalking me for days, even before the stag night. There was no mistaking who it was either, so I wouldn't be able to deny it. Briony will have a purple fit…or just leave, or both. How long could I keep this from her? I stared at the photograph, as the horrible reality of it sank in. This was the worst thing that could have happened to me – worse than the *Sex Shop Scandal,* worse than being wrongly accused of a heinous crime, even worse than drug-induced delusions with alarming conclusions. She's never going to believe it only happened once – just that one foolish moment of weakness.

'Aaaargggh!' I groaned out loud.

'Are you OK, Alex?' Raj looked over at me from behind the tall counter between us.

'No…I mean, yes…not really.'

'Can I help you?'

'No, Raj – unfortunately you can't. No one can.'

I walked back to the flat feeling wretched and humiliated. Everyone will think I'm an absolute cad. I decided to put off the evil moment of having to confess to Briony while I thought about my defence strategy, and that could take some time to formulate. I took a leaf out of Briony's book, just for tonight, and put the whole sorry affair in an air-concealed, imaginary box and nailed it down with a very big hammer.

Jacob rang me at work the next day. 'Mate – you're in big trouble. I just saw the *Stunner*. Have you seen it?'

'Yes, I have. I was in Raj's place last night. I only picked it up to check the football results.'

'What are you going to do?'

'Well, I'll have to tell her, or she'll hear it from someone else, won't she?'

'You can crash at my place if you want to.'

'Thanks, Jacob. She'll probably go to her parents' if she leaves. It was just one time, Jacob. The paparazzi just happened to be there at that moment. Can you believe it!'

'Kate's a great looking girl – I mean, you could do a lot worse…'

'That's not helping, Jacob. Briony and I are getting on really well, and now this! Just when everything is getting back on an even keel.'

'Why don't you tell her someone spiked your drink again?'

'She's not going to believe that, is she!'

'OK, well why don't you say that you assumed she was missing presumed dead, so you thought it would be OK to date someone else?'

'I really don't think that would go down very well with *anyone,* Jacob, not just Briony! I can't believe you're suggesting I say that.'

'Well, it's true, isn't it? You can't be left to rot like some sort of Miss Havisham character, until you've got one foot in the grave!'

'There are better ways to say it.'

'Well, I'm just trying to help you out.'

'Yeah, well, thanks for your advice.'

I suppose, in his own crude and inimitable way, Jacob has a point, but my problem is, how do I convey it to Briony, who will want to cut off my balls with a rusty saw?

Chapter 26

Harry called me at work in the afternoon, for two reasons; one, to sympathise over the compromising photograph which has now been dubbed 'kissingate', and then to tell me more about Robert McClegg.

'I thought it was a bit weird when Cleggy contacted me out of the blue like that,' he said. 'If I'd known what he did for a living, I wouldn't have invited him, I promise you.'

'It's not your fault, Harry. Anyway, we don't know it was him, do we?'

'Ah, well we do, actually,' he said, sounding pleased with himself. 'Briony was very clever, Alex. I won't spoil it for her – she can tell you. We've hatched a plan – a sting operation, if you like.'

All day, I've been worrying about what to say to Briony about Kate, it's eating me up. I decided I would have to just get on with it as soon as I got home and suffer the consequences. Imagine my shock when I came through the front door to find Kate sitting calmly on our sofa talking to Briony.

'Kate's been explaining things to me, Alex. I've seen the Sunday rag, so I know about the photo.'

'Right…' I waited to be pulverised by the pestle of all pestles, but it didn't happen. 'So, I'm not going to be hung, drawn and quartered, then?'

'No, not at the moment,' Briony said.

'I've explained to Briony,' said Kate, slowly, – 'that there was never anyone else but her for you, Alex, and that I was just a useful distraction. You were having a terrible time, and I was in the right place at the right time. I've tried to make her realise how hard it was for you too, and that you just needed someone understanding to talk to, and that it wasn't a serious thing between us at all.'

'Oh, um, well, thank you, Kate.'

'I'm going to go now, but I just wanted to wish you both luck and happiness – I do mean that, Alex.' She smiled and got up to go.'

'I'll see you out,' I said, feeling like a complete heel.

'That was incredibly generous of you, Kate…' I said at the door.

'Well, you both deserve to be happy, Alex. Anyway, I'm fine – my ex is trying to start reconciliation with me and Polly. It could work – I'm feeling positive about it. Sometimes things work out for the best. It was nice knowing you.' She squeezed my hand, and then she was gone.

Later, I discovered that Briony wasn't going to let it go completely.

'She was very pretty, Alex.'

'Hm?'

'I can see why you liked her…'

'Well, I was lonely and…you know…'

'Yes, I do know. But I didn't jump into bed with Findlay, did I?'

'Well. He probably didn't smell too good after several weeks at sea…'

'You don't have to joke about everything, Alex!'

'Sorry! I didn't do anything like that, and you know I didn't!'

'OK, well you nearly did…'

'I can't emphasise enough how glad I am that I didn't. OK?'

'OK, well, I suppose we're equal now, anyway.'

'Pardon?'

'At the office Christmas party last year, I let Andy Plunkett kiss me behind the Yucca plant by the lifts.'

'No! Not him!'

'Yes. Sorry.' I wish she hadn't told me that, because now I can't get rid of the image of Handy Andy snogging Briony's festive face off.

'I think I'd rather have remained ignorant.'

'Well, now you know, I feel much better.'

'I might want to punch his fat face when I see him.'

'No, you won't, Alex, because I'm not with him, I'm with you, and anyway, he's a terrible kisser,' Briony said, hooting with laughter. 'Let's just let bygones be bygones, Alex – OK?'

'Tell me about Robert Clegg,' I said later, when we were cooking tea.

'Oh, yes – Alex, you will be so proud of me! And it was so easy!'

She told me how she rang and spoke to Stacey Armstrong's secretary and fibbed about how Robert McClegg had advised her to contact them and offer them some explicit photographs of a well-known celebrity. The secretary didn't hesitate to respond – it was obvious that she knew exactly who Robert was and had often dealt with him. In fact, she joked about how he couldn't stay away these days. Briony pretended she wanted to know what the procedure was for selling such photos, as she was sure that Stacey Armstrong would be 'extremely interested'.

'We've got our man, Alex! The best thing of all is that Harry and I have devised a way to get Robert to stop harassing us or selling any more pictures to the tabloids.'

'I'm all ears,' I said, pouring us both a celebratory glass of wine.

'Well, Harry is going to invite him to the wedding.'

'What? Is he mad? That's a terrible idea! Why on earth would he want *him* to be there?'

'No, it's genius, Alex. Harry has asked him to take photographs of the wedding, so he'll bring his VERY expensive Canon – those lenses are worth a fortune. I mean, we're talking thousands, Alex.'

'And?'

'He won't suspect a thing. When he arrives, Harry and Patrick will put his camera somewhere for 'safe keeping' until it's needed, except they won't be giving it back for a while. The plan is to force Robert to make a statement – an affidavit, about what he did on that night. If he wants his camera back, he'll agree to it. Frank will witness Robert signing it, so we will have a legal document signed under oath to use as leverage. This is how we will discourage him from ever stalking us again.'

'But isn't that coercion?'

'Yes, a bit.'

'But it wouldn't stand up in court.'

'He wouldn't want it to get that far, Alex. There's no way he'd want it to be made public that he drugged someone just to get a story. You can go to prison for deliberately drugging people. There's no way he would want that to get out whether we can prove it or not. He'd never get another job again.'

'OK, playing devil's advocate here, but what if he calls the police and accuses Frank and Harry of theft?'

'We thought about that. Those cameras are very slippery in the wrong hands, you know. Accidents happen all the time.'

'What if he gets nasty?'

'Well, there's every possibility, but those stags are pretty unhappy about Robert's activities. He's massively outnumbered.'

'He's probably done his worst already, though, Briony.'

'Well, that's true, but it will be worth it to see the whites of his eyes!'

I hope this plan to out 'Cleggy', doesn't spoil Harry and Julia's wedding. This should be the happiest of days for them.

Anderson's Kitchens is going from strength to strength at the moment. Steve had the piece about us that was in the local paper framed, and it hangs on the wall next to our offices. There's one more thing I haven't done yet, and that's to tell Evangeline that I'm not going to be patron of her precious charity. I've been putting it off to be honest. I don't like upsetting people unnecessarily. Luckily, I've got some time in hand, so it can wait a bit longer. The infamous bust of Alfred Bedlington-Clarke will apparently take quite a while to be made, so the cupboard currently occupying the foyer is still bare, thank goodness. Alice is in her element, and it turns out that she's very good at running things around here, which means that Steve and I have more time to focus on designing. At the moment, we are just finalising Mr Anderson's home kitchen. I think he and his wife are going to be delighted with the finished result. I have to say, it's one of the best I've done so far. It'd be nice to think that, one day, I'll be able to design a kitchen for Briony and me in our future home together, when we can afford it. Now that things have settled at work a bit, I've had some time to think about a holiday for us both. I know she wanted somewhere quiet, but that doesn't mean it has to be dull, does it? I've got something in mind that I think will be perfect.

'Alex, I've got some girlfriends coming over this evening,' Briony announced, this morning.

'I suppose that means I'm banned from my own home, then?'

'Only for this evening…you wouldn't want to be here anyway, Alex.'

It's true, I really wouldn't want to suffer the indignity of a load of over-excited women drinking too much Prosecco, asking what other outfits I've got in my wardrobe and would I give them a 'sneak preview'. Last time they all came over, Mr Catkins bolted and went missing for *two* whole days. I decided to ask Jacob if he was free.

My office at work is really coming together now. I kept the tub chair – it sits in the corner, like a museum piece. The desk, however, has been cleaned up and polished and looks good as new. Steve, on the other hand, got all new stuff for his office – but each to their own, as they say. I like to feel connected to the past. Old Mr Anderson came in to see us today, to ask how we're getting on. He gave us some design tips while he looked over our latest ideas. He even drank coffee from the new machine and agreed that perhaps it was a good idea after all. We invited him to join us as a non-executive director, which he seemed to be very chuffed about. This was Frank's suggestion – as he said, 'us oldies have a lot to offer still', and I for one would agree one hundred percent. If I hadn't had Frank helping me these last few weeks, I don't know where I'd be now. If I asked her now, Briony would definitely agree with asking old Mr Anderson to contribute. She's mellowed somewhat now that she's reading 'Don't Throw the Baby Out', and I've noticed she hasn't called either of us 'fossils' since she's been devouring that particular book.

I got a 'surprise visit from my mother at work this afternoon. She decided to come and see for herself what all the 'fuss' was about. I haven't spoken to her since the day we fell out, and I wasn't sure what the reason for this unprecedented and unforeseen event was.

'Your Mum's here,' said Alice, on the internal phone to my office. I peered over the frosted glass partition to see her waiting at reception and chatting happily to Alice.

'Mum, how are you? Is everything all right?'

'Yes, of course it is, Alexander. I thought I'd come and see your establishment – I've been waiting for an invitation…'

'Oh, well, we haven't quite finished all the refurbishments yet. Obviously, you would have been invited, once it was finished.'

'Hm,' she said, not really believing me.

'Would you like a nice cup of coffee? I'll show you around.'

'Well, that was very interesting, Alexander,' she said, afterwards. 'I'm very impressed. I forget how old you are, sometimes – your father was about your age when he was expanding his own business, you know. By the time he was thirty-eight, he'd bought three shops…'

'Really? I never knew that.'

'Yes, well, I didn't always agree with his decisions, but in the end, they were usually good ones.' I wondered if this was my mother's peculiar way of apologising. I decided it was probably as good as I was going to get from her. 'I like your office, Alexander – it's very stylish. I didn't know you had such good taste.'

'Oh, thanks…'

'How's Briony?'

'She's resting, but hopefully she's going to be fine.'

'Oh, good. I've sent a little something over to her. I hope she likes it. Well, I'd better be going – Meredith Postlethwaite is expecting me. I'm looking forward to seeing her eat a bit of humble pie, now that you are in the clear! By the way, let me know what time you are coming to pick me up on Saturday, won't you? Oh, and I know you won't like me commenting, but I don't think facial hair is very professional for a businessman of your calibre – your father would not have approved. You're a CEO now, Alexander, and you need to set an example.'

'Your mum seems nice,' said Alice, as I waved her off.

'That's a matter for deliberation. The jury's still out.'

Alice frowned. 'You say weird things sometimes, Alex.'

After work, Jacob and I met up at the *Shovel* and dissected our week so far.

'It's been a crazy few days, hasn't it?' I said. Then I noticed how smart Jacob looked. 'So, what's with the suit then?'

'I got promoted to Sales Director.'

'Congratulations, Jacob! That's great!'

'Yeah, well, I've got a family to think about now, haven't I!'

'How's Lucy?'

'Getting bigger…she's fine, though. What about Briony?'

'Well, I've been feeding her up too! She was so thin, I thought she might snap.'

'What happened with Kate? I thought you'd be begging *me* for a bed that night!'

'It's OK. I've been forgiven too. We've both been given a reprieve, haven't we, Jacob? We should be grateful. I just want to move on from this whole sorry saga, to be honest.'

'Lucy and I have been invited to Harry and Julia's wedding on Saturday.'

'Oh, great! You know I've got to wear a kilt, don't you?'

'Hahaha, I bet those legs of yours will be as white as snow!'

'Oh, God! I hadn't thought of that!'

'Don't worry mate, you can always go down to Lucy's friend's spray-tan place.'

'I'm not that vain, Jacob. By the way, did you know about Harry and Briony's plan to nail that photographer?'

'No…'

'He's called Robert Mc Clegg – the guy who took the sex shop photos. He was with us that night – one of the hamburgers. He's actually an old school friend of Harry's. He's a paparazzi, would you believe it!'

'Cripes! Did Harry know?'

'No, he had no idea.'

'Blimey…So, what are they going to do?'

'Make him sign an affidavit.'

'An affa what?'

'It's like a statement – admitting what he did…'

'He won't just roll over, Alex.'

'They've thought of a way. He won't be taking any more photos or stalking me any more.'

'Haven't we had enough people going missing under suspicious circumstances?'

'Hahaha, don't worry – I'm not going to do anything heinous. I don't want to add to my already blemished record.'

'How long have you got that for, then?'

'I don't know, but I can get it expunged if I can prove Robert McClegg drugged me.'

'Some of those photos were pretty funny, though, Alex.'

'Yeah, as long as it's not *you* in them!'

'Fair point. But at least you'll be able to tell your kids you were famous once…'

'Not sure I really want to draw attention to this highly ignominious part of my life, thanks very much – and if I'm actually brave or stupid enough to produce any children, I'd thank you not to bring it up, EVER, in their hearing!'

'I think that works both ways, Alex!'

'Touché, my friend!'

Chapter 27

'I can't believe it!' said Briony, staring at the huge hamper that arrived this morning from Fortnum & Mason, along with a huge bunch of flowers. 'It's from your mother!'

'Oh, that's nice.'

'Did you know about this?'

'Not really. I didn't know what she was sending. Can we open it now? I bet there's some great things in there for breakfast.'

'Hands off! It's mine!'

'You can't eat all that by yourself.'

'I can try,' grinned Briony. 'Things appear to be looking up on the Philippa front.'

'Let's hope it lasts. Well, if I'm not allowed any fancy breakfast nosh, I'm off to work. I've got an early appointment anyway. By the way, do you think I should shave this beard off? Mother says it's unprofessional…'

'Hmm – well, these days beards are totally acceptable, so she's wrong about that. I haven't had time to adjust to it yet…I'll let you know...'

'Give us a kiss then!'

'Only if you save me a Florentine…'

I grabbed a banana on my way out. We're getting back to a place where things used to be good between us, and it feels like a weight has been lifted from my shoulders.

'You're very chipper today,' said Steve, as we got some coffees for our meeting with Gordon.

'Well, the police have dropped their investigation, the paparazzi have stopped harassing us and I got my girl back, so it's all good!'

We're tying up loose ends and planning our spending for the next six months. I'm glad we asked Gordon to keep us going forwards. I for one feel a lot more confident about everything with him guiding us along. My mother is right in a way – I don't think I'm anything like as business-savvy as my father was at my age, but I hope he's smiling down at me right now and feeling justified that all those extra maths lessons I endured as a child, weren't a waste of time.

'Ah, yes!' said Gordon, as he grasped a cup of the new coffee. 'This was definitely worth the investment.'

'Old Mr Anderson thought it was wasting money,' I said.

'Well, it's a loss-leader and it's hard to know whether we get many people coming here just because of it, or whether it helps to oil the wheels of sales negotiations – it's impossible to measure, but it's a small price to pay for customer comfort, isn't it! Anyway, I definitely appreciate it! So, let's get down to business, shall we!'

The main thing on our agenda, was social media. Basically, we don't have any.

'We don't have time to run social media platforms,' said Steve. 'We'll have to hire someone.'

'That's going to cost us quite a lot,' I said.

'Well, we can employ someone part-time to run it once it's set up.'

'We do have a website at least…'

'It's shit, though,' said Steve. 'I think we should scrap it and start again.'

'Yes, you're right. Briony's really good at this stuff, and she's not working at the moment…'

'Would she do it, do you think?'

'I'll see what she says.'

'Mrs Bedlington-Clarke has been chasing me regarding the position of patron, Alex…'

I sighed heavily. 'I actually can't do it, Gordon.'

'Why not?'

'Because I have a caution on my record, it wouldn't look good for them.'

'Oh…'

'I know.'

Steve was smirking. 'I bet you're really cut up about it, Alex!'

'She won't be happy,' said Gordon, gloomily.

'I know,' said Steve, – 'Hey! I've had a brainwave – why don't we ask Briony to do that as well?'

'Really?'

'Yes, Alex, it's purrrrrfect! She had to be rescued herself didn't she! So, that's the angle, plus she's famous now so that ticks the celeb box. Plus, she loves cats! I can see it now – Briony clutching Mr Catkins in front of some rugged, stormy coastline. He can be their poster rescue cat!'

'Well, I suppose it would be a much better choice than me. To be honest, I'm amazed Evangeline hasn't already dropped me like a hot brick – doesn't she read any newspapers? I mean, the trustees wouldn't want me if they'd seen those photos, Gordon. I'll have to ask Briony first, so don't say anything to her yet.'

'Do you think Briony will agree to helping?' Steve said.

'She's in a good mood at the moment, so I'll ask her this evening.'

'We need to decide on the Company charitable cause, as well,' said Gordon.

Steve came up with the obvious answer, which was staring us in the face. 'Well, it could be an environmental one – you know, planting more trees, etc. Then we can create some advertising around sustainability and conserving woodland. It's the way to go, Alex.'

'Yes, that's exactly what we need to do. It's a great USP. Hey – we're on fire today!' I said.

'Well, I'll look into the financial considerations and get back to you with a forecast, and we'll go from there.' Gordon said, closing his briefcase. 'I've got another meeting, so I'll see you next week.'

'How are we doing?' I asked him.

'Oh, just fine – you'll make the grade,' he said, smiling. 'I knew your father quite well, you know. There's a lot of him in you. I think he'd be very pleased that you have followed in his footsteps.'

'What do you think?' Briony was in the bedroom in front of our long mirror. She was wearing a very pretty cornflower-blue summer dress that I hadn't seen before, with matching shoes and a tiny little hat perched slightly on one side of her head. 'It's for the wedding!' she said, seeing the confusion on my face.

'Oh, yes! You look fabulous, Briony!'

'You don't usually say things like that, Alex! Do you really think so?'

'Yes – it looks amazing, absolutely beautiful, just like you!'

'Thank you, Alex!'

I cleared my throat, – 'So, I just wanted to ask you something…'

'Yes?'

'It's about a charity at work. We were wondering if you would consider being a patron for Mrs Bedlington-Clarke's *Fluffy Friends Cat Rescue* charity…' *(I suppose I should have realised that Briony can see straight through me by now.)*

'So, you think you can butter me up that easily, Alex Philpot?'

'Well, no, I mean maybe – anyway, what do you think? Could you consider the patron thing? I don't suppose it involves much work really – all you have to do is turn up once a year and cut a ribbon or give a tiny, tiny speech…It's really quite easy.'

'And you know that for sure, do you?'

'Well, maybe not entirely.'

'I'll think about it.'

'There's something else as well…'

'Right…' She turned to face me with raised eyebrows, hands on hips, and looked at me with her *what do you want now?* expression.

'Well, we need someone who knows what they're doing with social media and websites, Briony…'

'It's a lot of work, you know, Alex – organising all that stuff, plus it will need managing afterwards. You can't just do it and leave it to run itself…'

'I know, and that's why I'm asking you – you'd be paid properly for your highly skilled and professional assistance.'

'I'll sleep on it,' she said.

'I do actually think you look beautiful,' I said, – 'especially *without* the hat…the dress…and the shoes…and whatever's underneath…'

'Alex Philpot!' she said, gently pushing me away, – 'you're crushing my very expensive dress.'

'Well, you'd better take it off, then…'

'I haven't said 'yes' to your demands yet...'

'I'll throw in an Anderson's mug and matching coaster…'

'That sounds tantalising…how could I resist…'

'Alex,' Briony said later, 'I've agreed to do my first TV interview, on Friday morning, on Breakfast TV.'

'Oh, OK.'

'They asked if you would agree to be interviewed as well…"

'They've been asking me for weeks,' I said.

'I know – they said they got no response.'

'Why do you want to do one, Briony?'

'Because I want to tell my own story, and not have other people making stuff up – I want to set the record straight. Don't you?'

'I don't know. I think I just want to forget about it all and move on.'

'Well, I feel the same, but I want to have my say. Didn't the newspaper reports bother you, Alex?'

'I only read one or two, but they were pretty annoying. I deliberately avoided most of them – it was mostly nonsense, anyway.'

'Don't you want to have your say too?'

'I'm not sure. I suppose I'm worried that it might make things worse.'

'If we do it together, people will see that the media haven't managed to split us up and force us apart, but actually we're even stronger now than we were before – I think it would be good to go out there united against all that crap they tried to smear us with, Alex.'

'Well, that's fighting talk, Briony, but I'm not sure I've got the stomach for it.'

'I'd really like you to think about it. Also, do you think you could shave that beard off now? I think I preferred you as you were before…'

'OK.'

The thing is our lives are just getting back to normal and I really don't want to upset the applecart now. Trouble seems to have been following me around like the grim reaper, just waiting for an opportunity to trip me up. It's quite difficult to consider raking everything up again…but on the other hand Briony needs me to support her. I suppose the truth is, I can't duck out of it. It's going to be 'out of the frying pan, into the fire', as they say…

'Hello Alexander.' My mother was ringing to check Briony had received her gift.

'Oh, yes. Sorry, Mum – we've been so busy. We meant to call you yesterday…Briony loved the hamper. We've been enjoying the contents.'

'Well, don't eat everything at once, Alexander. You need to savour some of them.'

'Yes, mother…' *I rolled my eyes – she makes me feel about ten years old.*

Briony laughed. 'Is that Briony I can hear in the background?'

'Oh, yes – shall I get her?'

'No, no, it's fine – I can ask you – what is Briony wearing on Saturday?'

'A blue dress and one of those teeny tiny hat thingies.'

'That's called a fascinator, Alexander.'

'Oh, is it? Oh well, what do I know!'

'Plainly not a lot,' said my mother. Briony laughed again.

'What's wrong with Briony? She seems to be finding a lot of things funny today.'

'Oh, don't worry Mum, we're just in a silly mood.'

'Well, I hope you can pull yourselves together in time for Saturday. You still haven't told me what time you're coming.'

'Um, well, I have to be there extra early, Mum – I'm an usher, remember, so I can't collect you.'

'Oh, that's a shame.'

'I'll pick her up,' said Briony. It was my turn to raise my eyebrows and mouth '*really?*' Briony nodded.

'Mum, Briony says she'll collect you.'

There was silence, and then she said, – 'What time would that be?'

'About 11am.'

'Very well. Thank you. Oh, and Alexander, don't forget to hang your sporran correctly. Five inches from the top of your kilt. And I hope you remembered to buy Harry and Julia a wedding present?'

'Of course I did, Mother!'

'What did you get them?'

'Matching Kermit onesies and a disco ball…'

'You didn't!'

'What's wrong with that?'

'You should have got something useful, Alex. When people get married, they need practical things, not frivolous nonsense…'

'But Mum, everyone else will get them boring stuff like that…'

'Honestly Alex, I don't know where you get it from!'

'Don't worry, Mum, Briony bought them a Deluxe Lettuce Spinner.'

'Oh, good. At least someone's got some common sense.'

Briony was rolling about laughing when I came off the phone. 'Oh my God! Your mother is unbelievable!'

'Just be glad you didn't have to put up with her all through your childhood!'

Friday came, and I still wasn't sure this was the right thing to do, but Briony was determined, so I just had to bite the bullet. My mother wasn't keen on the idea at all when I told her.

'Why does she want to attract all that attention to herself?' she said. 'Why can't she just let the dust settle now?'

'What she really means,' said Briony, later, – 'is that she wants me to fade into the background and stop making an 'unseemly' fuss. Mainly because she doesn't want her posh friends asking her all about it again and embarrassing her.' I just nodded and said nothing. I've decided it's better to remain entirely noncommittal where Briony and my mother are concerned.

We arrived an hour early, as requested and subjected ourselves to the make-up and hair team. The interview itself went quite well, on the whole. Briony stayed very level-headed when the presenters asked her about Findlay.

'He was just a friend,' she said, resolutely and calmly looked them straight in the eye. 'He was an interesting guy and I liked him, but that was all. When things started to go wrong on the boat and we lost our bearings, I began to like him less and less. His mask slipped, to be honest – the veneer of happy-go-lucky charmer wore very thin quite quickly.' Then she moved on to me, which I was dreading.

'So, Alex, things went quite badly for you too, didn't they! Tell us about the newspaper stories and how that made you feel…'

'Um, well, you know, not great…well, pretty awful actually. The stories in the papers were complete bollo…I mean, rubbish. The reporters were literally making stuff up.'

'And what about the sex shop photos?'

'Well, obviously those were sort of true, but we were just joking around – I mean, we weren't actually *doing* anything indecent…'

'And scaling the statue in Piccadilly Circus….' They quickly interjected, in case I said anything offensive.

'Yes, also true. But that was just one night out on the town – my cousin's stag night. I mean, it was a bit wild – but aren't they all!'

'Do you think you perhaps should have sought some kind of counselling for the sake of your mental health? You were obviously indulging in some quite risky behaviours…'

'Didn't either of *you* have a wild stag night?' I said to them both.

The presenters looked at each other.

'No,' one of them said, firmly. 'I'm gay.'

'Oh, um…well, you can still have one, can't you? Aren't they called HAG nights or something?' Briony was looking at me slightly wide-eyed and I realised I'd strayed into unfamiliar and risky territory.

They tried again. 'It must have been a very difficult time for you, Alex – I expect you found it extremely stressful…'

'It was VERY stressful. I was going out of my mind at times, especially when I was falsely accused of murder. I actually thought I might be going mad. In fact, a lot of the newspaper articles suggested I was a crazy person, and some people believed it. Even people who know me started to think I'd done something terrible to Briony and Fin. It's been a living nightmare, I can tell you.'

'And how did your families cope with all of it? It must have been terrible for them not knowing if you were alive or dead, Briony?'

'My parents are just relieved that I'm home now. They found the whole experience pretty exhausting.'

'And have they forgiven Alex yet?'

Briony was quiet for a minute. 'Well, not quite, but it'll take time…'

'Why do they think it was all *my* fault?' I blurted out, instantly regretting it.

Briony did the wide-eyed thing again, and the presenters shuffled uncomfortably on their sofa.

'They…um, well, they thought you were getting cold feet – you know – because you wouldn't push for time off to go on holiday with me and …other stuff…' She responded, not wanting to elaborate.

I realised I'd put my cold foot right in it, as Briony continued to gaze at me with the eyes of Medusa.

'Well, all relationships have their ups and downs,' I said, trying to repair the damage I'd done. 'Briony and I are no different. We've both made mistakes in the past, and have regrets, but we're closer than ever now, and just want to look forward to our future together and be happy again.'

Briony seemed to relax, to my great relief, and the interview carried on with no more hiccups, thank goodness. At least no one mentioned Maggie, or the bondage debacle. Well, I suppose it was daytime TV, and they obviously wouldn't want to risk a discussion about inappropriate behaviour.

'Well,' said Briony as we left the studio, – 'that was nearly a total fuck-up!'

'Sorry, but I really don't understand why your parents can't just get over it!'

'Well, I did tell them you were a two-timing scumbag.'

'Haven't you explained that I actually wasn't and that the papers were printing nonsense?'

'Not really. I haven't had time. I will speak to them, I promise.'

'So, apart from that slight wobble, the interview went quite well, I thought.'

'The presenters were a bit disgusted by the puffin-eating, weren't they! I think they'll probably get quite a lot of complaints. Maybe I should just have stuck to talking about having to eat seaweed and limpets.'

'Well, people do what they have to do to survive, don't they! Anyone with half a brain knows that…'

'True, Alex, but there are a lot of people out there who aren't very sympathetic.'

'Do you think we did the right thing doing that interview?'

'I hope so. Anyway, I've got a surprise for you, later.'

'Really? I hope it's a good one!' I said, nervously.

'You'll like it, Alex, I promise you. Let's go and get some food.'

'This place is heaving with TV personalities, Briony…' I said, as we sat down outside in the sunshine.

'I know – the *Bluebird* is great for people-watching.'

'*They're* watching us as well…' I said, suddenly realising.

'Oh, yes! I hadn't thought of that. It won't last though, Alex. Once everyone gets bored of our story, we'll be forgotten about.'

'I'll drink to that!' I said.

'Well, we need to stay in the spotlight for just a bit longer…'

'Why?' I said, confused.

'Because…well, you need to meet someone…she's just coming…'

A tall blonde woman in a smart suit, suddenly arrived and plonked a large black bag on a chair. She smiled, took a seat at our table, and shook both our hands.

'This is Geraldine Porter, Alex. She's very interested in publishing your novel.'

'Really?'

'Yes, Alex! I absolutely love it!' she said.

'But you haven't seen it…'

'I have. Briony sent it to me last week,' she laughed.

'Alex, don't look so shocked!' said Briony.

'I'm just a bit lost for words…' I said looking at them both.

'Sorry Alex, we've been conspiring together. I hope you don't mind.' Geraldine smiled again and picked up the menu. 'By the way, please call me 'Gerry'. Shall we get some food and crack on? We've got a lot to talk about, haven't we!'

Chapter 28

'*Kill me now…*' texted Briony from her car, while she waited for my mother to re-appear. '*She's gone back in the house four times, Alex! FOUR times!*'

'*Oh dear…*' was all I could think of to text back.

'*AND…she said she thought my hair was very 'de rigueur…*'

'*Isn't that a compliment?*' I texted.

'*Not from your mother…*'

I rolled my eyes and told Briony to just ignore her.

Once I'd hung up, I finished getting dressed. 'Harry,' I asked, – 'do you think my sporran is hanging correctly?'

The church was packed and there was still no sign of Robert McClegg.

'I don't believe it!' said Harry, – 'he's bloody late!'

'Well, it's a good job he's not your actual photographer,' I said. 'Look, Harry – you need to focus on getting married. Patrick and I will think of something.'

'To be honest,' whispered Harry, – 'Julia wasn't too happy about our plan when I told her. She was worried it might spoil our day – especially if he got aggressive…'

'Hm, well, perhaps we need to think of something else, then.'

'Well, if he suddenly turns up, it'll have to wait until after the ceremony now,' said Jack. The *Wedding March* started up and everyone turned to see the beautiful bride floating down the aisle with a beaming father at her side and her three bridesmaids following behind, holding up her long, lacey train. Then I did a double take. One of the bridesmaids was very familiar to me. I looked across at Jacob on the other side of the church and caught his eye. He recognised her too, and I saw him visibly stiffen.

'That girl – the blonde bridesmaid,' I whispered to Patrick, who stood between me and the end of the pew, – 'do you know her?'

'Yes,' he said, – 'that's Maggie – she's one of Julia's old school friends. Why?'

'Oh, nothing – I just thought I recognised her…' I said, shrinking back behind him in case she noticed me. I looked across at Briony sitting beside my mother to see if she'd seen my sudden reaction. Luckily, she was looking the other way. What an unfortunate coincidence – fancy Julia knowing Maggie! This was really bad news. I spent the rest of the ceremony looking down at my feet and trying not to catch Maggie's eye. I breathed an inward sigh of relief when it was all over, and the Happy Couple turned round to go back up the aisle. Luckily, the bridesmaids were too busy gathering up the train, to pay attention to anyone in the congregation.

'What's the matter with you?' said Patrick, noticing my sudden preference for skulking behind pillars.

'I'll tell you later,' I said.

Jacob caught up with me on the way out.

'Christ, Alex! What the hell is she doing here?'

'I know! Can you believe it! She's an old school friend of Julia's.'

'What are we going to do?'

'I suppose we'll just have to brave it out and hope she doesn't cause any trouble.'

In the hotel, Jacob and I managed to avoid her for a while, but it was inevitable that she'd clock us, and when she did, she didn't hold back.

'Oi, Jacob!' she called out, as he tried to scoot past and dive into the gents' loos. 'I thought it was you!' she said, loudly. 'Where's your mate?' Then she spotted me as well. 'Oh, you look a right Bobby Dazzler there in that kilt, Alex! Are you wearing your SpongeBobs underneath, or going commando?' She hooted with laughter. 'Can I see?'

'Ssssh!' I said, trying to stop her.

'What have you got in your wee sporran, Alex?' she said, slurring. She stroked the fur and tried to unclip it.

'There's nothing in there!' I said, getting annoyed, and pushing her hand away.

'Oh, don't worry, your secret's safe with me,' she said, sniggering. She'd obviously had a few drinks by this point. Then I spotted Briony advancing down the corridor towards us. 'Is that your girlfriend, Alex?' said Maggie, grinning.

'Um, yes. Please don't tell her *anything!*' I hissed. Jacob had slipped away by now and left me to her mercy.

'Aw, she's a nice-looking girl, Alex,' she said, swaying on her heels and clutching my arm for support.

'Who's this?' asked Briony, joining us.

'Julia's old school friend,' I said, quickly. She's just a bit tipsy…'

'I think they're serving food soon, Alex. We need to get back to the tables.'

'Oh, yes, of course,' I said, eager to escape Maggie's clutches. 'See you later.' I took Briony's arm and swiftly walked away.

'She was being a bit over-familiar, Alex…'

'Oh, she's just had a few too many, that's all.' Briony eyed me suspiciously.

Frank and Lauren had had the foresight to seat my mother at a table with some of the other relatives, where she couldn't do too much damage. Half of them were as deaf as a post and the other half fell asleep during the speeches. Lauren had also had the good sense to put an old cousin between my mother and my mother's sister so they couldn't argue with each other. They go for quite long periods of time not speaking. I could see by their body language that they are currently in a cold-war situation. It's a shame really, because they have quite a lot in common, and if they didn't spend so much time trying to get one over on each other, they'd be fine. I looked around the rest of the room and saw that, luckily, Maggie was sitting several tables away with Julia's family. Jacob and Lucy were next to us, so he was safe for now.

'Why are you looking so on edge?' said Briony, pouring me some wine. 'You need to relax, Alex!'

'I will. I'm just wondering where Robert has got to. He was supposed to be here three hours ago.'

'Well, if he doesn't turn up, we'll just have to think of another way.'

'Maybe we should just let it go, Briony.'

'Are you serious? After all the trouble he's caused? No way, Alex!'

Well, so much for 'best laid plans'. Robert never showed up. Probably a good thing really, with hindsight. Anyway, it was bad enough having to dodge Maggie all evening. Jacob had the wonderful excuse to leave early due to Lucy getting tired, and managed to avoid any more embarrassing moments. My mother came and joined my table until she ran out of steam and decided she needed to go home.

'Have you enjoyed yourself?' I asked her as I accompanied her to her taxi.

'Well, it's been quite a day,' she said, elusively.

'Did you have a nice chat with Aunty Beatrice?'

'We've never got on, Alex – you know that! I've tried, but she's impossible. Do you know, she doesn't have a good word to say about anybody!'

'Has she gone?' asked Briony when I went back to the table.

I nodded. 'She's not speaking to her sister at the moment.'

'They're as bad as each other,' said Briony. 'Come on – we can let our hair down now and have some fun. This is my favourite disco track!' she said, as *Dancing Queen* came over the speakers, and the dance floor filled up instantaneously. By now, Maggie was too drunk to see straight, and I saw her being escorted out of the function suite.

'We should've got a room ourselves,' said Briony, as we watched her being helped upstairs. 'We'll probably have to wait ages for a taxi. By the way, Alex, I got chatting to Maggie earlier, when she was still reasonably compos mentis – while you were keeping your mother occupied. It was quite an interesting conversation…'

'Oh…'

Briony was looking at me with mock annoyance.

'And…' I said.

'She's been having a lot of fun with you and Jacob, hasn't she!' said Briony, laughing.

'What did she say?'

'Oh, just that you were a pair of chumps and easy to wind up.'

'Thanks!'

'*She* said it, not me! Anyway, she knows where Robert McClegg lives!'

'How?'

'He interviewed her for the *Stunner* when he was digging for dirt on you, and he used an old envelope to write on…'

'So?'

'It had his address on it!'

'Bingo!'

'Good, isn't it!'

'But doesn't Harry have his address?'

'No – only a phone number.'

'I wonder why he didn't turn up today?'

'Who knows! Anyway, apparently, he lives in Brixton.'

'We can't go harassing him at home though, Briony. We'll get into more trouble.'

'I know but we'll think of something. He can't be allowed to get away with it, Alex.'

Chapter 29

The following Monday, Briony got a phone call from the *Belfast Telegraph*. Apparently, a bottle was washed up on a beach near Ballintoy with her letters to her family and friends. A young boy and his dog had found it and taken it to the local police station. The Irish press want to interview her and have offered to pay for her flight over there, so she can be photographed on the beach with the boy. The letters are going to be published in the *Sunday Life* paper at the weekend, with a full-page spread.

'It's a bit weird,' said Briony, on Monday evening. 'I mean, I wrote those letters thinking I was going to die out there.'

'Did you write anything you regret now?'

'No, I don't think so…I'm a bit surprised they actually turned up somewhere. I thought the bottle would probably get smashed in the sea or on rocks. And do you know, the weirdest thing is – my family on my mother's side are from Ballintoy! Can you believe it! I've always wanted to go there – I looked it up once and it's really beautiful.'

Gerry was over the moon to hear about it. 'People are going to love this, Briony!' she enthused on the phone. 'It's heart-rending and a miraculous ending to your ordeal – it's like a romantic tragedy, but with a happy ending!'

'It's not really a tragedy of any kind,' I said to Briony after she put the phone down. 'I mean, you didn't actually die, did you? I take it that Gerry is planning on publishing your story too?'

Then Briony had to come clean about the whole thing. 'I've struck a deal with her – your novel for my story,' she admitted.

'Oh, I see…' I said, suddenly feeling pretty deflated, again. 'So, she wasn't really interested in my novel, then, was she?'

'Yes, she was, Alex. I promise. Look…what you have to understand is that the publishing world is very fickle, and it will be easier to sell your novel if people know who you are. We have to take advantage of your current high profile in the media. This is an opportunity to get your book noticed, and you should make the most of it.'

'But I want people to like the book on its own merit, not because I'm an accidental celebrity.'

'That's all very noble, but I think you should grasp Gerry's offer with both hands. It might be the only one you get, Alex.'

I must say, I felt quite disappointed by this state of affairs. People are bound to say I only got published because of our celebrity status. It's not what I'd hoped for, but maybe Briony's right – maybe this is my one and only chance of getting published. I might regret it for the rest of my life if I don't accept it.

'What do you think?' I said to Mr Catkins while Briony was in the shower. 'Should I swallow my pride and take the offer?' He looked at me, sighed, and jumped down off the sofa, stopping briefly to examine one of his paws, before walking nonchalantly away.

The next day, I asked Steve what he thought about it all.

'Go for it, Alex!' he said. 'Mind you, if it's crap, everyone will know.'

'Thanks a bunch,' I said. *He's right, of course – it'll be much more public if it flops and ends up in the bargain basement of all the book shops within three months of publication. What a horrible thought that is.* 'Don't forget,' I said to Steve, – 'I'm going away with Briony next week.'

'Oh, yes – where are you taking her, then?'

'I haven't quite decided.'

'Why don't you go to Disney Land?' said Alice. 'I love it there.'

'That's not really what I had in mind, Alice,' I said, – 'but thanks for the input.'

'I think he wants to go somewhere a bit more romantic,' said Steve, – 'like Paris, or a Greek Island…or Thailand…'

'My sister went there,' said Alice. 'She got bitten all over by mosquitos. She got Dengue Fever and was really ill.'

'Perhaps I'll avoid going there, then,' I said.

'Holidays are overrated,' said Steve. 'The last one I took my family on, cost me an arm and a leg. I'm still paying for it six months later.'

'Well, you're a right pair of gloom and doom merchants, aren't you!'

'What about Venice?' said Steve.

'No – not with all those boats and water…'

'Oh, yes – I forgot, sorry! Anyway, don't stay away too long, will you? Anderson's needs you! By the way, some places won't let you in with a police caution…'

'Oh cripes! I hadn't thought of that!'

'You're probably OK with Europe,' said Steve.

'How do you know about that?'

'My brother got into some scrapes when he was younger. Don't worry – it only stays on your record for six years.'

'That's six years too long,' I said, gloomily.

Later, I talked to Briony about how we were going to deal with Robert McClegg and get my caution lifted. Steve's revelation had brought it home to me – I mean, I hadn't really considered how frustrating the consequences would be. It could really affect my life. Six years seems like a lifetime at the moment. I'll be 41 before I can get rid of it!

'What are we going to do, Briony? That moron's ruining my life!' I said, over our dinner in the evening. I'd been googling about how a caution can actually have quite serious consequences. 'I won't be able to work with children or elderly people, or people with mental health problems, and I can't go to America or Australia if I want…AND, I can't be a Special Constable either.'

'Well, you probably won't *need* to do most of those things, Alex.'

'It's the principle.'

'You're not going to like what I'm about to show you, I'm afraid,' said Briony, getting out her laptop. 'Look at this,' she said, scrolling through the latest news stories. 'He's at it again. Harry told me earlier today. Robert was *actually* at the wedding, Alex! Can you believe it! He sneaked in and took some photos – no one noticed him. He got one of you with that girl – look at this…'

I stared, stunned to silence. He'd managed to catch a shot of Maggie's attempt to see under my kilt, and I happened to have a ridiculous expression plastered on my face – most likely acute embarrassment, but unfortunately, it looked like I was enjoying her advances.

'Why can't he just piss off and leave us alone!' I groaned. 'How come no one saw him creeping about?'

'He was probably in disguise – he's a professional paparazzi, after all.'

'You mean 'a professional degenerate',' I said.

'That girl seemed very interested in you, Alex…'

'She was drunk, Briony. Look, *(I was going to have to come clean now)* it was Maggie. It's a pure coincidence that Julia knows her from school. It was pretty awkward that she was there, after all the hassle I've had from her, and I didn't want to tell you because she's already caused enough trouble.'

'Hmm…you should have just told me, Alex! Anyway, he took some of me as well.' She pointed out a couple of photos of her dancing drunkenly, and very closely, with Harry and his friends. The caption to our pictures said: '***Alex and Briony's wavering relationship still at sea as Alex rocks the boat by telling close female friend to keep schtum'.***

'How the hell does he know what I said to her?' I said, angrily.

'He's probably paying her, Alex.'

'I don't know what we can do about him…'

'I've got another idea – sort of entrapment but without the risk of being arrested. We could write to him and say he was seen spiking drinks on the night in question, in a bar in Piccadilly, and that we can prove it.'

'But we can't…'

'That doesn't matter. If he did it, he'll be worried enough to take it seriously.'

'Oh, I don't know, Briony – we could get into trouble for blackmailing him.'

'Why would he report us if he's guilty himself?'

'But what if he isn't guilty?'

'Then he won't respond, will he! We'll do it anonymously, anyway.'

'What exactly do you have in mind?'

'We write to him asking him to fess up to the police, or we will do it for him.'

'He could go to prison, Briony. Why would he agree to that? I mean, what's his incentive?'

'If he hands himself in to the police and confesses his crime, his prison sentence will be a lot less. It could even be halved – that's his incentive!'

'It's a gamble, isn't it?'

'I suppose so, but it's low risk for us, Alex. He won't know who sent the letter – we'll make sure of that.'

Of course, I didn't mention Briony's unorthodox and risky plan to my police training buddies at the weekend. In fact, I try to limit the amount of information I tell them about what's been going on – Jim must think I'm really not Special Constable material after everything that's happened. He's probably revising his decision to let me carry on, especially after what he said the last time. I'm trying not to let it get me down, though. I was hoping that this weekend's session would take my mind off it all for a bit.

'Hey stranger!' said Sharon, when I walked into the training centre. Everyone was there, except Kate, of course.

'Ah, Alex! You're going to enjoy this session!' said Jim, enthusiastically.

'Am I?'

'We are taking a look at moral dilemmas…' I had a sudden sinking feeling, but it was too late to make a hasty retreat.

It turns out that there's a very thin line sometimes between a person being arrested or not, depending on a myriad of things. We've all seen those police reality shows where the offender could have got away with anti-social behaviour if they had just apologised and walked away from the scene, but nine out of ten times they can't help themselves. Jim gave us several scenarios to consider and debate, which certainly made us think. It made me realise that there's more to being a Special PC than arresting people.

'You're going to be taking on the role of a Social Worker for a large part of your job,' said Jim, – 'often the people you deal with need a compassionate ear and help with their basic needs. You will need to have empathy and understanding. You will need to be able to assess people and situations with critical but fair judgement.' I thought about PC Flannigan at this point and her less than sympathetic attitude towards me.

'For instance,' said Jim, – 'as a purely hypothetical scenario… *(he was looking directly at me with a mischievous glint in his eye)*, let's say, while you are out on the beat, you come across a seemingly drunk man, staggering about in the road. He has a deep cut on his head and is shouting at people. What do you do?'

'Tell him to pack it in,' said Theo.

'Arrest him for being drunk and disorderly,' said Rick, – 'I mean, he could cause an accident being in the road like that!'

'He should go to hospital,' said Sharon, – 'that cut on his head could be bad…'

'What else?' said Jim.

'Cuff him,' said Leo.

'But he's not physically threatening anyone…'

'Well, you could read him his rights, then.'

'Hmm…' Jim looked slightly bemused. 'Alex, what do you think?'

'Um, well…you should persuade him to get off the road first…'

'Yes…'

'Then you should talk to him to try and understand what's been going on, and then make sure his injuries are assessed by a doctor…'

'What about his demeanour?'

'He could be drunk, or he might have taken drugs…or he could have something wrong with him like an illness which is making him behave erratically…'

'Getting warmer. OK, anything else?'

'I know,' said Leo, – 'he might need to be restrained and put in a van if he resists arrest.'

'Right…OK, so you've all come up with a variety of thoughts. Now I'll tell you what actually happened. This man, who was registered blind, was out for a walk and was going along the pavement minding his own business when he tripped and fell into the road, losing his stick and badly hitting his head on the curb. He was shouting because he'd lost his stick and had no idea where he was, he had a head injury, and he was disorientated and distressed. None of you thought about witnesses, did you? Witnesses are very important to enable you to make an accurate assessment of a situation. So, the lesson here is to never jump to conclusions. Your job is to look at all the facts before making a judgement.'

'Can we get him on damage to Highways property?' asked Theo.

'I'm not sure you're entering into the spirit of things here,' Jim said to him. 'This class is about empathy and community-minded approaches to policing…'

'There's a screw loose with that bloke, Theo…' whispered Rick to me.

'How did it go?' asked Briony, when I got home later.

'Really interesting,' I said. 'Jim was showing us how we can jump to the wrong conclusion easily without knowing all the facts – I must say, it made me think about a lot of things. There's something I need to mull over, Briony. I've had a bit of an epiphany – the second one since all this newspaper stuff began. I think I might have a rethink about everything…'

'Well don't spend too long thinking, Alex! We've got things to do!'

Chapter 30

At work the next day, I got a call from Frank.

'Alex, have you got a minute?'

'Um, yes, of course…'

'Can you meet me for lunch today?'

Frank met me at one of our favourite Italian places in Surbiton, *Terra Mia.'*

'I'm paying,' he said, noticing me scanning the prices on the menu.

'That's very kind, Frank. Thank you.'

'Well, I think you might be contemplating an engagement soon, no?'

'Oh, well…um, I…er, haven't really…'

'I'm going to give you some advice, Alex. I've met that girl of yours now, and in my opinion, she's a smasher. Don't dilly dally any more – if you've got any sense at all, you'll get on with it and ask her to marry you.'

'I have been thinking about it…'

'The other thing is, never mind about your mother – I'll set her straight, don't you worry.' Frank was on a roll. He ordered two chilled glasses of Calvarino and Fettuccine Alfredo – our favourite lunchtime pasta dish. 'What you have to remember, Alex, is that she's only got you, and it's hard for her to let you go.'

'I'm not flavour of the month with Briony's parents either…'

'Well, that's going to be up to them to sort out. If I've learned anything in my life, Alex, it's this; you have to live your own life, not someone else's idea of it.'

'There's one thing that's going to get in the way of that, though.'

'What's that?'

'Well, it's this damn caution on my records, Frank…'

'Ah, yes – well, I was going to talk to you about that. I wrote to the police to appeal it and to try and get it removed. I thought we had a good chance since there was no criminal damage done to the monument, and you were under a lot of stress at the time, which would have affected your mental state. Basically, I appealed to them to take a sympathetic approach, especially given that your record up until then was unblemished. Anyway, I've got something for you...' Frank pushed an open envelope across the table. 'Open it,' he said.

As soon as I saw the words, "*...on this occasion, we have decided to make an allowance...*" my heart skipped a beat as I scanned the rest of the short letter. 'Oh my God – that's amazing, Frank! Thank you so much!' I said, beaming.

'I thought you'd like it!' said Frank. 'Let's toast to new beginnings and new adventures, eh! Just don't plan your wedding too soon – I'm still recovering from Harry and Julia's!'

It's probably my imagination, but that Fettuccini Alfredo was the best I've ever tasted. What amazing news! I felt so grateful to Uncle Frank – God knows what would have happened to me without his help. Over coffee afterwards, he also told me what he'd found out about Findlay Connor. I can't deny, my eyes were on stalks by the time he'd finished regaling me with the whole sorry saga. I decided to keep all this news to myself until I got home later.

'Mr Anderson came in while you were out,' said Alice on my return to the office. 'He left something for you. It's here,' she said, handing me a small package. I took it to my office, closed the door, and sat down to open it. There was a letter accompanying the parcel, which I read immediately:

Dear Alexander,

When I received this gift from Evangeline on the evening of my retirement, I was quite taken aback and, to be honest, most touched by her change of heart, which was quite unexpected.

Forty years ago, when I was of a similar age to you, and when Alfred and I set this business up, we were a formidable team, he and I – you might not imagine that now as I'm old and well past my prime! However, we were considered the best in the business at that time and won several awards, as you know. The one which we prized the most was the **UK Kitchen Designer of the Year Award**. *We won it for a design that I'd spent months on. Anyway, the long and short of it was that Alfred took it home and it stayed there all these years – Evangeline wanted it on her mantelpiece where she could show it off, and since she held the purse strings, I wasn't going to argue about it. So, when she finally returned it to me that evening, I was over the moon. I've had it sitting on my own mantlepiece at home these last few weeks. However, I've made the decision to give it to you for safe-keeping, Alexander. Put it in your office, where I hope it will give you the inspiration to remain true to the basic principles of Anderson's Kitchens – a bespoke design company of the highest calibre, honest and true in its aims, with integrity and quality at its heart.*

With Blessings,

Terrence Anderson

Steve knocked on my door and entered, curious to see what the old man had sent us.

'What is it?'

'A prized possession, Steve – look!'

'Wow! Can we keep it?'

I lifted the embossed silver plaque from its blue velvet casing and stood it up. 'He says we can…it's to remind us to stick to the design criteria that Anderson's is known for – a kind of talisman, I suppose…'

When I got home, Briony was busy in the kitchen. As I dumped my brief case on the floor, I noticed the fish tank was looking cloudy and grubby and I realised I hadn't cleaned it for ages – things have been so busy, I've been neglecting my poor fish.

'Sorry, chaps,' I told them, getting out the glass sponge.

'Are you talking to your fish again?' said Briony. 'You know you sound a bit mad, don't you?'

'Possibly, but I got used to talking to them when you were away – it's therapeutic, you know, to talk to your pets…'

'You had Mr Catkins. At least he can hear you…'

'He's quite judgemental, Briony – haven't you noticed? When I tried to talk to him, he gave me short shrift…I don't think he's a good listener…'

Briony sniggered, – 'Don't tell me fish are any better! By the way, why has the water gone all funny – it's full of bits floating around…hang on, is that what I think it is?'

'Good grief, Briony, you're right! It's hundreds of baby fish!' I said, squinting through the glass.

'So, there was nothing wrong with Xander, then!'

'Obviously not! What are we going to do with all of them, Alex? There are literally hundreds!'

'Um, well – I'll have to put them in the other tank, I suppose.'

'We could just give them away – we've got enough to think about right now…'

'Oh, well – you're probably right. They're tricky to keep alive by all accounts. Talking about fish, I had a very interesting conversation with Frank today…'

'Oh…'

'Yes – firstly, I no longer have a caution hanging over me – he's managed to get the police to drop the whole thing!'

'Oh, Alex, that's fantastic news!' she said, hugging me.

'It is, isn't it! Secondly, Fin is being extradited back to the UK to face a charge of – get this – multiple identity thefts, marine barratry (that's reckless damage to boats, to you and me), theft, forgery and fraud by false representation, amongst a load of other things…'

'Good grief!' Briony said, aghast, hand to mouth in shock, her eyes popping.

'Basically, there's a list of offences as long as your arm. Apparently, he has at least eight different identities – three of the people are actually dead. And, by the way, the authorities found your debit and credit cards on him plus your passport…'

'SHIT! That thieving scumbag! I thought I'd lost my bag during the storm when we had to escape onto the rocks.' Briony sat down on the sofa, her eyes filling with tears. 'How could someone do something like that, Alex?'

'I don't know, but they've caught him now – he'll go down for a long time, Briony, you can be sure of that.'

'Oh my God, Alex. I feel even more of an idiot now…'

'It wasn't your fault – he was a very good conman, Briony; he duped a lot of people.'

Well, it's been a crazy few weeks, all things considered. I've finally made my decision about where I'll take Briony on holiday. I think she'll approve – after all, she pretty much told me what she wanted to do, so it really is a no-brainer. Since the news broke the other day, about Findlay's extradition and his colourful exploits, there has been a resurgence of interest in us, and the paparazzi have been gathering outside our house again. It's been a week of decision-making – particularly with regard to our 'friend' Robert McClegg. I've persuaded Briony to agree to let the whole thing go since Frank got my caution lifted. We don't need the added stress of trying to tackle someone like him and his parasitic boss, Stacey Armstrong. Briony and I have come to the conclusion that life is too short to waste time and energy worrying about what they're doing.

'They'll soon get bored, Briony,' I told her – 'when they can't get any more uncompromising photos or juicy gossip. Let's just forget about them – we've got so much else to focus on now, and so much to look forward to…' She wasn't completely on board with this plan, but I'm hoping she sees the benefit of it in the long run. 'We need to move forward, not cling to the past,' I told her.

'You sound just like me,' she laughed.

The next day, I woke up early and full of energy. I felt excited for the future and all the possibilities that lay ahead. I told Briony I needed to go out and do a few things.

'Oooooh, intriguing!' she said, stretching and rubbing her eyes. 'You're up early for a Saturday. Actually, I need to get on too – I must hurry up and book my flight to Ireland to go and do the interview.'

'Um…don't do that yet,' I said – 'I'll explain later.'

She gave me an inquisitive look, – 'OK then…'

Outside, the early September sun was still warm, and I was on a mission to get things sorted. I gave Jacob a ring while I walked along.

'How's it going?' I asked him.

'Killing…Lucy isn't getting much sleep right now so neither am I…How about you?'

'Really good, thanks,' I said, feeling smug. I told him all my latest news and, to be fair to him, he seemed pleased for me.

'Good to hear things are going well, Alex.'

'I'm taking Briony away on Friday, Jacob, and, well – the other thing is, I'm going to propose to her…'

'What? Really?'

'Yes!'

'We thought you'd never get round to it!'

'Well, I'm ready to do it now.'

'What if she says 'no'?'

'Oh, well, I hadn't thought of that…Do you think she will…I mean, maybe I should wait for a bit…'

'No, Alex! Forget what I said – I'm sure she'll say 'yes'. Honestly, Lucy says she's been waiting for ages…'

'Did she? Have they been discussing it?'

'Of course they have, Alex. Blimey, I thought I was the stupid one…'

'Hahahaha! OK – well, thanks for the heads up.'

'Let me know ASAP won't you, mate?'

The travel shop was open, so I decided to book the holiday the old-fashioned way to make sure there'd be no chance of Briony seeing what I was doing on my laptop. I didn't want my surprise to be spoilt. Ballintoy looked perfect for a quiet and peaceful location. The old croft cottage I'd found on the edge of the beach looked idyllic. Briony would be able to go and do the interview from there, and then we would have time to just be together with nothing else to worry about – I couldn't wait! I just had a couple more things to do before heading back home.

'Mum, what are you doing this coming week?'

'Why?'

'Well, I need you to do me a favour…'

'And what might that be?'

'Would you be able to come to the flat this week and feed Mr Catkins and my fish, please?'

'Oh, where are you going?'

'On holiday – to Ireland. I'm taking Briony away.'

'It's cold and wet there, you know, Alex…Anyway, don't you need to be at work when you've got a fledgling business to run? I don't think your father would have gone off like this at such a crucial time.'

'I just need to know if you can look after the cat, Mum…'

'Well, all right. I suppose I can manage that.'

'Great, thanks Mum – you're a star!'

I wasn't going to let her dampen my enthusiasm – I've decided to take a leaf out of Briony's '*Don't Kill my Vibe'* book and let the 'arrows of negativity' bounce off me. I could now go full steam ahead with my plan and I must say, I was feeling pretty pleased with it.

In the evening, when I told Briony to go and pack for a week away, she looked a bit surprised. 'I know I'm not given to doing things on the spur of the moment, but I'm trying to be more spontaneous.'

She smiled and said that she knew something was up – my mother had rung while I was in the shower to ask her where she kept the cat food.

On the Six O'clock News that evening, the news about Findlay Connor broke, and we watched him being escorted onto a plane by two police officers and an official.

'He looks miserable,' said Briony.

'Well, it's the end of the line for him, isn't it? He knows he can't escape this time. He's cooked his chips. At least he can't do any more harm – for a while, anyway. Just think, Briony, if he hadn't been showing off to you, he'd still be running around, causing more trouble and ruining people's lives.'

In the morning, as we put our bags by the door, Mr Catkins sat glowering at us from his perch on top of the fish tank.

'Oh, he looks so cross, Alex!'

'He'll be fine, Briony. My mother's coming to look after him,' I swear that cat gave me an even more evil look when I said that. 'I'm afraid we've become a bit of a celebrity couple again,' I said to Briony, as we shut the front door behind us. 'There are quite a few paparazzi out on the street, just to warn you. Do you think we should say something to them to keep them happy?' I said, as we stood in the lobby, waiting to face the jostling throng.

'Like what?'

'Well, the sort of thing people usually say, like…I don't know – what about… *"I'd just like to say that I am extremely relieved that Briony is safe and well and back where she belongs with her loving fiancée, who's missed her more than he cares to admit…"* – Something like that…'

Briony stared at me for a moment. 'I'm sorry…what? Have I missed something?'

'Oh, yes, hang on…' I felt in my pocket for the little box I'd purchased earlier in the day on my way back from the travel shop. 'Briony, will you do me the honour of becoming my beautiful and long-suffering wife?'

'Oh my God! Alex, get up off the floor!'

'Well, what do you say?'

'You actually bought a ring!'

'Yes, I did. What do you think?'

'It's lovely, Alex! How did you know what to buy?'

'Well, I had a lot of time to think about it and, well, I saw some pictures of rings in your box of treasures…you know, the one that had the shark's tooth and gooey love missive. So, I took a chance and …well, I hope you like it.'

'You went through my stuff!'

'Not exactly – the police did. Anyway, is it a 'yes' or a 'no'? If it's a 'no', we'll just carry on as before, although I can't deny that I might never recover…'

Briony slipped it onto her finger and made me wait an eternity before answering.

'I think I'd better say 'yes', Alex.' She was grinning from ear to ear.

'You're the best thing that ever happened to me,' I told her, – 'and I never knew it until you'd gone. Please don't ever do that again.'

'I'll try not to,' she said, her big blue eyes brimming with tears. There was no turning back now – I knew what I wanted, and I wouldn't ever let her go again. I took her hand in mine and we stepped out to meet the swarming photographers.

'Let's give them a Front Page we can be proud of!' I said, taking Briony in my arms and kissing her, before we climbed into my car, smiling and waving goodbye to them. We drove off up the road, heading for the M25, full of excitement and anticipation for our new life together.

'We can face just about anything now!' said Briony. 'I'm so glad I'm doing it with you.'

ABOUT THE AUTHOR

Painting and writing have always been my main passions, but I've done all sorts of other things too; from being a Chambermaid, Cook, Barmaid, Driver, Gallery and Shop Assistant, Secretary and PA, Dresser for the Royal Scottish Ballet, Print Designer, Illustrator and Publisher, Singer in a Medieval Banquet, Events Organiser and teacher (to name but a few!) But most importantly I am a Mum to three of our own fabulous kids and Foster Mum to many more.

When times have been difficult, we've always retained our sense of humour as a family and tried to see the funny side of things and I am so grateful for all the wonderful experiences and interesting characters I've met along the way. Luckily, having such a lovely, chaotic, and hectic family life has inspired my first published series, 'Diary of a Stressed Out Mother', followed by my debut comedy romance, 'With Both Feet'. I very much hope there will be many more to follow as I've enjoyed every minute of writing these books and I hope my readers love them too!

For more about Nicola Kelsall:

Web: www.nicolakelsall.com
Facebook and Instagram: @nicola_kelsall
Twitter: https://twitter.com/StressOutMother

Printed in Great Britain
by Amazon

23416803R00195